NEVER A BRIDE

#3 in the At the Shore Series

A Contemporary Romance from NY Times and USA Today Bestseller Caridad Pineiro

Emma never dreamed that the happily-ever-after would change her life. . .

But as her two best friends find love, Emma worries about what her future will bring. She has seen all too often what happens once husbands and children arrive. She puts on a brave face because she wants her buddies to be happy, but as a wedding planner, she has seen one too many marriages go south. Not to mention her parents' bitter divorce which has soured her on the idea of marriage for herself. She can't imagine ever finding a man who can bring her a forever kind of romance.

He's been in love with her forever and can't understand why she can't see it. . .

Carlo da Costa knows why Emma avoids relationships and yet he can't help but wonder how someone who puts such love and care into others' dreams can't allow herself to believe in the fairy tale. He sees the yearning on her face when she spends time with him and his big boisterous family and knows that deep inside, she wants the same thing. Carlo hopes that one day he can provide her with that because he's sure Emma holds the key to his heart in her hands

Prologue

The bouquet shot toward her head like a spaceship launched at the moon.

Emma Grant had no time to deflect the missile. She tangled her fingers into the luscious petals of the peonies, roses, and hydrangea, rousing fragrant floral scents as the bouquet grazed her face. When she was in wedding planner mode, she would have taken the time to appreciate the freshness of the blooms, but tonight she was also a bridesmaid and best friend and totally unhappy about her current predicament.

Flowers fisted in her hand, Emma whirled to face her other best friend and maid of honor, Connie Reyes, who with a subtle hip check, had knocked Emma straight into the path of the flying tussie mussie. "I thought you were my friend!"

"Totally," Connie said with a broad smile and waltzed off to the side of the dance floor to where Carlo da Costa, Emma's caterer extraordinaire and longtime man crush, stood with some of his wait staff.

Her friends thought Carlo was the man to give Emma her happily-ever-after, except it wasn't possible that someone like Carlo could love someone like her. She was broken inside and had been for some time while Carlo was everything good in this world. A loving son and a supportive brother. A go-to-guy for her and so many others. But a lover? Even though her insides ignited at the thought of making love with the incredibly handsome Carlo, Emma knew it could only lead to misery on way too many levels.

He was her business partner of sorts and she valued how well they worked together. They had even talked about forming an event planning business more than once so Emma could leave the bridal salon where she currently worked and run her own company. Being partners would also allow

Carlo to expand his catering business to do more events. Not to mention that he was her best friend and she couldn't imagine not having him in her life, but she was certain that was what would happen if they tried to go from friends to lovers and it didn't work out. Just like her parents' marriage had turned into a total nightmare.

But Emma's fears weren't keeping Connie from trying to drag Carlo into the center of the dance floor for the next part of the wedding ritual. He protested at first and as all eyes settled on him as he balked, embarrassment engulfed her. His hesitation confirmed to Emma that changing the nature of their relationship was not necessarily something he wanted to do either.

Others soon joined in to offer Connie assistance and Carlo finally relented, although clearly reluctant. The handsome caterer stood with the other single men, and as the groom prepared his garter toss, Emma closed her eyes and mumbled a prayer beneath her breath.

"Dear Lord, please be good to me," she said and half-opened her eyes to watch.

Apparently God wasn't listening since the garter flew across the air, and like a horseshoe tossed at a ring, the circle of baby blue satin ribbon and beige lace landed on Carlo's index finger, earning hoots and shouts from all gathered at the perfect catch.

Emma groaned and popped her eyes wide open as Carlo stood there, dangling the garter for all to see. A stain of color marred his cheeks as he peeked at her with a chagrined smile.

The heat of a blush erupted all across her face and up to her ears. She half glanced at Connie who had returned to stand by her and Emma said, "I will kill you for this. When you least expect it."

Connie couldn't stifle her chuckle, and when the groom's brother and best man Jonathan Pierce strolled to her friend's side, Connie high-fived Jonathan. It had obviously been a conspiracy to get her and Carlo and together. Connie murmured something to him that Emma couldn't quite hear as the band launched into a sexy riff to continue the wedding tradition. Carlo sauntered over, garter dangling from his finger as someone placed a chair for her to sit on in the middle of the makeshift dance floor.

"The quicker you get it over with, the easier it will be," Emma thought, hurried out, and unceremoniously plopped onto the chair.

The sexy music continued as Carlo kneeled before her and mouthed "Don't worry." In deference to the fancy event being held at the Sinclair beachfront mansion, he was dressed in a tuxedo. The black of the tux emphasized the deep brown of his thick wavy hair. The electric white shirt was the perfect foil against olive skin that still bore the remnants of a summer tan. He smiled at her, his teeth toothpaste bright and perfect. The smile was brilliant and transformed the chiseled features of his face. Made his chocolate brown eyes gleam with a mix of amusement and awkwardness.

It was way too easy to picture him as the groom. *Her groom*, but that was an impossible wish. As his gaze locked with hers, she detected something different for a moment. Something dangerous that she tried to convince herself wasn't there. *There was no way that was there*, she told herself.

She silently pleaded with him not to make the situation worse. Ever the gentleman, he heeded her plea and kept it clean as she looked up toward the inky night sky to avoid watching him. His touch was deferential while he slipped the lacy fabric past her shoe and ankle, but even the faintest whisper of his rough palm against her skin had her trembling inside and heat racing across her body. He moved the garter up a little higher to her calf and paused, forcing Emma to look at him to find out the reason for his delay.

Carlo grinned sexily and the fire at her core ignited into a five-alarm blaze. He was just so damn gorgeous, and it was impossible not to imagine doing more with him. He inched the garter past her knee, his palm teasing her smooth skin, but stopped there despite the entreaties of the single men to go ever higher. He wagged his head, shook his finger in a no-way gesture, and tenderly draped Emma's gown back over her legs.

Emma met his gaze once more, thankful, but this time it was impossible to miss that his look was filled with yearning. With that emotion she had maybe hoped for and dreaded at the same time. And then Carlo did something totally unexpected and decidedly risky. He wrapped an arm around her waist, urged her to her feet, and slowly drew her close.

Her knees trembled and her heart pounded so loudly, she barely heard the music and cheers from those who'd maybe had a little too much to drink during the festivities. Carlo steadied her, keeping his arm around her waist as he cradled her jaw. Slowly he leaned toward her and tilted her face up with the gentlest pressure.

She could have backed away. Could have stopped him, but truthfully, she didn't want him to stop. She inched up on her tiptoes to meet his lips.

He kissed her like there was no tomorrow. His lips were hot, so hot. His mouth mobile against hers. His body hard everywhere as he held her near and she melted into him, letting herself savor the moment because it was one that could never be repeated. No matter how much she was enjoying it. No matter how much she wished it would be repeated. No matter how much she wished there could be more between them.

When Carlo finally ended the kiss, Emma stood there, dazed and a little unsteady, until Carlo bent and whispered, "It was totally worth the wait, *meu amor.*"

It had been, but she couldn't admit that, couldn't hope that things could change between them, so she playfully shoved him away to downplay what had just happened because Emma never intended to be a bride.

That prompted yet more catcalls from the single men, and with a shrug and a rueful grin, Carlo left the floor and started giving instructions to his catering crew again, while Emma stomped toward Connie who stood at the edge of the dance floor, clearly pleased with her accomplishment.

Emma thrust the tussie-mussie bouquet against Connie's chest and repeated her earlier warning. "You're a dead woman."

She whirled on one heel which dug down into the grass of the mansion's great lawn, making her wobble for a moment before she righted herself and strode toward the beachfront, needing some air and a moment to regain her composure before she had to face Carlo again. But as she marched toward the short boardwalk over the dunes, she couldn't help but reach up and run her fingers across her lips. She closed her eyes and remembered the kiss. The way his body had fit to hers perfectly. For a moment, just a moment, she let herself believe and then she took a deep breath and returned to reality.

She was a bridesmaid and a wedding planner, and as a friend and a professional, she had a lot to do before the night was over. But it was sure to be a night that she would not forget for some time to come.

Chapter 1

In some ways Sea Kiss was a typical Jersey Shore town. During the summer months the population swelled five-fold thanks to the invasion of the part-time residents and tourists that the locals referred to as Bennys. There were varying explanations for how that term had come about. Some said that in the early 1900s a now non-existent train line had run to Bayonne, Elizabeth, Newark and New York and the tickets had borne the initials of those towns. Still others claimed it was because those tourists would flash their cash in the faces of the locals, Benny referring to Ben Franklin on the tourists' $100 bills.

For many years Emma had been a Benny and it was only thanks to her friendship with her best friend Maggie Sinclair that the locals had befriended her at first. Maggie was a clam digger as the locals would say. The Sinclair family had deep roots in Sea Kiss, Emma thought as she strolled down Main Street toward the beachfront and the Sinclair home.

The early November day was glorious and unseasonably warm. As she walked down the street and the locals shared friendly smiles and waves with her, it was clear that after nearly nine years of living down the Shore, most townspeople had forgotten Emma's Benny status and accepted her as one of their own. That acceptance had its good points and bad, the latter being the intense interest that locals had about their fellow full-time residents.

As she neared the heart of Sea Kiss some of the shopkeepers were taking advantage of the nice weather to have some coffee in front of the bakery before opening their own stores.

"Hey, Em! Why don't you join us?" called out Sammie, the millennial owner of the town's surf and skate shop.

"Yes, please sit and chat," added Jesse, the young widow who owned the cheese shop adjacent to Sammie's store.

Emma paused, and smiled, their invitation appreciated. "I'd love to, but the ladies are waiting for me at Maggie's."

"To plan 'the most epic wedding ever' according to Jon," Sammie said with a chuckle. "Jon" being Jonathan Pierce, the self-made prodigal son surfer dude who had come home to Sea Kiss. Jon was bringing his start-up tech business with him as well as marrying her best friend Connie, she of the hip check that had started the whole bouquet/garter/kiss Carlo problem.

"That's what Carlo and I plan to do," she said with a nod, although worry lurked within that she and Carlo had been a little off lately.

"You always do, Emma. The two of you put together the most amazing weddings," Jesse said and lifted her paper coffee cup in a toast. "I know this one is going to be even more fabulous."

With a laugh and shake of her head, Emma said, "Not too much pressure considering the wedding's only weeks away."

"Is Connie handling it okay? I mean, with moving to Sea Kiss and the baby and all," Sammie asked, real concern in her voice.

Emma nodded. "She's doing great and it'll be nice to have her here. I'd love to keep on chatting, but I've got to go," she said and with a wave, continued the walk toward Maggie's oceanfront home.

But as she passed the bakery's front door, Carlo barreled out, his head buried in the leather notebook he used to keep notes. He stopped short as he realized he was about to plow into someone. Bright color stained his cheeks when he saw her.

"Em, hi . . ." he said and awkwardly mangled the notebook in his hands.

"Hi, yourself," she said and rose on tiptoes to drop a kiss on his cheek, only he had shifted, and she ended up grazing his nose.

"Sorry," they both said at the same time and did a little shuffle back and forth, almost as if trying to get back into step. It was typical of how things had been out of sync between them lately.

With a grimace, Carlo gestured with the notebook toward the bakery. "I was just dropping off an order for bread for a holiday lunch I've got to cater."

Emma nodded and motioned down Main Street. "I was just headed to Maggie's."

"Is that today? I'm sorry, I didn't –"

She laid a hand on his to both stop his apology and to reassure. "No, the planning meeting is not today, Carlo. We're just getting together for breakfast."

Beneath her hand the tension in his body relaxed and spread to the rest of his body. With an easy shrug, he said, "Sorry, again. I seem to be saying that a lot lately."

He did, but then again, so did she. Even their almost daily calls were filled with hesitant delays and off-putting interruptions instead of the fluid chatter and laughter that she had used to eagerly anticipate.

Wanting things to go back to normal, or as normal as could be given the change the kiss had begun, she squeezed his hand and said, "You never forget a thing, Carlo. That hasn't changed. It's why I know I can always count on you."

He sucked in a deep breath and held it for a second before slowly releasing it, his gaze locked on hers the entire time. "It is why you can count on me, Em. For anything."

She nodded. "For anything. So I'll see you tomorrow at Maggie's?"

He dipped his head. "Tomorrow morning. Nine sharp."

"Nine it is," she said and once again rose on tiptoes, this time landing a perfectly chaste kiss on his cheek. But then he shifted, moved downward and brushed a kiss across her lips. It was a barely there kiss that might have otherwise gone unnoticed, only it roused memories of that other kiss. The one that had curled her toes and had her leaning into him, wanting so much more.

Too much more, she thought as she jerked away, feeling the heat that had risen up to her cheeks and ears. Hating that with her pale complexion he was bound to notice the color.

His dimpled grin confirmed that he had, but he playfully tapped her nose and said, "See you tomorrow, *meu amor*."

"Tomorrow for sure," she said and hurried off. But as she took a quick peek back, she caught sight of his determined glance in her direction before he began to chat with Jesse and Sammie. Driving away thoughts of Carlo, she quickened her pace, already running late for breakfast with her friends.

On Ocean Avenue, bright sunlight gleamed off a sea as smooth as glass, but there was a slight chill along the boardwalk from a light ocean breeze.

A chill not unlike the one that would settle between her and Carlo at times ever since that wedding night kiss. A kiss that had unfortunately snared the attention of the locals for a good part of the summer and early fall.

She had been hoping that after the wedding the talk would turn to typical summer things. Which town had won the annual lifeguard contest. How many Bennys had to be pulled from the surf when they ignored the red flag warnings that said it wasn't safe to swim. Instead, "the kiss" seemed to have taken a life of its own for the better half of the summer since the locals were in love with love and eager to see two of their adopted own find their happily-ever-after.

Hopefully the locals would soon latch instead onto Connie and Jonathan's upcoming wedding, as well as the baby they'd be having sometime in late spring. She was looking forward to having Connie around more often in addition to Maggie and her other best friend Tracy. The women were like sisters to her, even though they all couldn't be more different in every which way.

Maggie, whom they teasingly called Mama Maggie, was their rock and the one who everyone went to for advice since she was normally level-headed and responsible. In part it was why her precipitous decision to marry Owen Pierce had shocked all of them. Luckily, it was all working out for her friend.

Connie was the crusader in the group, always watching out for all of them and anyone else who needed help. It was no wonder that she and Jonathan had fallen in love one summer. Everyone could see that Jonathan was like a ship lost at sea that had needed to find the right port to call home. Luckily after years apart Connie and Jonathan had found their way together.

Last but not least, there was Tracy. Drama Queen Tracy, a woman in love with being in love which had resulted in a marriage that had turned out to be a mistake of major proportions. Tracy had looked for love in all the wrong places.

And who are you, Emma? the little voice in her head prodded as Emma neared Maggie's home.

Emma wished she knew. Like Maggie she often found herself doling out advice to anxious brides and her friends. Like Connie she was there to try and fix any problems that came her way. And she hated to admit it, but like

Tracy, she was in love with love. All those traits made her a fabulous wedding planner and friend.

But still not right for Carlo? the little voice in her head challenged.

She ignored the voice as she neared the Sinclair and Pierce mansions which were nestled side-by-side on Ocean Avenue and on the beachfront.

Heart filled with joy that she'd soon be with her friends, she marched up the walk where mums in full bloom lined the path. The bright yellow and pink flowers complimented the joyful colors of the Sinclair's Victorian "painted lady."

Visiting the Sinclair home had always made Emma happy, maybe because it had become her second home of sorts. During her college years she and her friends had spent a great deal of time there with Maggie and her live-in housekeeper, Mrs. Patrick, who was a surrogate grandmother to all of them.

Emma was barely halfway up the walk when Maggie flung the door open wide. Her smile was as bright as the sun-filled day and her blue eyes gleamed with happiness. Connie stood beside Maggie, her smile just as radiant. A second later, Tracy's head popped up behind her other two friends, but there was no real joy there. Tracy's smile was forced and dark circles, like charcoal smudged across drawing paper, gave testament to sleepless nights.

"Hurry up, slow poke. We've been waiting for you," Maggie called out and urged her on with a sweep of her hand.

Emma picked up her pace and had set no more than a foot beyond the threshold when she was enveloped by the warmth of her friends' hugs, kisses, and laughter.

She joined in, chuckling and returning the embraces as they tumbled together like playful puppies toward the kitchen at the back of the house. "Did you ladies start drinking early?" she teased when they broke apart and Mrs. Patrick came up to hug her and drop a kiss on her cheek. The older woman smelled of vanilla and maple which boded well for one of her fabulous waffle breakfasts. Emma's mouth watered in anticipation.

"No drinkie for me, just happy," Connie singsonged and laid her hand over her belly.

"Me, too," Maggie said and at everyone's questioning look, she waved her hands and clarified. "Not preggers, yet. Just really really happy."

Emma joined the other women in helping set the table for breakfast in a routine that was as in step as a well-choreographed ballet after so many years. Of course, Mrs. Patrick was the choreographer, directing them on anything else that was needed for all of them to sit for breakfast while Maggie continued with her story.

"Not only do I have the most awesome new husband," she had to pause here so the other women could sigh, "but business is good too. Sales at my family's suburban stores are way up and the flagship store on Fifth Avenue is packed with families. The store restaurant doesn't have any empty dining reservations until mid-January. It's already paid off the costs of renovating and re-opening it," Maggie gushed without barely taking a breath, excitement in every word.

"That's such wonderful news, Mags," Connie said and hugged her friend.

"That is great," Emma and Tracy chimed in.

A tearful Maggie added, "I couldn't have done it without you ladies. You've been my bedrock through everything."

"We will always be here for you," Connie said and embraced Maggie again, a tell-tale glint in Connie's exotic green-gold eyes. Her hands were laden with the cutlery and napkins to help set the table.

"For each other," Emma stressed and twined her arm through Tracy's. Tension radiated from Tracy's body and it made Emma feel so bad for her dear friend. She glanced up at Tracy who whispered, "I'm okay."

Emma wouldn't press, but clearly all was not right in Tracy's world. It had been painfully obvious to all of them for the better part of a year that no matter how much she put a good face on it, Tracy's marriage was on the rocks and nothing was making it better–not the marriage counseling or the romantic vacations and date nights. It was part of Emma's worst fear—making what was supposed to be a lifetime commitment only to discover it was a colossal mistake. Just like what had happened with her parents.

But the little voice in her head countered with thoughts of Carlo, gorgeous amazing Carlo, and how well they worked together and the many ways he made her feel special and loved. It made her wonder why she thought it was impossible to trust—herself most of all. But she did have good reasons, she reminded herself. There was just too much at stake.

She tightened her hold on Tracy's arm in a gesture meant to reassure before they broke apart to finishing prepping for breakfast. As they worked, they chatted about Connie and Jonathan's surprise engagement just weeks earlier.

"Did you really propose to him?" Tracy asked, still disbelieving and Emma could understand. Connie had always been the most traditional of them not to mention the most career driven. That she had been the one to do the asking was totally unexpected and thoroughly romantic.

"I did propose to him and it was the hardest thing I ever did, besides quitting my job of course," Connie said as she laid out the cutlery.

Emma followed her around the table, placing a plate at each setting. "I never pictured you as the Sea Kiss township attorney, but then again, we've all been involved in a lot of the local projects, so it seems logical." Logical being the thing that lasting relationships were built on, not grand gestures and romance, Emma kept to herself.

Connie paused for a moment, considered the comment, and then nodded. "I never pictured it myself, but somehow it felt right. Especially with Jon so determined to move his corporate headquarters here to bring new blood into town. It's not often you get to be a part of something bigger than life and I'm excited about that."

Tracy set a tray with assorted fruit juices in the center of the table and asked, "Do you think all the house renovations you guys are doing will be done in time?"

With a shrug, Connie returned to her task and said, "I hope so. Jon's hired most of the contractors in the area to work on the headquarters, my new office, and the house. The holidays will be nice for those people."

"Lots of work for lots of people. That's a good thing for Sea Kiss and folks sure do appreciate it," Mrs. Patrick said and laid a plate piled high with waffles on the table. Maggie followed and added a dish with a mound of crispy bacon and pork roll and another smaller tray with syrups and a bowl of fresh berries.

"That's what I hear all around town," Emma said, hoping the locals would treat her friends kindly, but then again, the Pierce family was clam diggers also.

"That's the one thing that worries me. The locals and their talk," Connie admitted as she sat at the table. Connie being an outsider – a Benny—although she'd been coming to Sea Kiss for nearly the last decade and had worked on many projects to help the town through tough times.

"They don't mean anything by it," Mrs. Patrick said at the same time that Emma added with a shrug, "You get used to it." Emma took a spot beside Connie and soon everyone was seated and helping themselves to the delicious meal Mrs. Patrick had prepared.

"Did you?" Maggie questioned with a pointed arch of her brow in Emma's direction. That had Emma wondering if Maggie suspected that she and Carlo were still part of the gossip flitting around town.

"It's just talk and usually nothing major," Emma replied, trying to avoid where their discussion might go. Every one of her friends was squarely in the Carlo camp and let her regularly know that it was time she do something about him.

Maggie was about to follow-up with another question when Tracy said, "Well I have something major to tell you all. I'm divorcing Bill."

Momentary surprise created an almost deafening silence in the room, but then the silence was broken by a peppering of questions and comments.

"When?" Connie said.

"Are you sure?" Maggie added.

"I'm so sorry, my girl," Mrs. Patrick said and laid a reassuring hand over Tracy's as it rested on the table.

"We're here for you," Emma said, not totally surprised by the announcement.

Tracy sucked in a deep breath before the words shot out of her like a volley of gun fire. "When? As soon as you can draw up the papers, Con. Sure, Mags? Never more sure. I'm sorry, too, Mrs. Patrick, but I made a big mistake and nothing I've done has helped change that." With a pause to take another breath, she faced Emma and hugged her hard. "I know you'll all be here for me. It's what's keeping me together."

Connie and Maggie came over to join the embrace and held Tracy as her body vibrated with pain and tears. "You'll be okay, Trace. Everything will be okay," Emma said as she rubbed her friend's back and then glanced up at Connie and Maggie.

Worry etched their faces, but also determination. Together they'd help Tracy through this and in time her wounds would heal.

That's what friends did for each other, she thought, and ignored the little voice in her head that said her friends would be there for her as well if she took a chance with Carlo. She worried nothing could ever make things right if she dared to give in to her Carlo obsession and things didn't work out.

Coward, the little voice in her head shouted, but Emma ignored it as she did so often when it came to Carlo. At least a coward got to live another day.

Chapter 2

Carlo woke to darkness in the early November morning. He closed his eyes again and let himself linger beneath the warmth of the bedcovers. It was a quiet morning, but in the distance he could make out the ding-ding-ding of the NJ Transit bells warning that a train was pulling into the station followed by the toot-toot of the train. Beneath those sounds was the low murmur of the nearby ocean and the sharp bursts of a sea breeze as it buffeted his house.

He was almost always awake before the crack of dawn to take advantage of the peace and calm before the day got hectic. He would get in a quick workout before heading to his office to oversee what needed to be done that day for the events and catering orders his company had been entrusted to handle.

His company, he thought with a smile. He pillowed his head on his hands, stared up at the ceiling, and allowed himself a moment to appreciate all that he'd accomplished in the nearly dozen years since he'd left the family bakery. From one food truck he'd gone to three during the busy summer months with the help of his two younger brothers. A win on one of the food channel challenge programs had brought in a needed infusion of cash from the prize while the publicity had skyrocketed sales. That increase in customers had allowed him to open a full-time catering business. Long hours and lots of hard work had taken him to where he was today with an operation that employed over a dozen people full time and twice as many part-timers when needed.

Not bad, he thought as he slipped from the bed and stretched in the narrow space in his bedroom. The king-sized bed took up nearly the entire room, but he was a big man and couldn't imagine sleeping in anything smaller. He ambled out through a small hall to the kitchen where he prepped an espresso maker for his morning coffee and grabbed the remote to turn on the television just several feet away in the living room. With the push of a few buttons he was watching the financial news to see what the markets were doing and how that might impact his business. Many years earlier a big downturn in the markets had caused many of his customers in the financial sector to tighten their belts, causing him to lose business.

His mother would chide him for being a work-a-holic and starting his day that way. Carlo couldn't deny it, but he was fine with that because it had put him at a place in his life where he could consider doing something different. Like maybe the event planning business Emma and he had discussed some time ago. And maybe even something more with Emma although things had gotten a little awkward with them ever since the kiss months earlier.

He didn't regret the kiss. In fact, the only thing he regretted was having had it take almost nine years since the day he'd first met her and realized that she was the woman who'd be perfect for him. And maybe now, after that kiss, it was time to prove it to her, he thought.

Returning his full attention to the financial news, he was pleased with what he saw and lay down in the center of the narrow living room to do some quick pushups and crunches while the coffee brewed. The smell of it soon filled the small space and the sputter of the espresso pot warned him the coffee was ready. He headed back the few feet to the kitchen where he prepped his morning cup of *café com leite* for that much needed morning rush of caffeine and sugar.

As he sipped his coffee, a news story came on about tiny houses yanking a chuckle from him. Between growing his business and buying a prime lot close to the beach in Sea Kiss, he'd only been able to afford the compact mobile home he'd plopped on the lot to live in until he could one day replace it with a larger house. One that he'd intended to fill with a wife and kids, only the one woman with whom he wanted to share that home was more distant than ever.

For a moment he thought maybe he shouldn't have kissed Emma at the wedding, but he just hadn't been able to resist. He should have known better. He'd told himself that a thousand times since that night, but he hadn't stopped hoping she'd come around. Maybe after Connie and Jonathan's wedding and the holiday break that would follow, Emma would soften up a little and consider that maybe she was entitled to a little love in her life as well.

As *Squawkbox* came on the air, it drew his attention back to the television and he listened for only a few more minutes since he had to get going for a quick jog and shower before heading to work. He chugged down the coffee, dressed in sweats, and raced out the door. Barely an hour later, he was on his way to the warehouse housing his catering business.

He opened the front door and flipped on all the lights. Strolled through the reception area to the kitchens and work areas to make sure all was in order from the work the cleaning crew had done overnight to the walk-in freezers and fridges holding supplies. Then back to the stockrooms where they kept the china, cutlery, linens, tables, chairs, and decorations used for events. Finally, he sauntered toward the front of the building where he, his youngest brother Paolo, and their staff had their workspace.

In his office he perused the large calendar on the wall which was marked up with their events and orders for the upcoming months and smiled. Life was good. The business was doing well and would be busy through the holiday season with a wedding and various holiday parties. There was a slight break in January, which was normal, and then back to work for a number of February weddings. Lots of people loved the idea of a wedding close to Valentine's Day.

Yes, life was definitely good, he thought again, but then the little voice in his said, Except for your non-existent love life.

He drove that niggling idea away and went to work since he only had a couple of hours before an early morning meeting with none other than Emma, Connie, and Jonathan to go over their wedding plans. He had finished making notes for everything that needed to be done when Paolo strolled in for work, his face shadowed by a scruffy beard, hair bed-tousled, clothes rumpled as if he'd slept in them.

"Late night?" Carlo asked and arched a brow, worried that his youngest brother didn't seem to be settling down. Unfortunately, life at the Shore could include a lot of partying.

"*Sim*, but it's not what you think, *mano*. Lily got sick and I spent most of the night at the vet's."

Paolo loved the rescued pit bull that their *avô*, his mother's father, had given him, worried that the youngest wild child needed to become less restless and that maybe the responsibility of owning a dog might help him become more settled.

"I hope Lily will be okay," Carlo said because he liked the scrappy little dog.

Paolo tiredly dropped into a chair in front of Carlo's desk and dragged his fingers through the dark strands of his wavy hair, smoothing it into place. "She will. Vet managed to get out the blockage without surgery, but it was scary for a moment. Makes me wonder how parents handle things that happen like that with their kids, *sabe*."

"*Sim, eu sei. Mamãe* and *papai* had their share of sleepless nights with all of us," Carlo said with a shake of his head.

Paolo chuckled. "They did. Good thing we're all getting old and boring. Except Tomás, but at least he's back in the States for a bit."

Carlo was glad for that because he worried when his bad ass Army Ranger brother Tomás was on a mission. More than once he'd wished that Tomás would also settle down and leave behind his dangerous life.

"Let's hope Tomás finds time to visit his family while he's back," Carlo said and then shifted the talk to work and what needed to be done while he was at his morning meeting. After a quick chat, Carlo was satisfied that Paolo and his staff were ready to handle the chores scheduled for that day and left to go meet Emma, Connie, and Jonathan at the Sinclair mansion.

As he drove through town, he noticed that the Christmas decorations were starting to go up and some of the shops were already boasting holiday trimmings even though Thanksgiving was still a few weeks away. Sea Kiss was getting into the holiday season and he loved the change even if it was a little early. It always made him feel like he was home to see the Christmas spirit coming alive in the quaint Jersey Shore town. Funny considering how different Sea Kiss was from the urban Ironbound section of Newark where he'd grown up. Despite the differences, both places had that special something that made them unique, and Carlo was glad that he'd fled the nest and struck out on his own.

He'd needed his space and to make his own way and that wouldn't have been possible in the Ironbound where everyone knew him and his family and expected him to join the family business unaware of the fact that his younger brothers and he might not be welcome there.

With a sigh, he dispelled that sadness and focused instead on the happy decorations and what he hoped would be even more joyous gatherings. Connie and Jonathan's upcoming wedding was sure to start the holiday season right for all of them, and he had no doubt that it would be perfect.

Perfect was what he and Emma did together because they had a unique kind of alchemy that let them take the most basic idea and transform it into something golden and wondrous. Not that they hadn't had their share of near disasters like the time the baker's delivery truck had gotten into an accident on the way to the wedding. The crash had toppled the multi-tiered cake, but somehow in the few hours before the reception he had managed to piece it back together and hide the damage while Emma had raced out to the bakery for replacement cakes to feed the guests.

He was certain that Emma and he could be perfect together in other ways, whether it was being business partners or lovers. More than once he'd pictured making love with her and he was glad that he'd finally shown her just how he felt with the kiss. He knew they'd put things back to right soon. He missed their almost daily calls and the way they'd used to chat about what was going on in their lives once business was done. He missed just hanging out with Emma after a consult to share a bite and brainstorm ideas for whatever wedding they were working on. Most of all, he just missed seeing her, period.

Fifteen minutes later he wheeled his van into the circular driveway of the Sinclair family mansion and parked behind Emma's Sebring convertible. Connie and her fiancé Jonathan were staying in the Sinclair beach house while renovations were being done to the Pierce family mansion next door.

He glanced over at the newlywed's home-to-be which already looked so different than it had barely a month earlier. The bright colors welcomed and flowers lined the walk, inviting you to stroll up to the front door. That is if you could get past the carpenters, sawhorses, and lumber piled here and there along the walk and lawn. From inside the home came the sounds of whirring saws and men hammering away.

With Connie and Jonathan's wedding barely over a month away, Carlo hoped that the work here and at Jonathan Pierce's new corporate building would be done in time to host the ceremony and reception. Although they had talked about a Christmas wedding, everyone had decided to have the event the first week of December so the families could celebrate the holidays more peacefully.

Which meant he should get his butt in gear and head inside to go over what Connie and Jonathan wanted for their upcoming wedding. Especially since Emma was already here and he was eager to see her. He hopped out of the van and rushed to the door, and it swung open even before he could knock.

Connie stood there, smiling, looking more beautiful than ever with healthy color in her cheeks. Emma had told him during one of their almost daily calls that Connie had been experiencing horrible bouts of morning sickness during the first months of her pregnancy. Now into her third month, Connie looked positively radiant. He could understand how the saying about pregnant women glowing had come about. An aura of joy and peace surrounded her.

"*Hola*, Connie," he said and dropped a friendly peck on her cheek.

"How are you, *mi amigo?*" she said and hugged him.

With a quick glance at Emma as she stood beside the kitchen table with Jonathan, he said, "I could be better."

Connie tracked his gaze and nodded. "Don't give up on her." Wrapping her arm around his, Connie led him into the house. "We've been waiting for you."

They walked together through the parlor and into the kitchen where Emma and Jonathan stood by the table, seemingly in a deep discussion.

"Hey, Carlo," Jonathan shouted out and hurried over to give him a big bro hug and clasp his hand in greeting.

"Hey, yourself. I hope I didn't miss much," he said but it looked like Emma had only just started laying out wedding invitation samples on the table.

"Not a thing, but you know the world's best wedding planner is way anal," Jonathan teased Emma as he always did and returned to sit beside her at the table.

"I am totally anal – I prefer perfectionist by the way—because I'm so looking forward to ending your days of bachelorhood," Emma taunted right back and playfully poked him in the ribs.

"It will be my pleasure," Jonathan replied with a loving glance at Connie who slipped to her fiancé's side for a kiss that raised the temperature in the room by a few degrees.

"Break it up, kids," Emma said playfully, but then cursed as her portfolio fell onto its side and disgorged a mound of samples onto the floor.

Carlo bent at the same time Emma did and they barely avoided bumping heads as they gathered the invites into a pile. His hand brushed hers and heat blasted through him. As she jerked her hand away her gaze locked on his, full of confusion and yearning. It was a look he'd seen before on the night of Maggie's wedding. On the night of that kiss and after.

"Thank you," she said as they finished gathering the invites and rose together slowly. As their arms brushed, they jumped apart and quickly turned their attention to their two friends.

Jonathan and Connie were arm-in-arm and smiling, obviously in love.

"Time to get to work and plan the most epic wedding ever," Emma said and motioned for their friends to come look at the invitations.

"Yes, let's get to work," Carlo said in the solemn and measured tone he reserved for clients and wedding guests. A tone that he'd unfortunately found himself using way too much around Emma lately.

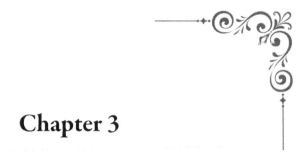

Chapter 3

Emma hated that Carlo could be so controlled, especially now when her own emotions were a whirlwind of need, confusion, and regret all crazily gyrating around him.

Connie must have sensed the vibes since she laid a hand on Emma's back and stroked it reassuringly. "Let's get this party started."

"Connie and I talked about this and we want to keep the wedding small," Jonathan said.

"Intimate," Emma suggested.

"Definitely intimate," Connie replied with a chuckle. "About sixty. Family, close friends, and some key business acquaintances."

Emma gestured with her head in the direction of the Pierce mansion. "Could we get a look next door to see if the space will work for that many?"

Jonathan nodded. "It will, I think." A second later, his cellphone chirped and after a quick glance at the screen, he said, "I have to take this."

He stepped away into the parlor while Emma said, "We'll be moving people to and from the new corporate center."

Carlo had noticed the brochures in the materials that had spilled out of Emma's portfolio and in sync with where she was going, he shifted them in front of Connie. "These are local companies that have trolleys we could use for the transportation. But I think we could also –"

"Showcase Jon's Pierce electric vehicles," Emma jumped in and Carlo smiled and put up his hand for a high five.

Emma grinned and slapped his hand while Connie shook her head. "I swear you're twins separated at birth with the way you think alike."

"Great minds," Emma said with a chuckle.

Carlo nodded and said, "I don't think you chose a theme yet—"

Connie shook her head and waved her hands. "Not a clue about the theme."

"The trolleys fit in with the quaint nature of Sea Kiss," Carlo said and Emma added, "As well as Jon's motor vehicle company."

"The old way of moving people and Jon's new way melding together," Connie said wistfully.

"Love the trolleys," Jonathan said as he walked back in and noticed the brochures on the table. "I remember riding in one with my mom as a kid. Unfortunately, Connie and I have to go. That call was from the contractor working on Connie's new office. He's got a problem and needs us there so we can make some decisions."

Emma shared a glance with Carlo and it was clear he understood what she intended. "If you guys trust us –"

"We do. Without hesitation," Connie said and Jonathan nodded in agreement.

"Totally, Em. Carlo," he said.

"Emma and I can take a look next door and come up with ideas," Carlo replied.

"Great. And after you do that, meet us at the corporate center. I'd like to talk to you about helping out with a press conference in about two weeks. It'll be a good test run for the wedding," Jonathan said.

Carlo peered intently at Emma, once again understanding even before she said it. "I'll have to check with Evelyn and Lucy about working on the press conference. I don't see why not, but the bosses will make the call."

"Which is why it's high time for you to think about your own company," Connie chided, but Carlo jumped in to defend her. "I'm sure Emma will work things out."

"Yes, I will. Thank you, Carlo," she said, reached out and squeezed his hand in gratitude, but that simple touch made his gut clench with need.

But Connie was like a pit bull and was about to say something else when Jonathan squeezed her waist gently. "Let's get going, babe. I'm sure Emma and Carlo can't wait to go next door to check things out and come up with epic wedding plans."

Connie met Emma's gaze and relented. "Yes, let's go. We'll meet you at the corporate center later."

Jonathan reached into his pocket and took out a ring of keys. "This will get you into the center. The men are at work next door and will let you in."

Carlo rose and snatched the key from Jonathan. "We'll see you later," Jonathan said and guided Connie from the room and out of the house.

When the snick of the front door confirmed that the couple had left, Emma chuckled softly and said, "Not too much pressure, right?"

Carlo shook his head and laughed. "To quote Jon, 'Gnarly.' But we've handled harder weddings."

She pointed a finger at him in confirmation. "Like Sidney the Bridezilla. Don't forget we've got to meet with her next week."

Carlo rolled his eyes. "How could I forget? How about we think about something more pleasant and go check out next door?"

"I'd like nothing better," she said, rose, and Carlo followed suit. As she walked to the front door, he placed a hand on the small of her back, the gesture both possessive and reassuring. She let herself bask in those feelings as they walked into the chilly ocean breeze and quickly crossed the lawn to the Pierce mansion.

The sounds of men working got louder as they approached the front door which was wide open. As they stepped inside one of the men installing flooring stopped working, stood, and looked in their direction.

The laborer was a hard-muscled young blond and a broad smile worked across his face as he saw them. "*Hola*, Carlo. What's up, *mano*?" he said and walked over to shake Carlo's hand.

"Miguelito. I didn't know you were working here," Carlo said and introduced the man. "Emma, Miguelito is an old friend from my lunch truck days."

He shook Emma's hand and flashed her a grin that might have been devastating if she was interested. But her sole interest was in the dark-haired, dark-eyed man beside her which must have apparent to the handsome laborer.

"How can I help you two?" Miguelito said.

Emma glanced around the space and worry speared through her. With only a month left before the wedding, it seemed like there was still a lot of work to do. Motioning to the space with her hand, she said, "Will this be ready by the first week of December?"

"*El Jefe* wants it ready, so it'll be ready," Miguelito confirmed with a nod. "We'll be done with the floor by tomorrow. After that, Jon wants us to build a dais where the kitchen island will eventually go. He started drawing something and left it over on the counter," he said and jerked his head in the direction of the vintage cherry cabinets. Connie had mentioned to her that Jon had salvaged them from an older Victorian home in town that was being torn down. The new owners wanted something more modern and township officials had been unable to certify the nearly two century old building as a landmark in order to avoid demolition.

"Watch your step," Miguelito said and gestured to the pipes near the cabinets where Emma assumed the island peninsula would go.

Emma and Carlo strode over to the kitchen area where assorted blueprints and papers sat on the white marble countertop. Emma flipped through some papers until she came to the partial design for the dais that Jonathan had hand drawn. She shifted the drawing so Carlo could see it.

"It looks familiar," he said and then quickly added, "Is that the back of Maggie's house?"

Emma sighed as she perused the partial design. "It's the balcony from Maggie's. When Jon and Connie first met he'd climb up the wisteria vine and up to the balcony to see Connie."

"Very romantic and the perfect theme. A summer romance, don't you think?" Carlo said. He turned, faced the space, and held his hands up like a movie director framing a scene. "The balcony dais will go right where we we're standing and we can have rows of chairs dressed in white with terra cotta pots filled with flowers at the end of each row."

His vision melded with hers as if often did. "Maybe even a grass runner down the aisle for a more outdoor look," she said. Stepping back to face the kitchen cabinets, she motioned to them. "We can ask Sylvia to paint a backdrop and place it here to make it look like the beachfront."

Carlo nodded. "For sure. And you have a wedding invite that opens like a garden gate, don't you? It would be perfect."

She smiled and hugged him hard. "This is going to be so epic!"

"It is, isn't it?" he said and prolonged the embrace, providing comfort that Emma hadn't really known she needed, but obviously did. While things were going well for her friends, except for Tracy, her life was still the same.

Some might say that was a good thing, but lately she had started feeling that it wasn't. Something was missing from her work life and of course, her love life.

But she had her friends and Carlo. That made it all bearable she thought as she savored the comfort of Carlo's embrace. Long seconds later they broke away from the hug, both laughing and smiling.

"This is going to be the most epic wedding ever," she said and hugged Carlo once again, caught up in wedding happiness, and wishing nothing but joy for her friends. She hoped that she and Carlo could deliver on their promise to provide a perfect event. She also let herself hope that she and Carlo could survive all the happiness without any further challenges to their relationship.

As they were walking toward the front door, Miguelito called Carlo over. Carlo excused himself and went to chat with the other man. It was obvious part of the discussion was about her, which was a little troubling. As Miguelito raised his hands in a gesture that said Hands Off/I Surrender, Carlo smiled, clapped the other man on the back and then returned to her side.

"What was that about?" she asked as Carlo once again laid a hand on her back, the gesture rousing emotions once more.

"One of our friends is opening a place in Asbury. The soft launch is tomorrow night and Miguelito thought we might want to go," he explained and guided her in the direction of his van at the curb.

"We? What kind of place?" she asked even though there was a little worry there about what going with him might mean. They'd spent a lot of time together in all the years they'd worked with each other. They chatted often, sometimes daily, but had never been on a real date.

"A new restaurant. Over on Bangs. What do you think?" he said as slipped into the driver's seat and wrapped his hands around the steering wheel, clenching and unclenching his fingers on it with obvious unease.

Saying yes was risky. Saying yes might change what was going on between them, much like the kiss that had shaken up the ground beneath their feet. But friends went to places together, she told herself. Things didn't need to change radically, just a little.

And maybe a little change was better than staying a coward and stuck in the same place where she'd been for so long.

"I think I'd like that. I can meet you there," she said with a reluctant smile.

Carlo chuckled, glanced in her direction, and grinned. With a nod of understanding, he said, "I'll meet you there, *meu amor*. How does eight o'clock sound?"

"It sounds wonderful," she said and tried not to acknowledge that something inside of her felt freer, more hopeful, than she'd felt in a long time.

CARLO LEANED AGAINST the brick wall outside of *Havana Lotus*, the Chino Latino restaurant his friend was opening. It was located on an avenue in Asbury Park that was on the edges of the ongoing gentrification of a city that some people were calling Brooklyn on the Beach. The restaurant's building looked like it had been recently renovated, but across the street and on the next avenue many of the buildings were still in various stages of destruction and construction.

He peered down the block one way and then another, searching for Emma, but she wasn't anywhere in sight. Instead bearded and tattooed hipsters, boomers, and gay couples strolled along the avenue, milled around the entrance to the restaurant, and drifted in and out of the building. As another group came around the corner, he recognized Miguelito and a few of the other young men he'd come to know from his days on the food truck route and his catering business.

While Miguelito was Cuban, the rest of the group was a mix of Colombians, Mexicans, and Peruvians from the area. As they approached and noticed him, they walked over and greeted him. "*Hola*, Carlos," one of the men said, forgetting that his mother had used the Italian form of his name because she'd had a thing for Italian actors when he and his brothers been born.

"*Hola*, Egecatl. How are you?" Carlo said to the short and stocky Peruvian. His burnished copper skin was a testament to his indigenous heritage.

"*Muy bien*. Miguelito here has me working for *El Jefe*," Egecatl replied and clapped the young contractor on the back. A second later, he and the rest of the group strolled into the restaurant, leaving Miguelito behind.

"*El Jefe*, huh?" Carlo said and eyeballed Miguelito.

"We can't all be best buds with the rich guys," Miguelito said and shrugged.

Carlo chuckled and shook his head. "Jon and Owen are good guys," he reminded his friend although wealthy, business types tended to be his customers and not his friends. But he'd felt immediately at ease around Jonathan and Owen Pierce, maybe because they had so many things in common. Much like the four very different women who were as good as sisters.

"They are, but they're not like us, *mano*," Miguelito said and jerked his head down the block where there was still no sign of Emma. "Did she stand you up?"

Carlo shot a quick look at his watch, but as he looked up, he noticed Emma rounding the corner. "And here she is, *mano*," he said and jabbed the other man in the ribs.

Miguelito snorted and said, "Another ten pounds and she'd be perfect, but you're still a lucky man."

Carlo chuckled at the old joke. His father would probably say Emma needed another twenty pounds, but he loved every lean and elegant curve of her body.

She walked up to them, a big smile on her face and bright color on her cheeks. Her green eyes glittered with excitement. "Have you been waiting long?" she said as she brushed a quick kiss on his cheek and then on Miguelito's.

"No," he said at the same time his friend mumbled "Forever." Which earned him another jab in the ribs from Carlo.

"You ready to go in?" Carlo asked and gestured to the restaurant's entrance with his head.

"Ready as I'll ever be," she said. They left Miguelito waiting for another friend and entered together. Immediately inside the door, the owner of the restaurant was greeting guests and smiled as he noticed Carlo.

"*Mano*, I wasn't expecting you," the man said and bro hugged Carlo.

"You should have let me know," Carlo chided and wrapped an arm around the shorter man's shoulder.

The owner seemed chagrined and dipped his head. "Wasn't sure a big celebrity chef like you –"

"*Mano*, stop that shit and let me introduce my . . . friend," Carlo said, hoping Emma wouldn't notice his hesitation.

Friend, Emma thought and wanted to cringe, but then again, it seemed like neither of them knew what to call their relationship. If they even had something you could call a relationship.

Recovering from the possible gaffe, Carlo laid a hand at the small of her back and urged her toward the young Chinese restaurant owner. "Emma, this is Eddie Lee. His family owns the best Cuban Chinese restaurant in all of Jersey. We've known each other since we were kids."

She shook the man's hand and said, "So nice to meet you and congratulations on the new place." Looking around, she noticed that the restaurant had a really Latin vibe with lots of dark woods, but brightly colored fabrics and paintings in a more Asian-style. In a far corner a trio of musicians in gleaming white shirts and panama hats were softly playing Cuban music.

"Nice to meet you, too. I've heard you and Carlo put on some amazing weddings," Eddie said and then held his arm wide in invitation. "*Mi casa es su casa*. Eat, drink, and enjoy."

"Thanks, Eddie, and all the best on the new place. I know we'll be back," she said and shot a quick look up at Carlo who nodded in agreement.

"Good luck, Eddie," Carlo said and hugged the man again before they threaded their way through the crowd inside the restaurant and over to the bar. A bartender was pouring samples of *mojitos, caipirinhas,* and *sangria.*

"White *sangria* for me," she said while Carlo went for one of the *cachaça*-based *caipirinhas.*

She raised her glass for a toast and said, "To friends."

Carlo grimaced, possibly recalling his earlier hesitation, but then raised his glass and tapped it to hers. "To friends and *to us*, Emma."

"To us," she added, hopeful for what that might mean for them.

As they shifted away from the congested bar, she realized assorted waiters were working their way through the crowd, offering food samples.

Carlo and she stopped and took the first offering which looked like an egg roll of some kind, but as she took a bite, she realized it was filled with a citrusy pork, rice, and black bean mixture. Almost like a burrito.

"Delicious," she said and finished off the tidbit. She leaned close to him to combat the noise in the place and said, "I've never had Chino Latino or Cuban Chinese food before." As a different waiter came by, she took another sample. Bacon wrapped around a sweet plantain.

Carlo grabbed a plantain as well and ate it in one bite. "You wouldn't get this in a Cuban Chinese place. That's either Cuban or Chinese food and not this fusion."

Emma nodded in understanding. "You said Eddie's family has a restaurant?"

With a dip of his head, Carlo snagged another sample from another waiter. A taco filled with a Korean style *bulgogi* and a daikon slaw. Dipping his head close to her ear, he explained. "Eddie's grandparents fled Cuba in the Sixties. They opened the restaurant in Union City and became customers of my family's bakery in the Ironbound."

"This is tasty," she said and murmured her appreciation of the small fusion taco. "So your family was already in Newark?"

Carlo nodded and sipped his drink. "We came here in the 1920s through Ellis Island. What about your family?" he asked and it occurred to her that in all the years they'd known each other, they'd never really gotten personal in this kind of way.

"American-style mutt here. My mom is Irish and Italian. Explains the strawberry blonde," she explained and sipped her *sangria*. The white wine was blended perfectly with citrus and sweet bits of strawberries and peaches.

"And your dad?" he asked and exerted some gentle pressure on her back to guide her to some seats that had opened up at a nearby table.

Her dad had been a dick and worse and she usually avoided talking about him if she could. Carlo must have sensed her hesitation since he expertly changed the subject. "So what do you think about the restaurant? Give you any ideas for Connie and Jon? Anglo Latino fusion stations during the cocktail hour?" he teased and grinned. His dark eyes were bright with humor.

The grin and glimmer warmed her insides so she took a sip of wine to cool the heat and after a pause said, "Like Cuban-style roast pork cheesesteaks?"

Carlo chuckled. "I like that idea. Baked potatoes with chorizo and manchego toppings?"

Emma smiled. "Yummy! I love *chorizo*."

Carlo raised his glass. "This dynamic duo is going to rock Connie and Jon's wedding."

With a slow deliberate motion, Emma lifted her almost empty glass and tapped it to his. "We are good together," she said and knew in her heart that it wasn't just about working with him no matter how much taking the next step scared her.

Carlo clearly understood. "So maybe we can think about being better together in other ways?"

"Maybe," she said with a hesitant nod, surprising herself and obviously Carlos as well. He narrowed his eyes to examine her, as if to judge if she was really serious. But a second later the band launched into a fast salsa beat and the couple next to them jumped up to dance, knocking into Carlos and shattering the moment.

Carlo slowly rose and held out his hand. "So how about we take that next step right now?"

Emma gulped and felt heat rush up to her cheeks. "Now? As in –"

"Dance with me," he said and wiggled his fingers in invitation.

Emma skipped her gaze from Carlo to the couples by the band. The trio had added a few more members who were playing a number of different percussion instruments and a trumpet player. There were several couples dancing expertly to the catchy beats, but also some who were doing the equivalent of the drunk dad dance, giving her hope that she could avoid being completely embarrassed if she tried.

She stood and grabbed hold of his hand but walked with a cautious pace until they reached the area where everyone was dancing. Carlo tugged on her hand to urge her near and placed his hand on her waist. "It's not that hard," he whispered in her ear.

But it seemed impossible to her as she struggled to find the beat and match his movements as he began to dance, fluidly and expertly. Especially as his muscular body teased hers, bringing thoughts of having him move against her as they made love.

"Just trust me," he said again and started to count out a beat, but when she stomped on his foot for the third time, she pulled away from his embrace. Self-conscious heat flooded her face.

Wrapping her arms around herself defensively, she said, "I'm sorry. I've got two left feet."

Carlo smiled and stroked his big hand down her back, the gesture reassuring. "Don't worry. Trust me, it'll happen."

As they walked back and found they'd lost their seats, Emma shot a rueful look at him. "Seems like we need to find another spot."

But the restaurant had gotten even more congested and noisy as more and more people came in to sample the free drinks and food samples.

"Maybe we should go," Carlo said and Emma had to agree. The intimacy she had felt at first with their small talk and getting to know each other had been replaced with the unease from the noisy crowd and the awkwardness of their dance.

On the sidewalk outside they weaved past the line of people waiting to enter and Carlo said, "I'll walk you to your car." She appreciated it since being on the fringes of gentrification also meant the area wasn't necessarily the safest at later hours.

She drifted close to him as he wrapped an arm around her waist and they walked, hips bumping occasionally. The pace comfortable and unrushed despite the chill of the November night and a breeze that swept up the avenues from the beachfront, forcing her ever closer to him for warmth until they reached her car.

At her driver door, she jiggled her keys in her hand and vacillated about leaving him until she told herself not to push. It was still too soon and despite their earlier assertion to maybe be better together, it was hard to lose years of fear and uncertainty overnight. But she wanted to end the night on a positive note, disastrous salsa dance notwithstanding.

"I had a nice time. Thanks for asking me to come tonight," she said and laid a hand on his cheek. His beard was rough against her palm and his skin slightly chilled.

He covered her hand with his and stroked it gently. "I had a nice time, too. Maybe we could do this again?"

"Go to another restaurant opening?" she teased and grinned.

"Or maybe a regular restaurant? When things settle down after all the weddings we've got scheduled?" he said and once again stroked her hand.

"I'd like that," she said, grateful for the slight reprieve that the few weeks until the weddings would give her time to adjust to a possible change in their relationship.

"Great. Text me when you get home, okay?" he said.

She nodded, unlocked her door and slipped in. He waited until she was settled before walking back to the curb and watching her drive away. As she glanced in the rear-view mirror and he got further and further away, his absence replaced the comfort she'd felt earlier in his presence.

It brought back the earlier fear she'd managed to force away. The fear of what would happen if things went wrong in their relationship and it drove them apart. If she felt his absence now, at just the start of something different, how much worse would it be if they truly became close?

She sucked in a breath and once again buried that concern. It would accomplish nothing and it was time she tried to be more positive about what could happen between them. It was the only way to heal what had been broken inside of her by her family's dysfunctional past.

It was only by healing that a man like Carlo could learn to love someone like her.

Chapter 4

Emma gritted her teeth and forced back a grimace as the bride lashed out at her husband-to-be as the couple sat across from her and Carlo in Emma's office at the bridal salon.

"William, we really need to be more conscious of what we're eating," the bridezilla said and glared at the finger sandwich in her fiancé's hand. Carlo had prepared the snacks for their final meeting as a sample of the appetizers the bridezilla had requested for the cocktail hour at the rehearsal dinner.

"I promise you that those sandwiches are about as healthy as you can get. It's whole grain bread and minced watercress with oil and vinegar. I hope it's just what you had in mind," Carlo interjected in a calming tone, obviously trying to defuse the situation.

"You had a wonderful idea having such light fare for your guests. So many people are health conscious now," Emma added, trying to placate the woman as well.

"Health is very important to me. To *us*," Sidney belatedly tacked on. She glared at her fiancé who joined in with, "Sidney is the queen at her gym—"

"Health and wellness center," Sidney corrected.

Blotches of red erupted across William's face and he stammered his apology. "O-of course, Sidney. Health and wellness are your life."

"*Our* life," the bride-to-be challenged again, earning another stumbling apology.

Emma was convinced nothing the man could say would be right. As Emma's gaze skipped across Carlo's, it was obvious he also felt sorry for the other man. He leapt to William's rescue in much the same way he came to her aid when things were going south.

"Emma and I understand how important being fit is to you both. We will work hard to make sure what we serve your guests is both nutritious and tasty," he said.

The bride-to-be did a once over of her groom's physique, but before she could utter another nasty word, Emma said, "Your fitness ethic is apparent in how wonderful you both look. You are going to be the most lovely couple we've ever had."

Sidney preened with the compliment, fluffing her hair with one hand. "Thank you, Emma. I'm so glad you understand how important it is for you to deal with all my requests."

"We totally understand, Sidney. We assure you this will be the wedding that everyone will be talking about for years," Emma said, although not for the reasons the bridezilla thought. If Sidney kept up her bullying routine through the ceremony and reception, there would be talk for sure.

"Let's just do a last review of all the details to make sure we're all on the same page," Emma said and Carlo seconded her request.

The discussion continued, but it was laced with barely laced barbs toward the prospective groom and Emma wondered why he would take it. But then again, hadn't her own life and her mother's been similar? Before he'd left for good, her father had hardly ever had a kind word for either of them. Even his praise had been nothing more than backhanded compliments and yet they'd suffered through them for years. Too many years.

Because of that, as Sidney's list of demands grew and grew together with her putdowns, Emma's temper rose until it was all she could do to hold back her anger. And then Sidney pushed her right over the edge.

"I have my own hairdresser and make-up people coming to assist me the morning of the wedding. I'm hoping you can get William some assistance so he looks properly groomed."

A BRIGHT PINK FLUSH was riding high on Emma's face and there was no mistaking she was about to lose it, Carlo thought. It was something Emma never did and he wondered at the reason for her upset. He laid a hand over Emma's as it rested on the table. She trembled with anger and he squeezed gently, attempting to calm her as he said, "We can assist William that morning although it's much easier for us gentleman to prepare."

Emma's color flushed a deeper rose and he squeezed her hand again to keep her grounded. "Both Emma and I," he began, with emphasis to reiterate their partnership and more, "will make sure all is in order for your wedding."

"I'm sure you will," Sidney said and cast a dismissive look at Emma. She slowly rose and William shot up out of his chair and followed the bridezilla from the room.

Once the door had closed, what sounded suspiciously like a low growl erupted from Emma before she said, "I despise that woman."

He understood. "Just think—in a few days it will all be over and we won't have to deal with her again."

"But he will," she said with surprising vehemence. "He will have to take that abuse day in and day out until it whittles him away to a big fat zero."

Carlo couldn't miss that there was something more going on that had nothing to do with the bitchy bride. "This is really bothering you, isn't it?"

She shrugged and looked away, but he cupped her chin gently and urged her back to face him. Her distress was apparent, both from the traces of color on her cheeks to the threat of tears shimmering in her gaze.

"Please tell me, Emma. Tell me why you're so upset."

EXPLAINING TO HIM WOULD open a crack in the walls she had erected to hide her pain and to keep her secrets. The wall had also served to keep him away but maintaining that façade had done nothing to erase the memories and bring her relief, so maybe it was time to share her past with him. Maybe by doing so she could let go of it and build a future free of that hurt.

"She reminds me of my father. Before he left us, he was always picking on my mom and me about one thing or another. If something broke, it was because we hadn't handled it properly. If I brought home an A minus, he was disappointed because it wasn't an A plus. We couldn't dress right, speak right, or do anything right. What few compliments he gave were bundled together with criticism," she said, the words rushing from her mouth as a torrent of tears slipped down her face, hot against her skin.

Carlo scooted his chair over and gripped her hand tightly. His gaze was pained and filled with sorrow as he reached up with his free hand and gently skimmed away her tears. "I'm so sorry, Emma. I didn't mean to make you sad."

She shook her head and wiped away her sniffles with the back of her hand. "It's not you, Carlo." It's never you, she wanted to say. He was one of the few things in her life that had been good and happy. Carlo, her mom, and her friends were bright points of light and joy for her.

"I wish . . ." He paused, clearly searching for the right words, but there were none. There was nothing that could change how her father had made her feel. Or the betrayal that had come later and made her so hesitant to trust a man and kept her from being able to love a wonderful man like Carlo.

"I know there's nothing that can change the past, but . . . Not all men are like that," he said, but she understood what he was really saying. *I'm not like that.*

"My mom told me once that he wasn't that way when they were dating or first got married. That it kind of just happened little by little."

Carlo, ever perceptive, cradled her cheek and said, "Which makes you wonder if it was something you or your Mom did to make him that way. But that's just making excuses for him, isn't it?"

His words were logical. Supportive even and yet she found anger rising up inside her again. "Don't you think I know that? Don't you think that I wish I could stop feeling like this and move on with my life?" Move on so that she could learn to love and trust a man like Carlo as both a lover and business partner.

Her words and their hurt vibrated in the air between them. She held her breath, waiting for a backlash. Waiting for rage like that which would erupt from her father if she challenged him. Instead, Carlo smiled tenderly and swiped his thumb across her cheek once more, the touch soothing and tender. He leaned forward, laid his forehead against hers and whispered, "I'm a patient man, Emma. I'll be waiting for you no matter how long it takes."

"What if it's never?" she wanted to say as he wrapped his arms around her and pulled her close. But for now, she let herself bask in the warmth of his embrace and let herself believe that he would wait. That he would be there if she ever got her act together. And if she didn't . . . .

She didn't want to think about that possibility.

Chapter 5

They survived the bridezilla rehearsal dinner and wedding because it turned out Sidney was like Jekyll and Hyde, full of charm and sunshine in public unlike the very nasty persona they'd seen during their private encounters. Emma recognized the pattern and was surprised she hadn't picked up on it before since her father had been much the same way. People would always tell her how nice he was because he hid the monster well.

The wedding ceremony and reception rolled along without a hitch with everyone smiling and enjoying the day, even the beleaguered groom. She hoped that his life with Sidney would turn out to be better than hers had been up until the day her father had left. Of course, her father's departure had caused even more havoc in their lives, but she fought back that unhappiness and plastered a smile on her face as the final guests left the ballroom of the country estate where the wedding had been held.

She did a slow spin around to check out the ballroom. Carlo was in one corner, directing his crew on what to do about the breakdown of the area. His team would have to cart away china, glasses, and cutlery as well as the decorations and flowers that had been left behind. In the morning she would run by his warehouse to pick up the flowers and drop them off at various assisted living and senior facilities where they would brighten someone's day.

She walked over to where he stood, finishing up the instructions for his staff. As his people walked away and he saw her, he smiled, his brown eyes glittering with joy as they settled on her. His smile warmed her, as it always did, and washed away some of the tiredness in her body and her soul.

"We did it," she said and hugged him. She lingered in his embrace, savoring the peace it brought.

"Yes, we did. Chalk up another one for the Dynamic Duo," he teased and swung her around playfully in his strong arms.

"Stop, you crazy man!" she said, but as he settled her on her feet again, their gazes met and the moment slowly morphed into more.

She reached up, cradled his cheek, and ran her thumb across the five o'clock shadow there and then across his lips. "Thank you for everything. This was a tough one."

"I know," he said and mimicked her action, his calloused fingers gentle against her face. He drifted his thumb across her lips in a touch as potent as any kiss and her insides twisted with need. Heat built inside her and she swayed ever closer and tilted her face upward, wanting more.

"Carlo," she began and rose on tiptoes, but was interrupted by Paolo, Carlo's younger brother, as he shouted out to snare Carlo's attention.

"*Mano*, we need you out back," Paolo yelled and stuck his head in through the doors to locate his brother.

A heavy sigh escaped Carlo and he wagged his head with regret as he eased out of their embrace. The absence of his comfort and strength came immediately. "I'm sorry. I have to go," he said and dropped a quick kiss on her cheek before he rushed away.

She watched him leave and whispered, "I'm sorry, too." As much as she needed to resist him until she could sort out her feelings, it was becoming difficult to do so. But it was also not fair to let their relationship founder like a ship tossed up against the Sea Kiss jetties, caught in the tides and repeating the same senseless pounding against the rocks until it broke apart and sank. If their relationship, business or otherwise, was to stay afloat, she needed to decide what she wanted.

Luckily, there was only one more wedding to go before a break for the holidays. After Connie and Jonathan's big day, she was going to have to find a way either to deal with her feelings for Carlo or go Carlo-free on a personal level for both their sakes. It was the only fair thing to do.

AS SOON AS CARLO PUSHED through the doors of the ballroom and they were out of Emma's sight, he playfully cuffed Paolo across the back of his head.

"*Cabrão*, didn't you see we needed a little privacy," he complained, frustrated at being interrupted just when Emma might actually be thawing.

Paolo rubbed his head and chuckled. "*Mano*, you never learn. She's just like Sasha. You're headed into another dark hole because Emma will never give you what you want."

Carlo grimaced at the mention of his old flame. They'd been involved for years and she'd expected him to join the family business so she would be set for life. For months after he'd decided to take a risk by buying his food truck, she'd bitched and moaned and complained, trying to get him to change his mind and be what she wanted instead of understanding his dreams. He'd finally had enough and ended the relationship.

"Emma is nothing like Sasha," he said and kept on walking toward the vans waiting to transport their equipment back to the warehouse.

"Sasha wanted what she wanted. Emma may not be selfish and impatient like Sasha, but she's a 'career woman,' who wants what she wants," Paolo said with some disdain and slapped Carlo on the back. "You need to find a nice Portuguese girl who'll be at home waiting for you with a nice *feijoada*. Make pretty babies so *mamãe* will stop complaining."

Carlos chuckled and shook his head, playfully nudging his brother with his shoulder. "You are a Neanderthal. And *mamãe* already has four gorgeous grandbabies."

"But not from her own sons," his brother said, digging up yet another painful part of his past.

Luckily, they had arrived at the vans and Carlo made short work of instructing the crew on how to get things packed. Unfortunately the over-the-top centerpieces the florist had made based on the bride's demands wouldn't all fit in the first load, so they'd have to do a second trip for those as well as some of the serving pieces they'd used for the elaborate dessert tables the bride had also insisted on.

Once his crew had returned to work in the loading area, Carlo hurried back into the ballroom to oversee the rest of the breakdown and hopefully return to where Emma and he had been when Paolo had rudely interrupted. Unfortunately, Paolo followed him and like a dog with a bone, his brother revived their earlier conversation. "Admit it, Carlo. You need to find someone else and soon. You're not getting any younger, *sabe*. *Mamãe* needs those *bebes*!" Paolo said and mimicked rocking a child in his strong arms.

Carlo stopped dead and jammed his hands on his hips. He faced his brother and with an exasperated sigh said, "*Mamãe* loves those grandbabies as if they were her own, just like she loves our older brothers as if they were her own."

"Half-brothers," Paolo corrected and then plunged on. "*Avô* never let us forget that *his* daughter didn't have us and that the bakery *wasn't* ours."

"*Avô* was a jerk. Papa would have gladly taken us into the business with Ricardo and Javier." And while that grandfather, the father of his father's first wife, might have objected, his two older brothers wouldn't have had a problem, or at least he had hoped not.

"Maybe," Paolo said with a shrug. "But don't tell me that isn't why you decided to start your own business. And don't tell me *mamãe* isn't dying for one of us to get married and start giving her more grandbabies."

"So I won't tell you," he said and pushed on toward the ballroom, not only tired of the discussion, but wishing that Paolo's words didn't bring to mind an image of his and Emma's future child, a fantasy he'd been having since they'd all found out that Connie and Jonathan were expecting. Which made him rush even faster toward the ballroom in the hopes of catching Emma before she left.

Unfortunately, she was gone, leaving him feeling empty inside. It was a feeling he'd had before thanks to Sasha's actions. But much like he'd hoped years earlier that Sasha would support him and love him for the man he was and not the man she wanted him to be, he knew that he had to do something to try and either move along the relationship with Emma or move along without her. In some ways Paolo was right that he was in another possibly hopeless situation. He didn't like being in that position again necessarily, but it also didn't stop him from smiling as he imagined a baby with Emma's strawberry blonde locks and beautiful emerald eyes and he dreamed of what could be.

EMMA STROLLED UP AND down the rows of gowns in the bridal salon's storeroom, searching for a few more wedding gowns that she thought Connie might like and which would suit her friend's body type and coloring. She had already selected her top three picks the day before, but she wanted to give Connie a number of gowns to choose from. She avoided anything that had too many ruffles, lace, or frou frou embellishments because that just wasn't her friend's style. Despite that, she did want something feminine and dreamy and elegant for her friend's special day. She ignored one section of the storeroom because the colors would not go well with her friend's olive skin and dark hair. After about an hour she had selected another three dresses that would best suit Connie and took them out to the consultation room. Connie would be there shortly along with Maggie and Tracy and Emma couldn't wait to see what the bride-to-be and her friends would think of her choices.

She had a personal favorite: a wedding dress in pale blush satin with textured organza that draped over a free-flowing asymmetric skirt overlay just below the bosom. The lighter and loose organza would do well to hide the baby bump.

She ran her hand lovingly over the fabric, picturing her friend in the romantic and elegant dress on her very special day. A day that Emma had never pictured given all the things that Connie had wanted out of life. Of course, the special day wasn't stopping Connie from her dreams, it was just giving her a whole new bunch of them.

Just like it might give you new dreams too, the little voice in her head chastised.

Shaking away that thought, she hung the dress on the center hook in the consultation room and did a quick once over of the other gowns she had chosen. They were all beautiful, but she could truly only picture Connie in one of them.

Determined not to show her preference, she set about prepping the room for when her friends would arrive. She laid out a tea service and an assortment of cookies that Carlo had made and brought over earlier.

Sexy and he can make cookies too! the little voice cajoled.

His pastry chef made them, she shot back, although they had still been warm when he had brought them over earlier that morning. Too early for his pastry chef to have been at work. She appreciated his thoughtfulness, but then again, they had promised to give Connie and Jonathan the most epic wedding ever and that also meant making all the little steps leading up to the big day perfect as well. That was why Carlo was being so attentive, she told herself although she knew otherwise. He was *always* attentive, and he knew how important it was for her to do this right for her friends.

She was determined to do it perfectly as well. For that reason, there would be beer and sandwiches for the guys later when they went to try on various tuxes and suits.

The sound of a footfall had her spinning around to where Connie stood, hands held over her mouth and tears glimmering in her eyes as she scrutinized the gowns hung up along the far wall. Maggie and Tracy were on either side of her. Maggie wrapped an arm around Connie's shoulders and smiled from ear-to-ear. Tracy was a little more reserved, but clearly happy for her friend.

"They're lovely," Connie said and hurried toward the gowns. She lightly danced her fingers over every dress before coming back to the blush gown in the center. "I think I like this one the best."

Maggie and Tracy murmured their agreement and Emma said, "I have to confess that's my favorite too. And we have some goodies for you all to nibble on while you decide."

"It sounds wonderful," Connie said and whipped around to hug Emma enthusiastically, rocking her side to side with glee and uncharacteristically girlish laughter.

Emma's heart warmed at her friend's joy and she grinned and hugged Connie back. "I don't think you'll be much bigger by your wedding day, but we'll plan for that. It's easier to take in than to let out so we can make adjustments at the final fitting," Emma said as she grabbed hold of the hanger and draped the skirt of the gown over her arm to walk it into the dressing room. When she exited, Maggie and Tracy were sitting on the antique upholstered divan slightly off center in the room and Tracy was pouring tea into the delicate bone china cups.

"I hope you've got something as beautiful for us," Tracy teased as she finished and laid the china teapot back onto the tray on the Queen Anne style mahogany table.

She did have equally wonderful gowns for her friends and grinned. "I have some waiting for you in the next room. As soon as Connie is done, I'll bring them in and we'll try them on."

Sitting on a wing chair beside the divan, Emma reached for the teacup and found her hands were shaking as she did so. The cup rattled against the china and Maggie reached out and laid a hand on Emma's arm to reassure her.

"It's going to be fine," Maggie said and Emma knew it was about more than the dress selection.

Emma had no doubt about how much Connie and Jonathan loved each other. It was obvious every time you saw them together. "I know. I just want it to be perfect for her. She deserves it."

"It *will* be perfect, Em. You're such an awesome wedding planner. And Carlo," Tracy paused as she nibbled on a shortbread cookie and then waved what was left of the treat. "Carlo is amazing. If he's the one who baked these cookies, don't let that man get away."

Emma was spared from having to reply as Connie walked out in the blush gown. Connie smoothed the skirt with her hands and glanced at herself in the mirror before facing her friends. A radiant smile beamed back at them from Connie's reflection in the mirror and her friend's gaze shimmered with unshed tears.

"You're so beautiful," Maggie said, her voice quavering.

"Gorgeous, Connie," Tracy added, her tone as raw as an open wound.

Connie glanced at Emma, obviously overcome with emotion. "Perfect. It's absolutely perfect."

Taking another moment to collect herself, Emma rose and guided Connie to the three-sided mirror at one end of the room so her friend could get a complete view of the gown. She smoothed the fabric and tucked in the excess so Connie would see what the final fit might look like. The barely-there pink brought out the best of Connie's skin and hair and made the color of Connie's amazing exotic green eyes pop brightly.

With slight pressure at Connie's waist, Emma urged her half around to see the back of the gown. "We could do a French bustle here that would let the organza fall naturally."

Nodding, Connie did a little back and forth twirl and said, "This is the one."

With a nod, Emma tousled Connie's shoulder length locks to fluff it out. "I know you're not a prissy kind of girl, so I was thinking of just some waves in your hair with a tiny floral tiara and a wisp of a veil. Summery flowers in the tiara to match the altar Jon designed."

"I like the summer theme for the wedding even if it will be December. It'll always remind us of what happened the magical summer we met," Connie said, way more romantically than Emma had ever heard. A sure sign that marriage did change women.

"I'm glad you said that, because I think you'll love the color I've chosen for the bridesmaids' gowns," Emma said, struggling to hide the emotion threatening to overwhelm her. "Now let's get you out of this so you can relax. It's a pretty good fit, but we'll get the seamstress to tailor it in a few weeks on account of the baby."

"The baby," Connie said with a sigh and then impulsively hugged and kissed Emma on the cheek before she rushed to the dressing room to get changed.

"She's so happy," Tracy said, although worry was laced with the joy in her words.

"She's going to be fine," Maggie reassured and placed her hand on Tracy's arm.

"She is," Emma said, but it was if she had to say it to convince herself as she sat.

That Tracy wasn't fully persuaded was evidenced by her next words which mirrored a lot of what Emma was feeling. "It's just so much change at once. A new job and home. A marriage. A baby," she paused, but then repeated, "A baby. Our Connie is going to be a mom!"

A mom and a wife. In Sea Kiss of all places. Not quite what Connie had envisioned nor what her friends had either. And even though Emma worried about how marriage would change things, having Connie in Sea Kiss hopefully meant she'd still be able to spend time with her friend.

Because of that, she said, "We'll be here for her if she gets too overwhelmed."

"We will," her friends echoed and to avoid going down a road to negativity, Emma jumped up and slapped her hands on her legs. "Now it's our turn."

She whisked away to the room they used as a prep area for consultations. Inside were the bridesmaids' gowns she had chosen the day before and she took them back out to where Connie now sat in the wing chair beside Maggie and Tracy.

As she laid out the three different styles all in the same color, she said, "I was thinking this pale seafoam was a perfect foil for the blush gown plus it keeps with the summery feel you mentioned earlier. What do you think?"

Connie grinned and clapped. "I think it's perfect. What do you ladies think?"

"Epic," Maggie teased with a wink, repeating Jonathan's favorite surfer dude compliment.

Emma smiled and shot a quick look at Tracy who nodded and said, "I agree. You've thought of everything to keep summer alive for Connie. Now you'll just have to make sure we don't have a blizzard."

Emma chuckled and shook her head. "We rarely have blizzards on the Shore," she said and hoped that Tracy hadn't just jinxed them. As the wedding planner there were a ton of things that Carlo and she could control, but the weather wasn't one of them.

Connie walked over and slipped her arm through Emma's. "But even if we did have snow, it wouldn't matter because Jon and I are getting married. Can you believe it?"

"Actually, no, but it is happening, so I'll make sure everything goes according to plan."

With a playful tug on her arm, Connie led her toward the settee and said, "You know that sometimes you've just got to let things happen organically without so much planning."

That statement was met with disbelief by all her other friends. "Connie Reyes is spontaneous said no one ever," Tracy said.

"Organic? That's Jon talk for sure," Emma added.

Smiling, Connie sat on the edge of the coffee table before her friends, earning a playful rebuke from Mama Maggie. "Tables are for glasses – "

"And not for asses," Connie finished and then plowed on. "I want you all to know how glad I am we're friends. I couldn't even begin to think about doing this – the move, the job, the baby – if I didn't have you all in my life."

"Shit, you had to go there," Tracy said, tears rolling down her face as she shifted to draw Connie into a hug.

Maggie and Emma quickly joined the embrace and Emma let herself savor the support of her sisterhood knowing that no matter what, they'd be there for her too.

Chapter 6

Emma didn't believe in being late for anything, but an unscheduled prospective customer at the bridal shop after her friends' departure had messed with her schedule. She'd had no choice but to spend some time with the possible new client.

But the change in her schedule meant that by the time she arrived at the men's shop Jonathan, Owen, Carlo, and Andy were trying on suits and tuxes. It wasn't the normal way it was done, but with so little time left before the wedding, she'd had to corral all the men together to pick their clothing and get fitted.

The men had already had a few beers, possibly more, and eaten most of the food. Jovial laughter filled the room as she entered and took note of the table with the remains of the beers from local microbreweries and the sandwiches. Her stomach grumbled at the sight of the small piece that remained of one of Carlo's famous pork and broccoli rabe sandwiches. Mouth watering, she hoped she could sneak a bite while the men tried on their clothes.

"I can see you're all having fun, but did you decide on any of the tuxes I picked out?" she said as she peered at Jonathan, Owen, and Andy, and wondered where Carlo was hiding.

Jonathan sauntered over, grabbed the last piece of sandwich, placed it on a plate, and handed it to her. "Eat. It's way past lunch hour and you're cranky."

"I'm not cranky," she said, but her stomach complained noisily, forcing her to add, "Just hungry."

"More like hangry," he teased. Grinning, Jonathan laid an arm over her shoulders and walked her to the leather wing chair beside a massive leather couch where Andy and Owen sat sipping beers. She joined them there and took a bite of the sandwich, nearly moaning as the flavors of the tender roast pork, bitter broccoli rabe, and sweet mozzarella cheese exploded in her mouth. Not to mention Carlo's secret garlicky tomato sauce, the game changer that had made him a champion on a network cooking show.

After swallowing, she glanced around the room at the men. "So what's up? Where are the tuxes I left out for you?"

"We decided we're not tux kind of guys. Well, Owen is, but the rest of us are just plain ol' suit types," Jonathan said as he sat on the arm of her chair.

She arched a brow. "And Carlo?"

Owen gestured with his beer bottle to the dressing room. "He's in there."

Wondering if Carlo needed help, she walked over and knocked.

"Come in," he said.

She did only to find Carlo standing there in nothing but his tidy whities and a white shirt that was too small for his broad shoulders. The shirt hung open in front giving her a glimpse of what lay beneath the fabric.

Her heart did a little stutter at the sight of him, all lean sculpted muscle and smooth skin with the remnants of a summer tan. Heat suffused her and her face warmed in a blush.

If Carlo noticed, he did his best to hide it as he fought to pull the shirt closed and said, "I never knew that the buttons on your suit sleeve said so much about a man. If they're real. Stitched. Horn. Who knew?"

She took a few hesitant steps until she was close to him and brushed his hands away as he struggled to button the shirt. "This shirt is absolutely the wrong size, but the style will suit you," she said and smoothed the fabric across his broad shoulders and chest.

At his ragged sigh, she looked up and met his gaze. The desire there was impossible to miss and she should have stopped touching him. She should have moved away, but she couldn't.

"You're not playing fair, Emma," he said, a rough grumble in his voice as he laid his hands at her waist.

"I'm sorry. It's just so scary to think about changing what we are," she said and finally stepped away from him and wrapped her arms around herself.

He raked his hands through his thick cocoa brown hair, tousling the ever-present waves. "I'm not your father, Emma. I would never hurt you. I respect you."

"I know," she said, but inside there was still too much fear and doubt. "I just need a little more time, Carlo. And you said you're a patient man, remember," she teased, trying to ease the tension in the room.

"I am, but I'm not a saint either. When you touch me . . . I want to touch too, Emma, but I can wait. Just promise me one thing."

She was afraid to ask what she had to promise but fought back her fear. "I guess it depends on what the promise is."

With another ragged sigh, he shrugged his shoulders, straining the fabric of the shirt. "I feel like a tool. Promise you'll make sure I look okay because I'm not a suit kind of guy."

She grinned and was about to reach out to smooth the linen over his shoulders again but jerked her hand away and locked it with her other hand behind her back to keep from touching him again. Meeting his gaze, she said, "I promise."

A WEEK AFTER THE MEN had selected their clothing, the Pierce brothers paraded before Emma in their custom fitted suits, doing a really bad imitation of runway models. With their blonde good looks the Pierce brothers actually could be models. Owen had the kind of refined air you'd see for a luxury watch or perfume ad while Jonathan was better suited for a 4x4 or sports ad. As they playfully posed, she laughed and shook her head.

"Come on, guys. Get serious," she said, but was happy to see that Jonathan was able to get his normally uptight brother to relax and have fun for a change. With both Maggie and his younger brother in his life, Owen had definitely changed for the better.

The snick of a door opening had her turning toward the dressing room where Carlo had been getting dressed.

Despite his denial last week, Carlo was definitely a suit kind of guy, Emma thought as he strolled out of the dressing room for a final fitting.

His body was perfection. His face all chiseled lines that a sculptor would envy. A five o'clock shadow darkened his look, making him appear dangerously bad boy sexy. Carlo would be everywoman's secret fantasy lover, which made Emma want to hide him all for herself. Undress him slowly, peeling away that elegant veneer to get to the raw power beneath

As he stopped to stare at himself in the mirror, he yanked at the suit's lapels and his full lips thinned before finally breaking into a smile that spread up into his chocolate brown eyes. Turning, he raked back a lock of tousled hair as it fell forward. He held his hands out as if to ask her what she thought and warmth suffused her as she remembered what was hidden beneath the expensive cotton shirt and bespoke suit.

"You look wonderful," she said as she tried to examine him on a professional level and pushed away her earlier fantasy.

The men had chosen soft charcoal grey color for the suits with brilliant white shirts. Jonathan's ensemble boasted a pale pink tie with tiny seafoam polka dots to match Connie's blush gown while the groomsmen had deep seafoam green ties with pale pink stripes to complement the bride and the bridesmaids.

As the four friends all gathered to stand together, it occurred to her they couldn't have a more handsome group of men. Even Jonathan's business partner Andy, whose look sometimes bordered on mad genius, had trimmed his hair and beard, revealing a strong jaw and bringing attention to his bright blue eyes.

But no matter how handsome the men, there was only one who made her heart stutter and her insides clench with need.

Carlo.

"You guys are rocking it," she said and chuckled with glee.

Carlo playfully tugged on his suit jacket sleeve and held it up to display the functional horn buttons with the playful seafoam thread stitching on the one buttonhole. "It's the buttons. They make all the difference."

"Get real. It's us hot guys. The ladies can't resist," Jonathan teased and nudged Carlo with his elbow.

"But we're all taken. Well, most of us," Andy said and shot a quick look at Carlo. A blast of pink flooded Andy's cheeks when he realized his gaffe and Emma felt her own cheeks flaming.

"It's good to see that the suits all fit so well. But let me just doublecheck. Jon," she said and he did an exaggerated stroll toward her, complete with a fake model's pout.

"Get serious, Jon," she said as she skimmed her hands across his shoulders. "We only have three weeks until the wedding so we need to get going. Turn around for me."

Jonathan grinned and did a slow pivot for her complete with another playful pout. "What do you think?"

Emma nodded. "Enzo did a nice job. If the fit on all of you is as good, he should be able to do the final tailoring and get the suits to you in no time."

She gestured to Owen and repeated her inspection with him and then Andy, smoothing and tugging to make sure the clothing fit properly. When only Carlo was left, their gazes met for a hesitant second before he sauntered over and she likewise gave the suit the once over. It fit perfectly across his wide shoulders and lean midsection. The fine wool fabric lovingly hugged his ass and muscled thighs, causing warmth to pool at her center.

Battling her reaction, she tracked her gaze down to his feet and realized he was in stockinged feet as were the other men.

"Shoes, guys. We need to see how the pants break with your shoes," she chided and clapped her hands like a schoolteacher rounding up errant students.

Jonathan, Owen, and Andy quickly went to slip on their footwear, but Carlo hesitated. When she shot him a questioning glance, he said, "We had to order mine because they didn't have my size in the style we chose."

"His *h-yuge* size. You know what they say about men's feet, right, Em?" Jonathan teased and winked at her.

What sounded like a low growl erupted from Carlo and he quickly retorted, "Says the man just one size away from the boy's department."

Jonathan jammed his hands on his hips and rocked them back and forth in a sexy motion. "Calling bullshit on that. Besides it's not the size of the wave, but the motion of the ocean."

"For God's sake, Jon! I *am* standing here and Connie *is* my best friend," Emma said, heat flooding her face.

Jonathan clasped his hands before him and lowered his head respectfully, suitably chastised. "Sorry, Em. You know I respect you and Connie."

"Then keep the locker talk between you guys. Now shoes," she commanded and snapped her fingers, making the men get in line before her so she could inspect the break on the pants legs. All were perfect until she got to Carlo with his unhemmed pants.

She skipped a look at his feet for fear of seeing just how big and moved her gaze up his legs, avoiding that dangerous spot and any thought about Jonathan's tease and what it meant. She'd already had a too short memory of how he felt against her from the night of their first kiss and Jonathan had been spot on about size.

H-yuge, the little voice in her head reminded.

"As soon as you get the shoes, we'll get Enzo to do the final measurement. No big deal," she said, her voice rough and more heat filling her face as she realized she'd made an unintended pun.

"No big deal," Carlo repeated, but totally tongue-in-cheek, unfortunately leaving her to recall things she was better off not thinking about as she dove into finishing up the fittings. The three weeks until the wedding were going to fly by and she had too many things to do to indulge herself with thoughts of Carlo and what could be.

Chapter 7

Carlo endured Enzo's crotch grabbing as the old Italian tailor measured the pants and hemmed the bottom for a cuff and the highly important break. The tailor muttered to himself around the pins held in his lips. Carlo looked down and said, "Something wrong?"

"*Staizii*! Stand up straight," Enzo grumbled and Carlo obeyed since the tailor's tone brooked no disagreement and the pins were dangerously close to some very vital parts.

After some more muttering and pinning, the tailor popped to his feet and with a dismissive wave of his hand said, "*Fini*. You can go now."

"*Grazie*, Enzo," he said, earning a smile from the wizened old man and another wave, impatient this time Carlo gathered. Italians clearly could speak with their hands, he thought and grinned.

But as he was about to heed Enzo's instructions, the old man surprised him by saying, "Go. Find that Emma and do the right thing by her."

At Carlo's questioning gaze, Enzo said, "I may be old, but I can still see quite well. She's softening and by the night of the wedding . . . Make your move, *ragazzo*. Have a wonderful time."

With a nod, Carlo went back into the dressing room to change and in no time, he left the tailor's shop just off Sea Kiss's Main Street. With a little time to spare before he had to return to work, he took advantage of an almost summer-like fall day and strolled around the block to the other businesses on the street. A luncheonette on the corner served ice cream year-round for souls who craved it even during damp winter days. The luncheonette was popular for its simple diner-style food and sat next to one of the town's real estate agents. There were a few along the street since beachside properties had regained their allure after Hurricane Sandy. A lawyer's office and hardware store came next and then his favorite surf and skate shop where he regularly picked up wax and clothing. Right next to the surf shop was a cheese shop that provided his catering business with a number of items for their events. He dropped in to check with Jesse, the owner, just to confirm that she would be ready with the platters for an upcoming party he was catering.

"Hey, Carlo! How are you doing?" Jesse called out as the bell on the door tinkled and announced his arrival.

"I'm doing fine. How are you? How's your son?" he asked, mindful that as a widow and mother of a young child who also ran her own business, she had a full load on her slim shoulders.

"We're doing well thanks to you. I can't tell you how much I appreciate the latest orders you placed. It was getting really slow around town," Jesse said. She sliced a piece from one of the cheeses and held the thin slice over the top of the small refrigerated display case for him to taste.

Shore towns like Sea Kiss were highly seasonal and even though Sea Kiss had a fairly large full-time population, the drop in business off season was hard to handle. Having Jonathan's company in town would help a lot with that since many of the Pierce company employees were moving into the area and Jonathan planned on having events to draw even more people to town.

Carlo took hold of the slice of cheese, munched on it, and nodded. "Love it. Sharp, a little grassy, but not too much."

"It's a new one I'm trying from a small South Jersey cheese maker. Artisan, organic, and of course, local. Do you think it will work for those platters I'm making for the party and for Connie and Jon's wedding?"

He nodded and smiled. "Totally. I'll bring the cash by tomorrow. I'm sure you could use the money for the holidays."

"Could I ever. It's been hard since . . ." Her voice choked up and tears shimmered in her eyes, but she dashed them aside. "It's been three years since Ed died and you'd think I'd be getting better about it. But it still gets tough around the holidays."

"We're here for you, Jesse. Just know that, okay?" He couldn't imagine how hard it was for her to have lost her husband so unexpectedly when a drunk driver had smashed into Ed's car as he was on his way home from work.

She braved a watery smile, sniffled, and nodded. "I know. I'll have everything ready. If you need anything else or extra hands . . ."

"If you're free to be a server –"

"I am," she immediately replied. "I can ask Sammie next door to babysit for me." The two shop owners often watched out for each other for things like deliveries, holidays, and babysitting. Sammie had just had a baby girl a few months earlier.

Although he had enough people for the upcoming parties and the wedding, he'd make room for Jesse and Sammie as well if she needed the work. "Great. I'll give you the details for the events and have Paolo reach out to you. Tell Sammie she's welcome to work as well if you guys can swing a babysitter."

With business settled, he did the short walk up the half a dozen or so blocks and across the busy state road to where his warehouse was located. As he entered, the sounds of laughter filled the space and he wondered what was up until he reached the reception area outside their offices and caught sight of the familiar figure in the Army service uniform and the distinctive tan beret that identified him as a Ranger.

"Tomás," he called out and hurried over to hug his younger brother. As he did so he noticed the cane his brother leaned on and the large metal brace on his left knee.

"You're hurt? Why didn't you call and let us know?" he said, his attention focused on the brace and the way his brother favored his good leg.

"He always was the clumsy one," Paolo teased and nudged Tomás with his elbow.

Tomás grinned ruefully and shook his head. "Because I'm embarrassed to say that it happened while I was training for a mission. Fell off the obstacle wall and landed wrong. Totally messed up the knee."

Carlo heard something in his brother's tone that he didn't like. "How bad?"

"Yeah, how bad?" chimed in Paolo, the baby of the three, his features wracked with worry. Tomás had dreamed of being a soldier since they were all kids.

"Bad. I'll be out of commission for at least another month in the brace and then PT for another few weeks. The Army doc is going to have to be satisfied that I can perform before I can rejoin my team."

"And you're not sure you can," Carlo prompted to get his brother to open up which could be difficult most times. Tomás preferred being the strong silent type.

"I'm not sure but I'm optimistic. In the meantime, you may be seeing a lot of me around here in the future. That is if you'll have me," Tomás said in a tone mixed with disappointment and hopefulness.

Carlo was surprised that his brother was willing to admit it and he wasn't the only one who had taken note of the unusual admission. Paolo wrapped his older brother in a hug and said, "The three da Costa brothers together again. Awesome, *mano*."

As he met Tomás's gaze over Paolo's shoulder, there was that mix of emotions again, but Tomás hugged his baby brother and repeated the wish in a determined voice. "The three da Costa brothers ride again," Tomás said.

Carlo smiled and slapped his brother on the back. "Let's find you an office and when you're ready, you can get to work. You can't believe how much we've got to get done in the next few weeks."

"Still the work-a-holic, *mano*?" Tomás teased.

"Always," Carlo confirmed and led his brother to a spare office down the hall, his pace measured in deference to his brother's slower speed.

At the door, he reached in and flipped on the light to display a desk piled with stacks of papers and files.

"Sorry for the mess, but we've been so busy I haven't had a chance to file these away," Carlo said.

Tomás nodded, walked to the desk, and shuffled some of the papers. "Perfect job for me. I'll get these put away for you."

"*Obrigado*," he said and started to walk away, but then stopped and turn. "I'm sorry you're hurt, *mano*, but I'm happy you're here."

Tomás smiled, eased off his beret, and pointed it in Carlo's direction. "Don't get soft on me, Carlo."

Carlo chuckled and as he walked away, he heard Tomás mumble, "I missed you goofballs too."

CONNIE HAD WANTED TO forego the traditional bridal shower and bachelorette party because of the limited time before the wedding, but Emma and her friends wouldn't let Connie miss such rituals for all the money in the world. With only a little over two weeks to go before the wedding, the large living room of the Sinclair beach house was filled with friends and family, mounds of gifts, and an assortment of fabulous finger foods prepared by Carlo and his staff. His brothers Paolo and Tomás were part of the crew keeping food available and champagne flowing along with a number of other servers, including Jesse from the cheese shop. The young woman looked like she was almost back to normal.

Emma couldn't imagine what it would be like to lose your husband so tragically and with a young son to support. It had been a tough few years for Jesse, but everyone in town had banded together to help her in one way or another. From babysitting to watching the shop to buying local, Emma was proud of how they'd all pulled together for one of their own and in the nearly three years since that loss, she and Jesse had gotten to be friends.

While Connie opened gifts with Tracy and Maggie helping her, she took a moment to seek out Jesse as she took a break from serving.

She hugged the other woman and said, "You're looking good."

Jesse offered up a soft smile. "Thanks to all of you. How are you holding up? It seems like there's so much to do in a couple of weeks."

Emma chuckled. "That's an understatement, but we'll get it done. And now Carlo has Tomás here to help out also," she said and motioned toward where the da Costa brothers were busy working. Paolo was instructing one server on what to do while Tomás poured more champagne into the punch bowl. Carlo was wheeling in a cart with pastries for the party goers.

Jesse looked over in their direction as well, her gaze seeming to linger on Tomás, but then the other woman quickly shifted her glance to Connie. "She looks so content," Jesse said.

"Yes, she does. I'm so very happy for her," Emma said, but peered from Jesse to Tomás, wondering if she'd imagined there had been something different in that look.

"And what about you, Em? How are you holding up?" Jesse said and glanced toward the brothers again, but this time the young widow's gaze settled firmly on Carlo.

Emma glanced over longingly, the joyous emotions of the day making it difficult to contain her emotions. "I'm . . . struggling with it all," she confessed, trusting the other woman's friendship and discretion.

Jesse patted her on the back and then laid her hand on Emma's shoulder. "I get it, Em. You're afraid of losing him as a lover and a friend, but remember that old saying?"

"It's better to have loved and lost—" Emma began, but cut off abruptly as she realized how inappropriate it might be considering what Jesse had suffered.

"Yeah, that one. Believe me, I know. But even if I'd had a clue how it would end with Ed, I wouldn't have changed a thing," Jesse said, her voice shaky and the glimmer of tears in her eyes.

Emma hugged the other woman and said, "Thank you for that, Jesse."

She broke away from Jesse as Maggie, Tracy, and Connie called out for her. "Come on, *chica*! We need you up here!" Connie said and with a broad swipe of her hand waved at Emma to join them in opening the gifts.

"Duty calls," Emma grinned, and hurried across the room to where her friends were gathered amidst piles of presents. Tracy had a notepad and was keeping track of who gave what while Maggie had been handing Connie the gaily wrapped items. That left Emma taking over from Connie's cousin Katrina who had been selecting ribbons, paper, and bows to make a hat for Connie to wear.

As box after box was opened, the hat grew way too big and Emma and Katrina started making a bouquet. With nimble fingers and a light heart, Emma created a brightly colored bouquet and smiled as it was her turn to hand it to the bride-to-be while Katrina tied the outrageously immense hat on Connie.

The friends all gathered around Connie and Carlo did them a favor by snapping photos on their cell phones to commemorate the event. When he was done, Connie faced her friends and they exchanged a big exuberant group hug.

"You *chicas* are the best," Connie said, rocking all of them back and forth jubilantly.

Which prompted a happy exchange of "No, you are," between the friends who laughed and hugged again before sitting to watch the guests mingling.

"Did you ever think you would be doing something like this with me?" Connie said and eyeballed her friends.

Her comment was met with resounding agreement.

"Never," Maggie said with a strong shake of her head.

"No way," Emma said.

"Absolutely not," Tracy said, but then quickly added, "But stranger things have been known to happen, like my moving to Sea Kiss."

Stunned, Emma leaned forward to scrutinize her friend's face to see if she was really serious and surprisingly, it seemed she was. "You're moving here? To Sea Kiss?"

With a shrug, Tracy said, "With all of you here . . . I want to start my new life surrounded by friends and finally do what *I* want to do."

"Which is?" Maggie and Connie said at the same time and with similar puzzled looks.

With another shrug and a hesitant chuckle, Tracy said, "I'm not really sure."

A long pregnant moment filled the air, but then Connie hugged her and said, "We're happy to have you here with us. It is going to be totally epic."

Emma chuckled and shook her head, "Jon is truly rubbing off on you."

With a sniffle, Maggie said, "You guys make me want to live here full time."

Connie laughed and rubbed her baby bump. "Maybe when it's baby time for you."

Maggie rolled her eyes. "Believe me, we're trying."

Which prompted raucous laughter from her friends. "Yeah, it must be rough to make love with the uber hot Owen Pierce," Tracy said with a roll of her eyes.

"I'm with you, Tracy," Emma chimed in.

"Totally rough," Maggie said with a self-deprecating laugh. Pointing her finger at Emma and Tracy, she said, "But just wait until it's your turn."

Tracy waved her hands back and forth. "No way. I'm done with men for a long time. Maybe forever."

Emma slapped her legs with her hands and shot to her feet. "I second that thought. And I think it's time for me to see how things are going."

She walked away quickly, but not fast enough to avoid hearing her friends' disbelieving laughter and comments

"I say she falls hard on my wedding day," Connie said.

"For sure," Maggie and Tracy chimed in.

No way, Emma thought as she walked into the kitchen and caught sight of Carlo patiently instructing a young server on proper procedure. The teenager smiled at him and swung up the tray with the finger foods to head out to the guests.

It was way too easy to picture him being that patient with a young child. Their child. One with dark hair with some of her reddish color, hazel eyes that blended his dark chocolate with her green, and Carlo's olive skin so the poor kid would never have to worry about blushes or sunburn from a day spent on Sea Kiss beach. A real mix of the two of them.

With a sigh, she held that thought for a moment, then released it to drift away like a soap bubble in the wind. Joyful, but ephemeral.

As Carlo sensed her presence, he looked her way and smiled, and a bubble of hope built inside her. She walked over and wrapped her arms around him. "Thank you for everything. You made it so special for Connie."

She sensed the surprise in him at the spontaneous gesture, but he relaxed, returned the embrace, and said, "*We* made it special, Emma. And you know I'd do anything for you. Anything."

"I know, Carlo. I know you would," she said and nestled against him tighter, savoring the peace and comfort of his arms. Thinking that it would be amazing to feel that all the time. Thinking that her friends were right that it was getting harder and harder to fight what she felt for this amazing man. And that she was an idiot for doing it.

"Hey, Carlo," Paolo called out and came rushing into the room.

Carlo mumbled a curse beneath his breath and eased away from her. "I'm sorry, Emma."

Me, too, she thought as Carlo hurried away and cuffed his brother playfully on the back of the head as the two of them walked out the door.

As Maggie called out to Emma, she lingered for just a moment to store the memory of him and their embrace and then returned to the party.

Chapter 8

Carlo's mind was so set on getting through Jonathan's press conference in a week and the wedding the week after, that he hadn't done anything to get ready for Thanksgiving which was only days away. That meant making a few dishes for his mother, going home with his two brothers for the always over-the-top table piled with food and the assorted relatives who would drift in and out over the course of the day. It also meant asking Emma to join him as she had for so many years.

Since her mother lived in Edison, only about thirty-five or so minutes away from Newark, she'd usually have an early meal with her mother and then come north to join him and his family. Or at least that's what used to happen only she was sending so many mixed signals lately that he didn't know what she was thinking.

And he suspected what some members of his family were alternately thinking. Paolo was all for cutting Emma loose and not having a repeat of Carlo's prior disastrous engagement. Tomás seemed to be on the fence and lost in his own thoughts revolving around his military service and possibly Jesse. You'd have to be blind not to see that there was a connection between the two of them. As for his father, mother, and his half-brothers, they were all aboard the Emma train, but they only saw her at family events when she plastered on her happy face and everything seemed good between them.

And maybe it was all good, he thought as he hesitated, his fingers poised on the speed dial number for Emma, and then pressed it. He listened to her cheery pop ringtone until she picked up and breathlessly said, "Sorry. I was just finishing up a consult. Is everything okay?"

"Everything's going great if you don't count that this Thursday is Thanksgiving and I still need to cook a bunch of dishes," he said in a teasing tone.

The rustle of papers came across the line followed by a mumbled curse. "I get it. I can't believe it's Thanksgiving already. It's just been so crazy the last few weeks."

"I get you. M*amãe* called to remind me about what to bring," he said and paused. Before she could say anything, he jumped in with, "And to ask if you'd be coming to join me . . . join us again."

An uneasy silence filled the air before she said, "There's still so much work for Connie and Jon's wedding and I'm so tired. . ."

He shut her down to save himself the embarrassment of a rejection. "It's okay, Emma. There is a lot going on with all the events and I bet you could use a little down time by yourself. Plus I know that if you came we'd probably end up talking about the wedding and stuff so you couldn't really relax."

"Yeah, we probably would," she said with a sigh filled with sadness that he suspected had nothing to do with Connie and Jonathan's upcoming marriage.

"I guess I'll see you next Monday to finalize the press conference plans," he said and when she quickly agreed, he ended the call.

A knock on the glass door of his office dragged him back to work as he noticed Tomás standing by the door. He'd been wearing civvies since coming back, but the brace was ever present on his left leg. "What's up, *mano*?" he said with a quick jerk of his head.

"I was going to ask you the same thing, Carlo. You look like the day we had to put down Spottie," he said, referring to the beagle they'd had for over a dozen years as kids. They'd found the beagle with only a stub of a tail rooting through the bakery's garbage one morning and taken him in as a pet. Carlo, always the sucker for the lost and wounded, had bonded with Spottie more than any of them.

Carlo shook his head, unable to deny his mood. "Feeling close to that bad, Tomás. How are you doing? Leg doesn't seem to slow you down all that much."

Tomás glanced at his balky knee and made a face. "I'm trying not to let it, but there's a part of me that says I need to consider what I'll do if I can't go back to the Rangers. You know what I mean, right, about considering what to do if things don't work out?"

Tomás's question surprised him since it seemed to move him into the Paolo Cut-Emma-Loose camp. "I know what you mean, but maybe I'm just not ready to take that next step."

"Me, either, *mano*. But I have to say that all this wedding stuff and being in Sea Kiss has me wondering what it would be like to be here all the time. Get up in the morning and go surfing or fishing. Take a stroll with a beautiful woman through town or on the boardwalk. Maybe even have a kid or two, you know. Things I never imagined I'd want."

The wistful tone in his younger brother's voice was impossible to miss and a surprise since he'd always been All Action Guy. "It's 'cause we're getting older. *Mamãe* already had the three of us by this age."

Tomás blew out a rough laugh. "*Caralho*, I'm only thirty. Don't make me feel sixty."

"Sometimes I feel sixty," Carlo admitted with a heavy exhale, although he was only two years older than Tomás. "It would be great to have you here, helping out. It would give me more time to relax."

Another laugh erupted from his brother, but it wasn't harsh. "You, relax? If I know you, you've got plans all done up for expanding the business. Lord knows you've probably been hoarding away everything you make to do it."

He smiled. "You know me too well. But if you're staying, I'd be glad to have you here with us full time. Maybe I'd finally have the time to use some of those dollars I saved to trade my mobile home for the one I've thought about for years."

His brother arched a dark brow and said, "Are you sure you want me around here? Paolo mentioned you and Emma had talked about going into business together."

He shook his head. "Paolo talks too much," Carlo chided, but without any sting.

"But is it true? You and Emma together? Business-wise that is," Tomás clarified.

Carlo nodded. "We had talked about it and I hope it'll happen someday. Right now Emma is a big maybe in that plan, so let's leave that for another time. As for you, would that beautiful woman and child you mentioned before be Jesse and her son by any chance?"

Tomás looked away and his lips tightened into a thin slash. "She intrigues me and it's not just that she's beautiful. She's strong, but I see the sadness there too. I'd like to take away that hurt and make her really smile again."

Carlo nodded and leaned back in his chair, steepling his hands as he considered his brother. "She's had a rough time. I'm sure you heard her story already."

"I knew Jesse before she married Ed. We dated a few times the summer you came down here to start the business and I was helping you out. It was nice, really nice, but it just wasn't what I wanted back then. And now . . . the last thing I want is to take advantage of someone who might still be vulnerable, but that's jumping the gun considering that I don't know if I'm staying or going."

Just like Carlo didn't know if Emma was staying or going in his life, so he understood his brother's predicament. "When it's the right thing to do, you'll know."

"So will you, *mano*," Tomás said and with a wave, walked out the door to get back to work.

As Carlo watched him go, he hoped his brother was right.

THE AMBIANCE IN THE room at the upscale inn was subdued and elegant. Antique tables and chairs were efficiently laid out around the wood-burning fireplace where a nice fire tossed out welcome warmth. The tables were set with fine linen, china, silver, and crystal for the well-heeled patrons who chatted in hushed tones over Thanksgiving meals. On walls of an indeterminate shade of white an eclectic mix of paintings hung discreetly. The artwork was from a gallery in town that specialized in up and coming local artists.

The vibe couldn't be any more different from the raucous get together that would be going on at Carlo's family home, but this Thanksgiving treat had become a ritual with her and her mother once they'd managed to put their lives back together after her father's betrayal.

Emma raised her wine glass for a toast and as her mother did the same, Emma said, "To strong women."

Juliana repeated the toast, but there was something different in Emma's mother's gaze. The haunted look that had been there for so many years as they'd struggled to get back on their feet was finally gone and replaced by a brilliant sparkle in green eyes so similar to her own.

"You look . . . really happy," Emma said and thought that this new shine took years off her mother's face. She could pass for a woman in her mid-forties although she was sixty. Plus her mother kept herself in good shape and had always managed to look fashionable even when they'd been dead broke.

"I wish I could say the same about you, Emma. I can see you're troubled," Juliana said and set her glass back on the table.

Emma shrugged and sipped her wine. "I've got a ton of work to do for the next few weeks. Just worried about making sure it all goes right."

"Connie's wedding?" Juliana asked and Emma nodded.

"That and a press conference for Jon's company, not that I'm complaining. More work means more money in my pocket." More money being of utmost importance since the day they'd discovered that her father had not only run off with another woman, but emptied all their bank accounts, including the one intended to pay for Emma's college tuition. Since then she'd always been careful with her finances. It had let her buy her home in Sea Kiss and after that, she'd started setting aside money to open her own business one day. Maybe even that event planning business with Carlo.

Her mother raised her glass, hesitated to peer at Emma over the rim, and took a sip before deliberately setting the glass down once more. Juliana avoided Emma's gaze as she said, "I never thought I'd say this, but money doesn't make up for not having someone special in your life."

There was a tone in her mother's voice which both surprised and worried. "Why do I get the feeling that there's something you want to tell me, mom?"

Juliana's head shot up as if in surprise, but then she met Emma's gaze directly. "Because there is, Em. I've met someone and we've been seeing each other."

Emma jerked back almost as if struck by the news. During all of their weekly talks and occasional dinners, her mother had never mentioned a man. "How long have you been seeing him?"

Juliana's hand shook as she reached for a piece of bread and broke off a slice in a nervous gesture. "About six months –"

"Six months!" Emma said in a strained whisper and leaned toward her mom. "Six months and you never said anything in all the times we talked?"

Her mother's surprise announcement was almost like a deception in her mind. They'd always been close and that she'd kept it a secret for so long . . .

With a pained sigh, Juliana said, "I was worried you'd react just like this, Em. I know I made a lot of mistakes with your dad."

"You weren't the one who made the mistakes, mom," she said and laid her hand over her mother's as it rested on the table, concern overriding her initial anger.

Tears shimmered in Juliana's green eyes, but she corralled the tears much as she had for so long during her marriage. "I shouldn't have let him berate us the way he did. I should have stood up to him and I should have paid more attention to what was happening. I should have seen it coming."

"Mommy," she began, sounding too much like the scared seventeen-year-old whose world had totally been turned upside down overnight.

Her mother cupped her face from across the narrow width of the table and smiled. "It's okay, Emma. We survived. It made us stronger, but sometimes I worry you equate being strong with being alone. I know I felt that way for a long time, but then I met Scott."

Emma's throat was tight with emotion, but somehow she managed to squeak out, "Scott? Is that his name?" At Juliana's nod, she asked, "How did you meet him?"

"At work," her mother said and Emma started to pick at her meal as she listened to her mother's story about how Scott had been hired in another department and they'd run into each other at a party for a colleague's birthday.

"He's nothing like your father," Juliana said and forked up a bit of turkey and stuffing from her plate. After she chewed and swallowed, she continued. "I think I care for him and I'd like you to meet him."

Her mother with a man. Emma never could have imagined that this day would come. She'd kind of pictured the two of them alone together against the world and that word leapt at her again as it had when her mother had said it.

Alone. Not that she'd seen her mother and her going all Grey Gardens, but she'd never pictured a man in their lives.

Not even Carlo? the little voice chastised.

With that weird kind of mind reading that moms seemed to possess, Juliana said, "Since you're so busy with work, I assume you've been seeing a lot of Carlo. How's he doing?"

"Fine. Busy," she mumbled around a mouthful of cranberry and turkey.

"Hmm," Juliana said thoughtfully, but it was obvious her mother wasn't buying it. "I guess you're going to his family's house like you usually do?"

"No," she said and focused on the meal in front of her, avoiding Juliana's intense perusal.

"But you always go there –"

"I've got too much work to do. Besides, things change, mom. Just look at you," she said and hated the anger and upset in her voice, and immediately apologized. "I'm sorry. I'm very glad you've found someone who makes you happy. I really am. I just need to get used to the idea."

"You will, but I need you to promise me something," Juliana began and as Emma met her gaze, her mother continued. "Don't be afraid to take a chance on Carlo. He's a good man. One who will respect you and love you with all his heart."

Her brain knew that to be true, but her heart, a heart that had already experienced too much pain, was finding it hard to take the next step. But she knew her mother couldn't be happy if she thought that Emma was miserable and so she relented.

"I'll try, mom. I promise I'll try."

Chapter 9

Carlo had endured a minimum amount of ribbing about Emma's absence since Tomás had made it clear to all the brothers that the subject was off limits. His brother had also playfully reinforced that instruction with a threat about the kind of pain a Ranger could inflict and all of the brothers had listened.

Carlo was grateful for that since it made it a little easier to deal with the situation. But as he sat there eating tasteless food that was anything but tasteless, he told himself to get over it and Emma and enjoy this time with his family.

He was clearing off dinner plates from the table when the doorbell rang, surprising everyone in the room since the da Costa family had an open-door policy on holidays which meant you were invited to just walk right in. Carlo was closest, so he shoved the plates he held at his older brother Ricardo and went to see who would be knocking, ignoring the way his heart knocked unevenly as he hoped it might be Emma.

He jerked the door open to find her standing there, nervously clasping her purse. "Emma?" he asked, surprised, but pleased.

With a sharp jerk of her shoulders, she said, "Mom and I got done early and I wasn't ready to go back to Sea Kiss yet. I hope you don't mind that I changed my mind about coming. I'd understand if it was too late to visit."

"No, it's not too late at all. We were just cleaning up and getting ready for the next round of food. You know how we love food and company. Come in. *Por favor*," he said and held his arm out wide to invite her in.

EMMA PEELED OFF HER jacket and handed it to Carlo. He walked into the front parlor and casually tossed it on top of the pile of coats already on the sofa.

Carlo laid a hand at the small of her back and guided her to the dining room table which had been cleared of a traditional Thanksgiving meal of turkey and other American dishes. Years earlier Carlo had told her that when his grandparents had come from Portugal they'd insisted that the family learn to be American and honor American customs and traditions. For that reason, the da Costa family went all out to make sure their Thanksgiving was as American as the apple pie that would shortly be brought out for dessert. The only concession to breaking tradition was the assorted Portuguese pastries which graced every holiday table.

A stilted silence settled over the normally boisterous clan as she entered the dining room and Carlo glared at all of them, clearly commanding his family to behave with his look. It was obvious that they hadn't expected her to come that night.

His mother was first to act. She jumped to her feet, walked over to Emma, and hugged her enthusiastically. "It's so good to have you here, Emma."

"It's good to be here. I'm sorry I missed dinner, but I already ate with my mother," she said and laid her hand over her stomach.

Ricardo jumped into the discussion. "If you ask me, you could use a little more meat on your bones. My brother too," he said and poked Carlo in the ribs.

"I think you've been eating too many of your own *pasteis de nata*, Rickie. Javi, *tambén*," Tomás kidded. As Emma snuck a quick peek at Carlo's brothers, Ricardo and Javier, it was obvious they were sampling a great many treats at their bakery and getting a bit round.

"*Basta*," Carlo's father called out, drawing her attention as he sat at the head of the table like a king with his subjects.

"Seems to me the Army must be pretty desperate to take a runt like you," Javier kidded and wrapped a beefy arm around Tomás's neck to give him a loving noogie.

"*Por favor*. We have a guest," their mother chided and slipped in between Tomás and Javier as they began to good-naturedly scuffle.

Carlo's father slapped the table in jest and in a booming voice said, "*Por favor*, Rosa. Boys will be boys."

Rosa rolled her eyes and Carlo did the same, dragging a laugh from Emma. "Some things just don't change, do they, Em?" Carlo said.

Having experienced many a holiday with Carlo's family, she was glad that things had returned to the da Costa version of normal so quickly. She always loved being with his family. Even though things sometimes got loud and animated as it had before, there was no doubt they all loved and respected each other. It was such a difference from her own family and many a time it had made her wonder what it would be like to be a permanent part of a family like this.

And being a part of her own family with Carlo, the little voice chided.

Carlo's family hauled out dish after dish of assorted Portuguese desserts. Rice pudding. Custard tarts. Flan. Carlo's favorite *bolo de bolacha*, a cake-like dessert made with ground tea cookies, coffee, milk, and sugar. A few different baked *bolas* from his family's bakery. Pots of espresso and bottles of port completed the dessert portion of the meal.

Carlo grabbed a *bola de berlim*, the Portuguese equivalent of a custard-filled donut, and offered it to her. His arm brushed against hers as he reached for the dessert and his tension was impossible to ignore. Emma shot him a nervous half-glance, smoothed a hand down his arm, and offered up a smile.

"This is your favorite, isn't it?" she asked.

"It is," he said and she took a bite. After she murmured her pleasure, he placed the rest of the *bola* on her plate and cut slices of the *bolo de bolacha* for the rest of the family.

"I remember this one too," she said and motioned to another dessert that his mother passed over to them. "It's like *tiramisu*," she said and forked up a piece of the sweet.

"You could say that," he said and ate a big piece. "You did good, *mamãe*. It's delicious."

"*Obrigado, milho*. You'll have to take some of it home with you," his mother said with a satisfied smile.

"I won't argue with you," Carlo replied and for the next half an hour or so, the meal passed with playful banter and the eating of a ton of the desserts.

Carlo and she passed on the sherry since they were driving, but not Paolo and Tomás who were Carlo's passengers for the ride to Sea Kiss. Emma hoped the brothers' trip home would not be punctuated with comments about her surprise appearance because that would only make the situation between them that much more awkward.

As dessert wound down, Emma shifted uneasily in the chair and considered whether to make an exit as abrupt as her arrival. But she owed Carlo more and dutifully sat beside him while they chatted over dessert plates virtually licked clean and the glasses of sherry which were refilled a few times for the others while Carlo and she lingered over their demitasse cups of espresso.

When his mother rose to start clearing off the dishes, Carlo also stood and Emma popped up beside him, knocking elbows with him as they both reached for the same dish on the table. They chuckled good naturedly and adjusted, picking up other plates to bring into the kitchen where his sisters-in-law were busy packing away the leftovers and making doggie bags for people to take home.

After they had finished, Emma stood by her chair awkwardly and said, "I guess it's time for me to go home. Thank you all so much for a lovely night."

"It's late. I'll walk you to your car." Carlo placed his hand at the small of her back as they strolled to the front door. He scooped her coat off the pile in the parlor and helped her slip it on. They were about to head out the door when his mother bustled out holding two large storage containers filled with the desserts as well as some turkey and stuffing.

"Don't forget your goodies and *obrigado* for coming, Emma. I know Carlo was very happy to see you," Rosa said and bright color flashed across his face with embarrassment.

"*Obrigado*, Rosa. It was my pleasure to be with all of you tonight," Emma said graciously and accepted the containers from his mom. As always, she had truly enjoyed her time in the warmth and love of Carlo's family.

ROSA POKED CARLO IN the chest and said, "Take care of *minha nina*."

He feigned injury and kidded, "Ouch, *mamãe*."

His mother wagged her finger in his face before she waddled away to join the rest of the family in the dining room.

They stood in the foyer awkwardly for a moment before Emma said, "I should go. It's a long trip back to Sea Kiss."

"It is and we've both got tons of work to do in the next few days," he said and opened the door. When she stepped out, he followed and strolled with her down the steps to the sidewalk. Almost reflexively he ran his hand across the *azulejo* of the Lady of Fatima worked into the retaining wall by the steps. Murmured a short prayer that Emma's unexpected appearance was a good sign.

Emma was silent as they hurried down the sidewalk and he could see Emma's Sebring parked toward the end of the block. They were silent as they walked and at her car, they stopped and stood there uneasily again. He shrugged his shoulders against the slight chill of the late November night and said, "Thank you for coming. My family was really happy to see you."

She narrowed her gaze and hugged the plastic containers to her midsection. "Only your family was happy to see me?"

With a rough shift of his shoulders, he said, "Me, too. I'm glad you came. It felt really weird without you."

Emma nodded. "It was really weird not to come and I felt bad that your brothers might be busting your chops about it."

"They were relentless, so *obrigado*," he said, placed a hand over his heart and did a little bow of gratitude.

She chuckled and smiled. "I couldn't let that happen to a friend and we are friends, right?"

Caralho, he was being friend-zoned, he thought, and his heart plummeted with disappointment. "We are. Friends," he said hesitantly, unsure of whether he could accept being only friends with her.

She must have sensed his disillusionment. With a small smile, she cradled his cheek and stroked her thumb across his face. "It's a start and not an ending, Carlo."

A start to what? he thought and at her shocked look, it occurred to him he had said it out loud.

"To something more," she replied.

He also wanted to believe that it could be something more. "I want that too, Emma. Friends . . . and maybe more," he said and turned his face to drop a kiss on her palm.

A powerful blush erupted across her face and he grinned, pleased that she was not unaffected by his kiss. He reached past her to open her door and then they stood there again awkwardly. "Please text me when you get home. I worry about my friends."

She smiled and said, "I will. You do the same, okay? I worry about my friends too."

He nodded. "I won't be too late, but I've got to pry Paolo and Tomás away. It's hard to do when they've had way too much sherry."

Her smile faded a bit and she glanced back up the sidewalk toward his family's home. "How is Tomás doing?"

He mimicked her action and considered his statement before admitting, "I'm not sure. He seems to be handling it, but he's always so . . . controlled. Regimented which is why the Army is such a good fit for him."

A chuckle escaped her. "Controlled seems to be a da Costa trait."

He laughed, but then something dark inside of him made him say, "You seemed to like it when I lost control at Maggie's wedding."

Bright red color swept up her neck and painted her cheeks and ears. "I think I did," she admitted, surprising him.

He decided to take that small victory that said maybe more was truly possible. Leaning toward her, he whispered a kiss across her lips. "Drive safe. Think of me."

"I will," she said and kissed him back, surprising him. But before he could follow-up, she got in the car, shut the door, and started the car. Flashing him a hesitant smile, she drove off.

He stayed there watching her car until she turned onto Ferry Street to head toward the Turnpike. Grinning, he strolled back toward his family's home, feeling very thankful for all that had happened that night.

Feeling hopeful about what might be happening with Emma.

Chapter 10

Emma stood beside Connie, Maggie, Owen, Tracy and Carlo, of course as they gathered close to the stage set up for the press conference. To her other side were Andy and the remaining partners in Jonathan's company. Jonathan kissed and hugged Connie and then walked up to the center of the stage. A week later the stage would be converted to a dais for Connie and Jonathan's wedding. Today would be a good test run.

She reminded herself one step at a time as one of Jonathan's assistants handed him a microphone so Jonathan could begin the press conference.

Today was all about the launch of the new Thunder electric SUV and giving the media a first look at the work that had been done to create the new Pierce research and development center as well as Sea Kiss and all it had to offer. As she glanced around the room, things seemed to be going fine. Once they were done here at the center, Jonathan, Connie, and the Mayor of Sea Kiss intended to take the press members for a tour of the town's many small businesses, restaurants, and recreational areas.

The lights flickered off and on in warning that Jonathan would soon begin his presentation and introduce the new SUV plus an updated model of the Lightning which so far had been selling well despite its six-figure price tag. Seconds later, the lights in the room dimmed completely and a spotlight fixed on Jonathan as he stood in the center of the stage.

"Ladies and gentleman. Welcome to the new Pierce Research and Development Center and to Sea Kiss, the home of my heart and the Jewel of the Jersey Shore."

Smatters of applause greeted his intro, but then the lights pulled back from him and in the center of the display area, laser lines danced and shot scatters of dots until they coalesced into a hologram of the new Lightning model. As Jonathan read off the specifications for the vehicle, the hologram obeyed. Doors opened and closed followed by enlarged images of the cockpit, dashboard, and interior, earning oohs and aahs from the attendees.

There was a burst of light and then darkness for long seconds. Expectation built as Jonathan said, "And now, I want to introduce you to the new Thunder electric SUV."

A flash of light, like a bolt of lightning, illuminated the center of the room before a loud rumble erupted and the hologram of the Thunder burst into the center of the room. As Jonathan had before, he ran through the specifications for the vehicle, including a nearly 300 mile range and a price tag that placed it solidly in the bracket of your average luxury vehicle.

"The Thunder is friendly to the environment and to your pocketbook while wrapping you in luxury and safety. A win-win for consumers and we hope you'll think so as well," Jonathan said from the shadow at the podium. "But I don't think you came here just to see some fancy light shows," he added, earning laughter from the attendees.

The image of the hologram disappeared as the lights snapped on in the room, almost disorienting at first after the darkness. The brightness revealed the two vehicles draped with shiny metallic cloth. At Jonathan's prompting, several Pierce employees surged forward and in an almost choreographed dance, removed the cloth, revealing the vehicles.

The two cars were in the same shade of metallic red, but couldn't look more different, Emma thought.

The Lightning was every man's wet dream of a sports car while the Thunder would be the envy of soccer moms everywhere. As the reporters pressed forward to inspect the vehicles, she took hold of Carlo's hand and peered up at him. He didn't need any further urging to know it was time for them and their staff to get to work.

As she passed Connie, she hugged her friend and whispered, "He nailed it."

"Yes, he did," Connie said, pride evident in her tones. Jonathan approached his fiancée and wrapped an arm around her waist. "Please join me for the photo ops," he said and walked her to where the photographers waited along with reporters who wanted Jonathan to answer more questions about the automobiles.

Emma slipped away to join Carlo in the back room which would one day be a cafeteria for Pierce employees. Carlo's crew had laid out the spread they'd discussed for the reporters. Paolo and Tomás were finishing up the beverage service while waitstaff was coming in from outside with trays of appetizers to offer to those gathered in the main display area.

"It all looks good," she said, grateful that it was going smoothly.

Hands on his hips, Carlo examined the setup and nodded. "It does. Why don't you go back outside and keep an eye on things? Keep me posted via the coms," he said, referring to the communication devices they used for events like this.

"Will do," she said and exited to the display space to make sure things were in order. Everything was running exceptionally well and it was amazing how much work Jonathan's people had gotten done in the short time since he'd bought the historic building. She'd always been partial to it with its unique clock tower and 1920s architecture. The main floor was completely restored, but also renovated with modern features. The two other stories and clock tower still needed work and hopefully it would all be completed by its anticipated Memorial Day grand opening date. A date which unintentionally coincided with Connie's due date. The grand opening had been scheduled before her friends had realized Connie was pregnant and couldn't be re-scheduled.

Even though they hadn't even gotten past the wedding, her mind started whirring with ideas for a baby shower and a grand opening party for Jonathan's new building.

For the next hour or so the reporters and guests mingled back and forth between examining the vehicles and peppering Jonathan, Connie, and the mayor with questions, and taking breaks to sample the foods and beverages available. As she stood there watching the activity, she was proud of her friends and all that they had accomplished.

A short burst of noise came across her com device before Carlo said, "Trolleys are here to take the reporters on the tour. Whenever Jonathan is ready."

The use of the trolleys was a great test run for how they would move guests during the wedding, she thought. She tracked down Jonathan who was standing beside his wife-to-be and her new boss, Sea Kiss Mayor Welding. "We're all ready for the tour. Just say the word."

Jonathan smiled and deferred to the politician. "It's your call, Mayor Welding."

The mayor immediately rushed to the podium on the stage and tapped on the microphone to draw attention to that area. Once the attendees quieted a little, he said, "Ladies and gentlemen. We're so very proud that the Pierce company has chosen Sea Kiss for the home of their new research and development center and we'd love to show you why. If you please, we have transportation available to give you a quick tour of our wonderful town."

The mayor, Jonathan, and Connie went out the door first to where the trolleys waited. As soon as they were filled, the operators would take them on a narrated drive around Sea Kiss, showing them the quaint town that as Jonathan had mentioned, some thought of as the Jewel of the Jersey Shore.

She hung back and watched through the wall of glass windows as the last of the reporters boarded the vehicles. Satisfied everything was operating efficiently with that part of the event, she did a quick check with Carlo via the com. "How's it going?"

"We're prepping for a second wave and Paolo and Tomás have everything under control," he said from right beside her.

She jumped. "Shit, you scared me."

He grinned, reached up, and brushed away a lock of her hair that had come loose from her french braid. "I love how focused you are when you work."

So focused she hadn't seen him nearby which was a shame. In deference to the big event, he had worn a suit. A new dark blue one that had clearly been custom made. She shifted her hands across his shoulders and said, "You lied to me, you know."

His smile faded and concern filled his dark gaze. "I don't lie."

She smiled and trailed her hands down the sleeves of his suit to grasp his hands with hers. "You said you weren't a suit kind of guy, but here you are rockin' these new threads."

A touch of color painted the sharp lines of his cheeks. "I didn't think I was, but when I saw how I looked . . ." He chuckled and lifted his arm to proudly show her the buttons on the sleeve. Real buttons with stitched buttonholes, one in a different color, and the top one undone. "Just like Owen taught me."

She didn't have time to wonder what other information the men had shared since Carlo jerked his head in the direction of the last trolley sitting outside. "We have time to sneak a ride."

"Let's," she said and they hurried out, hand-in-hand, and climbed into the warm interior of the trolley. They took a seat on one of the shiny wooden benches and Carlo tucked her into his side and wrapped an arm around her shoulders to keep her close. Feeling the comfort he always provided, she relaxed into his embrace, letting herself imagine how nice it would be to share moments like this more often.

The operator waited only another minute or two and satisfied they were the last people out of the building, he began his tour, but Emma didn't really pay attention. It was all too fairy tale, sitting beside him and driving through Sea Kiss. A gentle snow fall had begun, dusting the town like powdered sugar on a sweet. After the end of the Thanksgiving weekend a barrage of holiday lights and wreaths had gone up in the business areas and it was truly like looking at a picture-perfect holiday postcard.

Serenity filled her and she let herself bask in the feeling since she hadn't felt that way in such a long time. Not since. . .

She stopped that thought midstream, unwilling to let the past enslave her again. It was long overdue for her to put aside what had happened and her aloneness to live once more. To believe, as hard and scary as it was, that a life with the love of a good man was possible.

A good man like the one sitting beside her, she thought and snuggled closer to him. "It's beautiful, isn't it?" she said as they drove along Ocean Avenue and the gentle snow drifted to the sand and disappeared. It would take a lot more snow to create any kind of accumulation on the beach, but on the roofs of the beach houses and small cottages, a thin layer of white frosted the buildings.

"It is beautiful. Maybe even magical," Carlo said, a wistful tone in his voice.

Magical? she wondered and risked a glance at him. He was staring out the trolley windows, smiling, but shot a quick look at her and it was impossible to miss the peace in his gaze as well.

"Yes, magical," she repeated, slipped her hand into his, and sat back to savor the rest of the ride in blissful silence.

Their last to leave trolley was also the last to arrive, but as Carlo had indicated, Paolo and Tomás along with the rest of the crew were handling the return of the guests with aplomb. The media people were taking final photos and plying Jonathan and his partners with the last of their questions.

Connie peeled away from the gaggle of press people and came to their side. "This went well. Everything was perfect."

"I think Jonathan and his people put on quite a show. So did you and the Mayor and of course, Sea Kiss. Hollywood couldn't have scripted the day any better," Emma said.

Connie smiled with pride and contentment, but then she peered at Emma pensively. "No, it couldn't have. And did I maybe notice a change between you and Carlo?"

Although she was reluctant to admit it, Connie was always determined and wouldn't let go until she got what she wanted so Emma nodded and said, "I took your advice and talked to my mom."

"And?" Connie prompted with the arch of a dark perfectly plucked brow.

"It was . . . enlightening. It made me reconsider some things," she admitted.

"Like Carlo?" Connie pushed.

"Like Carlo and my life and what I want out of it," she said and before Connie could lead her to reveal more, she shot her hand up to stop any further discussion. "That's enough for now. It's all too new and I'm not really ready to share."

With a wry grin, Connie wrapped an arm around Emma and hugged her. "Well I'd say that's a good start."

FROM THE CORNER OF his eye Carlo caught sight of Emma and Connie as they stood off to the side of the room. Emma seemed way too serious, but Connie was smiling, so he hoped it was all good, just as it had been all good during the rest of the day. From the set-up for the event, to the event itself, trolley ride, and this last whirlwind hour as things wound down, he couldn't have asked for a better day.

As he stepped outside to check on how the crew was doing with loading the Cambros back into their van, he noticed Tomás helping Jesse unload a tray of dirty dishes. With his knee brace his brother had some mobility issues, but it hadn't kept him from being an immense help with some of the lighter chores. And although he sensed Tomás wasn't trying to show any favoritism, he had seen him helping the young widow more than once during their latest jobs.

Jesse and Tomás shared a laugh and a smile before Jesse returned to waitressing. As his brother hefted the tub with the dirty dishes onto a cart, Carlo's gaze crossed with his brother's and he realized there was a new light there. In all the years that his brother had been off in the military, Tomás had grown harder and more distant, but since he'd been in Sea Kiss the last couple of weeks, he'd loosened up. Carlo hoped that it meant that even if his brother's knee could take the strain of another enlistment, Tomás would choose to stay home.

"Yo, bro, stop daydreaming and get to work," Paolo called out and slapped him on the back as he wheeled a cart loaded with empty food trays down the sidewalk toward the van. As Paolo moved away, he heard him mutter, "Put a fancy suit on a guy and his hands get soft."

Carlo chuckled and shook his head, but for a second he wondered if maybe hanging out with the rich folks was changing him. Making him think that he was a suit kind of guy, but he quickly banished that thought. Jonathan might be a billionaire, but he had the callouses on his hands to prove how hard he had worked for that money. And Connie was a lot like him. The granddaughter of immigrants who'd fled Cuba, Connie had studied and worked to earn her law degree.

Emma . . . Emma had not had an easy time to get to where she was. Although she'd grown up in an upper middle-class town, he knew that money had become an issue for her family. She'd never said why and he hadn't asked because much like talking about her dad, he'd sensed that it was a topic that was off limits. Shaking his head, he acknowledged there was a lot about Emma that she kept hidden, but her latest actions were promising.

The chill of the snow landing on his face reminded him it was time to go back in and make sure that everything was set for the wedding that would take place in just over a week.

Inside, Connie and Jonathan stood arm-in-arm as did Maggie and Owen. Tracy was beside Emma and they were all chatting and smiling, their mood much more relaxed now that the media had left. For a second, he felt like an outsider looking in, but only for a second since this diverse group of people had welcomed him without hesitation.

They were as much family as his own family and now that work was over, he joined them in celebrating the day's success.

Chapter 11

The fire was toasty warm as the four friends lazed about in front of it, exhausted after the long day. An early rehearsal dinner had led to their bachelorette party of sorts while the men had gone off to have their own last celebration before tomorrow's wedding.

Emma sat on the floor and leaned against the sofa while Maggie sprawled above her on the seat cushions. Tracy had draped herself crosswise in a comfy side chair while Connie lay on a plush area rug in front of the chair and smoothed her hands down across the long loose Mets nightshirt she wore.

A week earlier, Connie's belly had suddenly popped out a little like one of those old-fashioned stove top popcorn makers. It wasn't a big bump yet, but in her current position it was decidedly noticeable. Not so obvious in the gown luckily, not that people seemed to pay much mind to that kind of thing lately. She'd seen nine-month pregnant brides waddle down the aisle with nary a raised eyebrow.

"I feel so weird," Connie said and ran her hands across the small mound, but there was a dreamy, slightly puzzled look on her face that was evidenced by her next words. "I never quite pictured myself like this."

"Neither did we, but it looks good on you. You're . . . glowing," Tracy said and leaned down to rub a hand across Connie's belly.

Connie sat up on her elbows and peered at herself. "Glowing, huh? Must be the firelight."

Maggie rolled onto her side and examined her friend. "Nope, it's not the firelight. I've never seen you happier."

Emma had to agree, but it wasn't just happiness she saw. There was serenity there. Peacefulness. Something she'd never seen in all the years she'd known Connie and her friend had been chasing a partnership in a big New York City law firm.

Connie narrowed her gaze thoughtfully, considering the statement, and with a shrug said, "I am happy. Amazingly so. I wouldn't have thought it, but I feel like . . . I feel like I'm finally where I was meant to be. Jon. The baby. Sea Kiss. My new job. Normally I'd be freaking out about all that, but now . . ."

She didn't need to finish because they all understood. Maggie maybe moreso since in the months after renewing her vows with Owen she too had seemed to find peace in her life.

"I totally get it," Maggie said, confirming what Emma had thought. "Things got off to a rough start with Owen and me, but lately everything is so good. It's nice to have someone who understands me and supports me."

"And it doesn't hurt that the Pierce brothers are both gorgeous men," Tracy said teasingly, trying to lighten the mood that was becoming too maudlin.

"It's tough, believe me. Sometimes I roll over in bed and see him . . . I feel sorry for this poor little one and what she has to endure," Connie said with a laugh and a pass of her hand over her belly.

"You think it's a girl?" Maggie asked, an almost wistful tone in her voice.

With another shrug, Connie said, "Yeah. I can't think of her as anything else so you better hurry up and give her a playmate, Mags."

Maggie chuckled and rolled her eyes. "Again, we're trying. All the time. It's like we never stop."

Tracy waved her hands fanatically. "Please, ladies. The next thing you know you'll both be soccer moms and I'll be the scrappy, wise cracking, old maiden aunt visiting for the holidays."

"You and me both," Emma added, shaking her head.

Connie huffed out a laugh and reached for the glass of sparkling apple juice she was having instead of the wine the rest of them had been drinking. "There's nothing maiden aunt about either of you too, puleez," she said and sipped her drink. Still holding the glass, she gestured with it toward Tracy. "You just made a mistake."

Tracy jumped in with, "A big one."

"So what? No one is entitled to a mistake?" Maggie said. "I sure have made more than a few in my life."

"And you," Connie continued, shifting her attention to Emma. "You've got Prince Charming right in front of you."

"I'm not some fairy tale princess who needs to be saved, Con," Emma shot back. "I'm a grown ass woman who can save herself."

"You go, girl," Maggie and Tracy both shouted out playfully and raised their glasses of wine in a toast.

Connie chuckled and lifted her glass. "That's right. You go, girl. Right to Carlo if you have a lick of sense."

"OMG, Con. Some things change, but you obviously don't. I still love you though," she said and nudged her friend with her stockinged foot.

"And I love you, Em, and Mags and Trace. You're my best friends forever!" Connie picked up her glass again and they all toasted for what most have been the hundredth time that night since Emma was starting to feel a buzz. A very pleasant buzz that wasn't only from the wine. Especially as Maggie shifted closer to the edge of the couch, reached down, and hugged her.

Emma returned the hug with a one-armed embrace and relaxed back against the sofa, content to just sit and sip as her friends chatted about all that had to get done in the morning to be ready for the wedding. Hair, make-up, dressing, and so many other everyday things, but her brain was adding all the things she had to make sure were ready since she was the wedding planner. Luckily she trusted that Carlo, despite his groomsman duty, would likewise keep things in mind so that as promised, they would give Connie and Jonathan the most epic wedding ever.

THE TWO PIERCE BROTHERS were in rare form, Carlo thought, as he watched them hoist up yet another glass of the aged bourbon Andy had brought for their bachelor party in Andy's new Sea Kiss home. It was a big Victorian that had once been an inn and was located just off Main Street in Sea Kiss and across from the boardwalk and beach on Ocean Avenue. Andy's wife had been nice enough to vacate the house until later that night and the men were sleeping there so the ladies could prep in private at the Sinclair home for the wedding.

"To Maggie and Connie, our lovely wives," Jonathan and Owen shouted out in slightly disjointed harmony.

"Not your wife just yet, Jon," Carlo reminded.

Jonathan grinned in response and said, "It's 'cause I can't wait. I love her, dude. Really really love her."

Owen slapped his brother on the back so hard Carlo winced, but Jonathan didn't flinch. Maybe because the bourbon had done a good job of numbing him.

"It's because she made you wait so damn long," Owen said and snorted a laugh.

"Says the man who fell in love with his wife at six," Jonathan parried.

Owen laughed good naturedly and nodded. "I always knew a good thing when I saw it and may I say, I agree with your choice and yours, Carlo."

Caralho, Carlo thought.

Jonathan plopped onto the sofa beside him and draped an arm around Carlo's shoulder. "No pressure, dude. But just remember that if you hurt Emma you'll have to answer to me and since I really like you that would be gnarly, dude."

Carlo shook his head. "I won't hurt Emma. I lo . . . I care for Emma."

"You love Emma," Owen said, slight disbelief in his tone, and sat down on his other side while Andy took a seat opposite them. "He loves the Ice Queen. That is gnarly," Owen added, mimicking Jonathan's favorite surfer expression.

Carlo chuckled. "That's what my brother Paolo calls her and yes, it is gnarly," he confessed.

Jonathan nudged him. "Hot guy like you is going to melt that ice."

"Yeah," Owen said and elbowed him as well from the other side, causing some of his bourbon to slosh from his glass onto Carlo's jeans.

"You guys think I'm hot, huh? I have to warn you I'm not into threesomes," Carlo said, hoping to shock his friends out of the discussion.

"What?" Jonathan said at the same time Owen shot him a puzzled look and a "Huh?"

"What he's saying is lay off him and Emma not to mention that it's time to hit the sack. Alone of course, unless you are into threesomes. Except for me of course since Sarah should be home soon," Andy said and to drive the point home, peered at his wristwatch.

"Tell me you're not pissed, dude," Jonathan said, finally realizing he might have stepped over a line with his comments about Emma.

"We mean well. You're our friend. Emma too," Owen said, his tone serious despite the alcohol-induced haziness of his gaze.

Carlo nodded and shot a look from brother to brother. "I know you mean well, but it's complicated. I'm asking that you leave it alone, okay?"

To make sure they understood, he rose, faced them, and held his hands up in pleading. "Leave it alone or you'll make things worse. Trust me."

Jonathan saluted and Owen nodded solemnly.

"Great and like Andy said, it's time to get some sleep. I need to be up early to meet with my crew and then get back here to make sure you all don't look like shit. Like you do now. We don't want the ladies to get one look at you and run away," Carlo joked, loosening up in light of the two brothers' slightly drunk and hangdog expressions.

"Sure thing, dude," Jonathan said.

"Maggie will kill me if I mess up tomorrow," Owen added and hiccoughed.

"Great. Glad to hear so get going," Carlo said and met Andy's amused gaze as the two brothers stumbled up the stairs to the bedrooms.

"I have to confess I've never seen Jon quite like this," Andy said with a chuckle.

"Me, either, but that's a good thing, isn't it?" Carlo said, smiling.

"Yes, it is. He's been way more happy and creative since he's been with Connie and that, my friend, is a thing to behold," Andy said and gave him a bro hug.

"The right woman can do that to a man." An image of Emma popped into Carlo's brain, causing his smile to broaden.

"Keep that in mind tomorrow, Carlo," Andy said with a nudge.

Carlo rolled his eyes and shook his head. "Not you, too, Andy."

With a shrug, the man walked away, but as he did so, he said, "I may be an old married dude, but I'm not blind, you know."

"Yeah, I know," he said, but didn't follow the other man up the stairs, needing some time to himself.

He sat on the couch and picked up his barely touched glass of bourbon. Took a sip and leaned his head back against the top of the sofa as he thought about all that he had to accomplish tomorrow as well as how to survive what was going to be an emotional day for everyone. Especially him and Emma. He had no delusions about that. Walking down the aisle with her was going to be tough for both of them. And contrary to what the guys were urging, he had to stay cool and let Emma set the tone for the day.

No matter how much he hoped that the change that had happened lately would continue, he wasn't going to push because like thin ice on the top of a lake, breaking through the surface could be dangerous.

Chapter 12

C arlo rested his hands on his hips and did a slow turn to take in the conversion of the research and development center's display area into the space for the cocktail reception which would take place before the wedding. Smaller table rounds were laid out through the space and had already been dressed with linens and centerpieces for the event later that afternoon.

Once the trolleys, carriages, and Pierce vehicles transported the guests to the beachside home for the wedding, they'd return to the R&D center for the reception once the ceremony was over. His crew would have to do a quick turnaround to get the area ready which would mean changing linens, adding cutlery and glassware, and chairs. The florist in town had designed amazing centerpieces which would combine the smaller cocktail ones into more elaborate decorations for the evening.

Which had him thinking about the flowers down at the beach house and whether everything was going well there. He whipped out his cellphone and dialed Emma, but it was Connie who breathlessly answered.

"Connie? Everything okay?" he asked, worried that something had gone wrong if the bride-to-be was answering.

"It's beautiful, Carlo. Everything is absolutely perfect! ¡*Tan lindo*!" she said and there was no mistaking the joy in her voice which brought relief.

"That's great. Is Emma around?" he said and held up his hand as Tomás walked toward him.

"She's kind of busy with a slightly hungover Maid of Honor and bridesmaid. Good thing I can't drink or it might have been three of us," Connie said with a laugh.

Carlo chuckled. "Totally get it. I'm not sure the guys are out of bed yet." He hoped the bourbon had worn off and had not left too many nasty reminders of the night before.

"*Carajo*, Carlo. What are you waiting for? Get back to Andy's and wake my man up! I'm waiting for him!" she teased and ended the call.

He laughed, shook his head, and Tomás said, "I guess everything is going okay?"

Carlo nodded. "You could say that. You doing okay?" He'd noticed a more pronounced limp in his brother's gait that morning.

Tomás grimaced and rubbed his leg. "I feel like an old woman when I say this, but weather's changing. I think snow is on the way again."

Carlo blew out a pained breath both because his brother was hurting, but also because of the possible snow. He'd heard it on the weather report on the way over this morning and had been hoping they were wrong. It would complicate moving everyone around. They normally didn't get much snow so close to the shore, but this winter was proving to be different so far.

He grasped his brother's shoulder and squeezed reassuringly. "Sorry you're hurting and if you're old, I'm ancient because I suspect that even in your current condition you could still kick my ass."

Tomás laughed and nodded. "I could. You're getting soft, *cabrão*." He poked Carlo's midsection and feigned surprise. "*Caralho*. You're all skin and bones."

Carlo yanked up his t-shirt to reveal his lean ripped abs. "All muscle, *mano*."

"You'll look good in that suit," his brother said with a rough exhale. "My brother in a suit. Never thought I'd see that day."

"You're just jealous 'cuz I look so good. Now get to work. I've got to wake up the men and make sure their ready."

"To meet their doom," Tomás teased in a horror movie kind of voice and held his hands up like scary claws.

The men walked outside and paused to look up at the sky. Thick clouds with dark streaks hung heavy in a leaden sky. Chilly air had that smell that just screamed snow.

Tomás patted his back and said, "Relax. It's nothing the da Costa brothers can't handle."

He nodded and said, "Yes, we can handle it. See you later."

As he walked away, Tomás sent him a parting shot. "I'll be sure to have my phone for some photos so *mamãe* can see you in your new duds. You look damn good, *cabrão*."

Carlo waved him off and got in his van for the drive through Sea Kiss and to Andy's house. Even with the threat of snow there were still a few early morning risers strolling through the shops. A news crew van was parked on one side street. Probably to try and get some shots of the "celebrity" wedding.

He turned away from Main Street and drove past Andy's house just to make sure it all seemed okay at the Pierce family home where the wedding would take place. The circular drive was already lined with the luminarias and floral arrangements would greet the guests as they arrived. The front door entrance was likewise decorated with flowers, ribbons, and lights. As Connie had told him earlier, it all looked beautiful and he trusted everything was going well inside also.

Relaxing a little, he turned back around and located parking near Andy's. In no time he was inside where Andy was doling out aspirins to Owen and Jonathan along with immense glasses of water.

Feeling like a little payback was in order for last night's Emma pressure, he made sure his voice was on the loud side as he heartily slapped the brothers on the back and said, "How's it going, dudes? All set for the big day?"

Both men winced and Jonathan glared at him. "We're ready. No thanks to you. Why didn't you stop us last night?"

Carlo grinned wryly. "I distinctly remember someone saying there was no stopping the Pierce brothers when I suggested you might reconsider having more alcohol. Do you remember that, Andy?"

Andy draped his arms across his chest and nodded. "I'm pretty sure that's what I heard."

Andy's wife Sarah waltzed in at that moment, walked up to her husband, and hugged him. With a playful tousle of his now short hair, she looked at him and said, "Thank you, Carlo. He looks so much better without all that mad scientist hair and that scraggly beard."

"But you love me anyway," Andy said and kissed her.

"I do and I may have to keep an eye on you today and fight off all those other women now that you're so handsome," she said before dropping a quick peck on his lips and hurrying out again with a wave.

A flush worked across Andy's normally pale cheeks. "I think she loves me."

"You're a lucky man and today, I'm going to get lucky also," Jonathan said cheerfully, but winced again at the loudness of his own voice.

Owen laughed and grimaced at the sound, but still managed to say, "Considering the bride's knocked up, I'd say you got lucky already."

"Sweet Lord, I never thought I'd be the one to have to reel you two in. Are you still drunk?" Carlo said and laid a hand on each brother's arm to take them into a large parlor where their suits were hanging on a portable garment rack Emma had brought over days earlier along with the clothing.

"Get your shit together, get upstairs, get clean, and get dressed. The photographer and videographer are going to be here in an hour," Carlo said.

"Shit, dude. Where's your client voice?" Jonathan groused as he massaged his temples with his fingers.

"Right now, I'm in friend mode. Get moving," he warned and was relieved to see the two of them comply despite their mumbled complaints. The brothers grabbed the garment bags with their suits, shirts, and ties, but fumbled with the shoeboxes.

"I'll get those upstairs for you," he offered and Owen and Jonathan left to get ready.

Carlo breathed a sigh of relief. Everything was under control here. Paolo and Tomás were in charge of his crew. Emma . . . things were going well with her also, so it was time he took the advice he had given the Pierce brothers and also got ready for the big event.

EMMA HAD TOLD HERSELF she wouldn't cry because it would mess up her make-up, but it was tough not to do as she watched the photographer shoot the final pre-wedding photos while the videographer hovered behind them, capturing the moment for posterity. Connie was radiant as Jonathan's little pup Dudley yipped excitedly with all the activity and weaved his way around the people gathered there, almost tripping up the photographer. The pup had a jaunty little seafoam bowtie with pink stripes around his neck because he was going to be a part of the bridal party also.

In a little while the first of the guests would arrive from the R&D center where the cocktail reception had been held. According to Carlo, who had phoned just moments earlier, everything had gone off well except for one of the horses leaving road apples in front of the building. That and the hangovers for the bridal party were simple enough to handle.

Luckily letting Jonathan and the other groomsmen mingle with the guests combined with the food had helped them fully recover from their bachelor party. Her friends had likewise gotten past their slight overindulgence of the night before. Mrs. Patrick and Emma had prepped a light breakfast for them that morning which had helped Maggie and Tracy's recovery.

Everyone looked great, she thought as the photographer snapped off family photos of Connie, her mother, and Connie's grandparents.

"Come on, one last girls' photo," Connie called out and held out her hand to urge them over after her family had stepped away.

A last photo, Emma thought and tried not to let those words pain her. Just because Maggie and Connie's lives had changed, that didn't mean their friendships would also change. Tracy must have sensed her upset since when they stood together for the photo, she made a point of squeezing Emma's waist reassuringly and whispering, "It's going to be all right."

It was going to be just fine, she told herself as the photos wound down and a chirp in the earbud she wore warned that Carlo or one of his brothers was in communications range. A second later, Carlo's voice came across the line. "We're here. Is it clear for us to come in?"

Emma clapped and called out to her friends. "Ladies. Time to let the men and guests get settled." She motioned to the room that would soon be Connie's home office and was doubling as a bridal suite.

Maggie and Tracy entered first and when Connie followed, Emma picked up the train on the dress to help out her friend. Connie called out to Dudley and he followed them obediently with jaunty steps and a playful bark. Inside the room Maggie and Tracy sat, but Connie paced with Dudley following her. Her nervousness was apparent as the sounds of guests arriving filtered in from beyond the closed door and Dudley drifted over to the entrance to sniff and whine. He must have sensed Jonathan's presence.

Emma rose and hugged Connie. "Hang in there. It won't be much longer."

Long minutes later Carlo's voice snapped across her earbud as he said, "Everyone's in place. Ready when you are."

Emma took a deep breath and splayed a hand across the nervous butterflies in her own midsection. She faced her friends and said, "It's time."

"Don't worry. Everything is going to be fine," Connie said and hugged her.

"I know. I just need to make sure everything's under control," Emma replied, her voice cracking with emotion.

Connie drew her in tighter and laid her cheek against Emma's. She stroked one hand down her back to soothe her. "Don't worry, Auntie Em." she teased.

"Dear God, please do not call me that, although with all of you married, I do feel like I'm lost in some other world," Emma confessed.

"Nothing will change, Em. If anything, you're going to get to see more of me for sure since we'll be neighbors."

"There is that," she said grudgingly.

"And you know Maggie will be coming down more often too. And Tracy will be needing us with all the changes in her life." Connie shot a look back at her friend who was clearly battling to stay chill even though she had to be hurting.

Emma glanced toward Tracy. "Yes, she'll need us, and we'll be there, right?"

Connie nodded and joined Maggie and Tracy at the far side of the room.

Emma stepped outside into the foyer to doublecheck that all was ready. As she stood there, the front door opened, letting a sharp gust of cold air blast into the foyer. Carlo hurried in, brushing snowflakes off the dark fabric of his suit.

Her mouth went dry and her heart skipped a beat at the sight of him, smiling so freely. His dark brown eyes glittered with happiness and as a lock of thick cocoa brown hair fell onto his forehead, he raked it back.

She imagined brushing away that hair as they made love. Sifting her fingers through the thick strands and then down across his cheeks to those full lips.

An inferno of need blazed to life and the heat spread across her skin. She sucked in a ragged breath and hurried to his side where she brushed some more snowflakes from his suit.

"Great. Snow. What else will go wrong today?" Emma groused and shook her head.

"The drivers said not to worry. It's only flurries and I checked the radar. It won't get worse," Carlo said.

"Everything will be totally fine today, because I'm getting married, Em. Getting married! Can you believe it?" Connie said as she walked to the door of the room but stayed out of sight of the guests.

"It's been a long time coming," Emma said and then grabbed Carlo's hand and dragged him to the front of the group of people waiting for the trip down the aisle. "Let's get this show on the road."

Connie gave a quick flip of her hand to Dudley who raced out of the foyer and up to the makeshift altar where Jonathan already waited. The dog launched himself into Jonathan's arms and after a playful tussle, Jonathan placed him on the floor where the pup dutifully took a seat. If Emma didn't know better, she'd say the dog actually had a smile on his face.

At the altar beside Jonathan was the priest from the local Catholic parish in deference to Connie's Cuban family. Her grandparents were already seated in the front row and on the opposite side were Jonathan's father and his mother who had only recently become a part of the men's lives together with a special needs brother who wasn't able to attend the wedding.

She peered around the room, trying to locate Connie's mother Lilli who was going to walk Connie down the aisle. Lilli was talking to Connie's grandparents at the front of the room. She looked beautiful in a rose-colored gown that worked perfectly with the seafoam and blush colors of the bridal party.

A cello player sat not far from the altar, softly playing classical music until it was time to switch to something suitable for the march down the aisle. She motioned to Lilli who excused herself and walked toward the foyer where Carlo had rounded up Owen and Andy.

"Maggie and Tracy. I need you first. Connie you wait until you hear the cello stop. Then count to five and join your mother in the middle of the foyer. Count to five again and once you hear the cello start –"

"I'll control myself somehow and sedately stroll down the aisle," Connie said and wrung her hands nervously around the bouquet Maggie had handed her.

"You'd think you hadn't seen him in weeks and not just a day," Tracy kidded.

Connie shrugged. "What can I say? He makes me happy."

"I know the feeling," Maggie added with a contented sigh.

Carlo walked over and laid a hand on her waist. "We're ready to go, Em."

With a shaky nod, Emma motioned Maggie to join her newlywed husband. The smiles on their faces as they walked down the aisle were so joyous that it filled the room with brightness despite the growing gloom of the snowy early December day visible from the wall of glass.

With another wave of her hand, she directed Tracy over to Andy who was grinning from ear-to-ear. Tracy was smiling also, but she knew her friend too well not to see that the smile on Tracy's face was strained and didn't quite reach up into her hazel eyes.

And then there was no avoiding Carlo any longer. After mouthing, "Count to five," at Connie, she walked to the center of the aisle and met Carlo there. His dark good looks were a perfect foil to her pale skin and reddish hair and as they walked down the aisle together, she could no longer fight her feelings for him. It just felt too right and for this day, she was going to enjoy this amazing man and whatever the day – or night—would bring.

At the altar, Jonathan stood beside Owen, Andy, and the priest, a broad smile on his face and his sea blue eyes glittering with joy. As she and Carlo reached the altar, they paused for a moment and their gazes collided. In that heartbeat the yearning on his face and the love was impossible to miss. It filled her with optimism she normally didn't have. Or maybe it was all the joy and happiness surrounding her on Connie and Jonathan's very special day.

As she took her spot, she cued the celloist with a subtle nod. The young woman acknowledged her with a smile and the tiniest dip of her head. A few seconds later the celloist wound down the sonata she'd been playing, set her bow hand on her leg, and glanced toward the foyer.

Emma trained her gaze on that spot as well and as she counted down in her head, Connie's mother took her spot in the foyer. Lilli held her hand out, and a second later, Connie stepped out and joined her mother.

Her friend was stunning. The blush of the dress was a perfect complement to her dark hair and exotic gold-green eyes. As Emma had thought, the cut of the gown and overskirt hid the slight baby bump and wonderfully showed off the rest of Connie's curvy and toned body.

Her friend's thick brown hair fell in artful waves to her shoulders and the floral tiara and barely there veil framed her gorgeous heart-shaped face. But as with Jonathan, it was her iridescent smile and the gleam in her eyes that made her beauty truly shine.

As Connie and Lilli linked arms, the celloist began an adaptation of Pachelbel's Canon. In sync, mother and daughter took the first step down the aisle, but despite Emma's earlier entreaty and Connie's promise for a sedate walk to the altar, her friend hurried to meet her husband-to-be who couldn't take his eyes off Connie.

When she neared, Jonathan stepped forward to take Connie's hand from her mother, but he apparently couldn't wait another minute to show her just how much he loved her. He wrapped his arm around Connie's waist and kissed her, earning applause and laughter from those gathered for the ceremony. Dudley barked excitedly and raced around them in a circle, clearly joyous for his pet parents.

After Jonathan released her, Connie reached up and wiped away the traces of her lipstick from his mouth and Dudley took a spot between them. This time there was no mistaking the joy on his puppy face.

"You're very impatient, Mr. Pierce," Connie said, smiling.

"And you, soon-to-be Mrs. Reyes-Pierce, are irresistible," Jonathan said, grinning.

"Which means we should start this ceremony and get you both wed," the priest said with a stern but playful glance.

"We definitely should," her friends said in unison, joined hands, and stood close together as the priest began the introductory rites for the wedding celebration.

Emma had been to so many weddings, she could recite the vows in her sleep and yet hearing her friends recite them roused deep emotion from within. Especially as the priest offered up a blessing for them and took a moment to speak about the wonders of marriage and the commitment to love one another through all the challenges life would bring them. Like the baby that would soon join them although the priest was astute enough not to mention that as he joined their hands together to continue with the ceremony.

The priest smiled and said, "Do you Jonathan Frances Pierce take Consuelo Maria Reyes as your lawfully wedded wife, to have and to hold, from this day forward, for better or for worse, for richer or for poorer, in sickness and in health, to love and cherish until death do you part?"

Jonathan had been so focused on his wife-to-be as the priest spoke that Connie had to squeeze his hand to prompt him for the traditional "I do."

"Do you Consuelo Maria Reyes take Jonathan Frances Pierce as your lawfully wedded husband, to have and to hold, from this day forward, for better or for worse, for richer or for poorer, in sickness and in health, to love and cherish until death do you part?" the priest asked.

"I do," her friend said strongly and without hesitation, making Emma's heart clench with joy.

Jonathan grinned and Owen leaned forward to hand him the ring. Jonathan's hand shook as he slipped the wedding band on Connie's finger, and Connie's hand was none too steady either as she eased the ring on Jonathan.

The priest continued with the blessing of the rings and after, her friends recited the Lord's Prayer together before the nuptial blessing.

Emma waited, expectant, until the priest finally and happily said, "You may now kiss the bride."

Jonathan did, dragging Connie tight against him and digging his fingers into her hair to hold her tenderly as he kissed her. She kissed him but pulled back at the priest's warning cough. Smiling, Connie said, "I love you, Jon. As long as we're together, we will always be home."

Grinning, he nodded and said, "Always, Connie."

Emma's throat choked up at the tender scene and she prayed that every day of her friends' lives would be as happy as today.

As the newly married couple faced their guests, loud applause and cheers greeted them and for good measure, Jonathan grabbed Connie and kissed her again. When they broke apart, the celloist started to play and the bride and groom sashayed down the aisle to the foyer.

Once they were a few feet away, she met Carlo in the center of the aisle. Caught up in the moment much as she was, he was smiling and offered her his arm. She slipped hers through his and took hold of his hand, trying to keep hers from shaking. Trembling, she hurried down the aisle until they reached the foyer and it was time to go into wedding planner mode.

But as she walked away, Carlo kept a hold of her hand and dragged her close. He cupped her cheek and said, "Relax, Emma. Everything is going great."

"It has to go great, Carlo. Connie and Jonathan deserve the best," she said.

With a small smile, he said, "So do you." And then he leaned in and kissed her. Just a quick short kiss that so surprised her she had nothing to say when he stepped back and tugged on her hand to pull her toward the trolleys and Pierce vehicles waiting out front.

"Come on. We've got the world's most epic wedding to finish," he said.

Chapter 13

Carlo stood with Paolo and Tomás in the prep room where servers were busy whisking in the guests' dinner choices. So far everything had progressed perfectly and he and Emma had had little to do since his brothers had kept everything running smoothly.

"Are you sure you don't need me for anything?" he asked again, worried that maybe things were going too well.

"*Mano*, go enjoy yourself. We've got it all under control," Paolo said, confidence in his tone.

Since his youngest brother sometimes shot from the hip, he looked at Tomás for confirmation. "Seriously?"

Tomás swung an arm over her shoulders. "Seriously. Everyone is pitching in so you don't have to worry. Paolo's got the meals moving along. Jesse and me are helping the wait staff keep up. Cake is ready for later along with the pastries for the dessert table. Coffee is brewing and water is heating for tea."

He hated to say it, but it did sound like his brothers had everything taken care of which meant he could head back to the dais and just be a guest for once.

"I'll see you guys later," he said, but Tomás shook his head and steered him toward the door to where the reception was being held.

"*Mano*, we don't want to see you for the rest of the night. The only thing you have to worry about is what you're going to do about the Ice Queen because from what I can tell, she's quickly melting thanks to many glasses of champagne."

Many many glasses, Carlo thought. Since the first toast when Connie and Jonathan had shared their first kiss and welcomed the guests, Emma had been downing the bubbly and while it had made her relax, he was worried she was getting way too relaxed.

"Go forth and be her Knight in Shining Armor," Tomás teased and faked dubbing him with a sword.

Carlo glared at him and said, "Don't think that just because you're injured, I won't kick your ass."

"As if you could, but seriously. She needs someone to take care of her and who better than you? Don't delay because I've seen a number of the single dudes eyeing her." His brother gave him a playful shove out into the reception area, giving him no choice but to go forth as his brother had kidded.

Emma was sitting beside Tracy, sipping another glass, and smiling as she chatted with her friend. As the two laughed and Emma's nose crinkled, she looked almost pixiesh, especially with her creamy white skin and strawberry blonde hair. When she glanced away from Tracy and noticed him heading her way, a big smile came to her face and she waved at him, a little too loosely and unsteady.

Too much champagne, he thought, regretting that her ease around him was alcohol-induced.

As he reached the table, the singer for the band wound down the song and asked the guests who had been dancing in the center of the room to return to their tables for dinner. A second later his wait staff streamed from the prep room, trays laden with covered dishes with the meals.

"Like clockwork," he heard Paolo say through his earbud.

He couldn't disagree and so he sat beside Emma who smiled at him again and leaned toward him. "Like clockwork," she said, repeating Paolo's words. She tried to snap her fingers to confirm it, but they didn't seem to be working.

With a laugh, he took hold of her hand and teased, "Just how many glasses of champagne have you had?"

She held up four fingers on her other hand and then stuck up a fifth. Squinting her eyes, she searched for a way to put up another few fingers, but he was holding on to her hand. Shaking her head, she said, "Maybe too many."

"Maybe," he repeated as Jesse placed their dishes in front of them with a grin and a wink.

Carlo gestured to the plate. "How about we get some real food inside you? Maybe it will help you feel better."

"I feel great and so do you," she said, leaned against him, and nuzzled his jaw with her nose.

Any other time he would have welcomed her playfulness, but not this way.

Once more he pointed to her plate with the perfectly done filet mignon with red wine demi-glace, smashed fingerling potatoes, and grilled asparagus. "Eat, Emma. Now."

With a pout that made him want to kiss those delicious lips, she relented and ate. But her murmurs of appreciation had his mind and body working overtime as he imagined her murmuring to him as he made love to her. He had hoped that tonight would have been the first step toward that since pre-bubbly Emma had been slowly opening up to him.

Now his one hope was to get Emma sober enough so that the night he'd hoped for would get back on track. As a waiter approached with a fresh round of champagne, he glared at the young man who quickly detoured away. The young server was intercepted by Tomás who handed him a smaller tray with glasses. Hopefully sparkling cider, Carlo thought as the waiter returned and replaced their empty glasses with the new drinks.

Carlo swallowed his bite of the tasty and tender steak and picked up the glass. With a sip he confirmed his suspicions. Sparkling cider, but as Emma took a sip, she luckily didn't seem to notice the difference.

He breathed a sigh of relief and dug into his meal, hungry after the long day filled with so much emotion and activity. The steak filled his belly and as he gazed over at Emma, she seemed to be a little more alert.

"That was delicious. You did an amazing job," she said and sipped her drink.

"*We* did. *We* should be happy with the work *we* did," he said and cradled her cheek.

"*We're* good together," she said and narrowed her gaze to skip it over his features, as if surprised at her words.

"We *are* good together, Emma. We get each other," he said and rubbed his thumb across the smooth skin of her cheek. He shifted it to her full lower lip and smoothed it across the soft edges of her mouth.

"You think you know me –"

"I do, Em. I know you," he said to allay the sadness that had crept into her emerald eyes.

"You only think you do." She covered his hand with hers, turned her face just enough to drop a kiss on his palm. Then she gently eased his hand away and twined her fingers with his, giving him the courage to believe she wasn't totally retreating from him.

His crew came around to efficiently clean away the dishes and prep for the final service of the night. As they finished clearing the dinner plates, Tomás and Jesse wheeled the table with the multi-tiered wedding cake over from where it had been sitting by the front dais and the wedding singer announced that it was time for the cake cutting.

Connie and Jonathan stepped down from the dais hand-in-hand, blissful smiles on their faces. As they reached the table, Jesse handed them the silver cake knife and the photographer and videographer swooped in to commemorate the event. Lights flashed as the first cut was made and after, as the cake was plated and the ecstatic couple fed each other.

Carlo's gut warmed at the thought of what would come next and the possibility that they'd have a repeat of what had happened at Maggie and Owen's wedding several months earlier. As he glanced at Emma from the corner of his eye, he noted the pleased smile on her face.

"Are you ready for this?" he asked.

With a chuckle, she said, "Never." She arched a reddish blonde brow and added, "And you?"

He laughed and shook his head. "Never."

"Come on, Emma. It's time for us single girls," Tracy said and popped out of her chair, wobbling as she stood.

Great, he thought and wondered how he'd take care of Tracy as well.

Emma rose from her chair, locked her arms with Tracy, and the two women supported each other as they joined the group of single women on the dance floor. Connie pointed to both of them and winked, making it clear who she wanted to catch her bouquet. She turned, held the bouquet up in the air, and waved it mischievously, the ribbons on the bouquet dancing around her hand as she did so. The wedding singer began the countdown, and Emma and Tracy inched forward, allowing the rest of the women to shift to a better bouquet-catching spot.

The countdown ended and Connie tossed the flowers up and over her head. The bouquet soared through the air, past Emma and Tracy and into the hands of two women. After a little tussle that sent some of the bouquet flowers scattering, one woman emerged victorious and waved the bouquet over her head in victory.

Carlo breathed a sigh of relief mixed with disappointment. As Emma and Tracy returned to the dais, Emma peered at him and said, "It's your turn now. Get up there."

He glared at her jokingly but did as she commanded. He watched as Jonathan teased Connie while he removed the garter. After he stood and waved it in the air, the groom pointed to him much like Connie had gestured to her friends earlier.

"Who me?" he mimed and pointed at himself.

Jonathan repeated his gesture and turned, but as he did so, Carlo moved as far off to the side as he could. The garter flew through air and straight at Paolo's head as he walked by with a tray loaded with plates of cake slices. Somehow his brother managed to swat it away and over to one of the young men in the crowd of energetic garter seekers.

Relief flooded him again and he hurried back to the dais. Emma smirked at him as he sat. "I saw you sneaking out of there," she teased, steadier than she had been before.

He leaned close and whispered in her ear, "And you avoided the toss like a champ."

A sharp burst of laughter escaped her. "I did, didn't I? Maybe I prefer for our kiss to be more private."

He jerked as if she'd hit him and pulled back to gaze at her, surprised. "Our kiss? More private?"

She smiled, her gaze clearer, and laid her fingers against his lips. "It is what you were hoping for, isn't it?"

He kissed the pads of her fingers, reached up, and grasped her hand gently. He ran his thumb across her knuckles and said, "I don't lie, remember."

"So?" she pressed.

"I want to kiss you in private. In public. I want to kiss you everywhere, Emma."

A wry smile lifted one side of the lips he so wanted to savor. "What's stopping you?"

Chapter 14

Did I just say that? Emma thought and waited expectantly, her heart pounding so loudly she worried he might hear it.

He squinted and considered her carefully. "Please tell me that's not the champagne talking."

"You mean the cider you slipped me with dinner instead?" she said with an arch of a brow.

A chagrined smirk erupted on his lips. The lips she so wanted against hers.

"I didn't think you'd notice," he admitted and brushed back a few wayward strands of her hair that had worked free of the braid and floral headpiece at the crown of her head.

"I'm not that drunk," she shot back.

"Just half-drunk? Maybe I should wait until you're full sober for that kiss," he said and raised her hand to brush a tender kiss across her knuckles.

She hated that he was right. "Maybe," was all she could muster with a shrug and looked away from him.

The heat of his breath spilled across the side of her face a second before he whispered a kiss across the sensitive skin there. A tease of what she could expect when they finally did whatever it was they were destined to do.

But as much as she wanted tonight to lead to more, a part of her worried what that more might be and if she was truly ready for it. Which had her reaching for another glass of champagne as it came by rather than pushing it away. As she met Carlo's gaze over the rim of the glass, she almost dared him to stop her, but he raised his own glass and tapped it to hers.

She was about to take a sip when the band launched into a fast-paced salsa piece and Carlo rose and offered his hand to her.

"Me?" she squeaked and shot a quick look at the dance floor where the newlyweds and several of Connie's family were expertly moving to the beat.

"You," Carlo confirmed and wiggled his fingers in invitation.

Tracy nudged her with her elbow. "Go. It's not as hard as it looks."

Peering at the dancers, she thought it looked really hard and she wasn't much of a dancer as she'd proven the night at the China Latino restaurant. But with Carlo waiting there, his gaze expectant, she couldn't refuse.

She slipped her hand into his and shot to her feet. At the edge of the dance floor, he took hold of her hands, leaned close and whispered, "It's just an easy four/four beat."

Maybe it was only she couldn't seem to think straight much less count out the beats with him so close. All she could think about was the feel of his calloused hand in hers and at her waist, guiding her. Strong hands, but so gentle at the same time. The smell of him enveloped her, something light and citrusy.

As he stepped forward on the one beat, she stomped on his foot and mumbled an apology. He smiled and said, "Relax."

She found herself doing just the opposite, intently looking down at their feet and trying to count out the one-two-three and then rest beat in her head. As she trod on his foot again, she mumbled a curse.

"*Meu amor*, look up. At me. You can do this," he urged, the tone of his voice soft and soothing.

Emma met his gaze and forced a smile. She wanted to relax and give herself over to the music but couldn't when she was so hyper aware of everything about him. From the flecks of gold in his dark brown eyes to the slight dimple in his right cheek as he smiled to the smooth way he moved his hips in time to the salsa beat. Everything about him was perfect, but as she mangled his foot once again, she realized she wasn't.

Disappointment slammed into her and in the back of her brain, she heard her father's condemning voice telling her she wasn't good enough. That she could never do anything right. Luckily the song ended at that moment with a loud crashing beat of the drums and she was able to make her escape, not that Carlo wasn't wise enough to see her upset.

"It's okay, Em. You just need to trust your partner," he said and rubbed her back as they sat at their table once again.

She wanted to trust him about so much more than a salsa dance, but worried that maybe she never could and that if she did, she'd disappoint him anyway. Which had her reaching for her glass of champagne. She sipped the bubbly. Had a second and third glass but the liquor did nothing to improve her mood. It didn't stop her from having more until her head was whirling and she cursed herself for not using better judgment. Especially as she rose to join everyone as they walked out to the front of the building where a limo waited to whisk Connie and Jonathan to a private jet waiting to fly them to a week's honeymoon at a private tropical isle.

She wobbled unsteadily and Carlo was immediately there, wrapping an arm around her waist to steady her as her newlywed friends waved to everyone and climbed into the car. As they walked back in, her high heeled shoes slipped on the snowy ground, but Carlo supported her. With the ocean nearby, snow rarely held on for long unless it was a major snowfall. But as she looked up at the night sky, the snow was still coming down.

"So much for your radar and only flurries. It's going to be a big one," she said.

"So much for science," he said as he walked her back inside and to the dais. "Set yourself here while I see how we're doing."

Since her head was whirling, she didn't argue and plopped down beside Tracy who to her chagrin was way more sober. "Why did I do this?" she murmured and massaged her temples.

"Because you're afraid of what might have happened so now you're going to take my advice," Tracy said and took hold of Emma's hands.

Maggie came over and sat on her other side. Laid a hand on her thigh and said, "Are you okay?"

"Fine. Just fine," she said although she really wasn't.

"Maybe it's time we took you home," Maggie said, but Tracy held her hand up to silence her friend.

"Carlo can take her home. It's time for you and Owen to go home and I'm going back to my room at the inn," Tracy said.

"No way. Come on, Emma. We'll take you home," Maggie said, but Emma shook her head.

"I'm okay. Besides, I'm the wedding planner, remember? I have to make sure Carlo and his people don't need my help," she reminded her friend, not that she could be much help in the condition she was in. But she had to try.

Maggie and Tracy looked at one another, obviously doubtful of her claim, but then they relented.

"You can go, Mags. I'll stay with Emma until Carlo comes back," Tracy said, but she didn't have long to wait since a few minutes later, Carlo returned to the dais.

"Everything okay?" Emma asked.

"Totally under control. My brothers have things running smoothly and any breakdown we don't finish tonight on account of the snow can be done in the morning," he said and rubbed her shoulder in reassurance.

She looked up him. "Are you sure?"

He smiled supportively. "Never more sure. Let me take you home."

She relented and rose slowly, mindful of every action and step to try and convince everyone that she was okay. Only she wasn't on so many levels.

Maggie and Tracy walked with her to the doors leading to the parking lot where they'd left their cars earlier that day in anticipation of the end of the night. Owen joined them by the door and hugged Maggie to him.

"Ready?" Owen asked and kissed his wife's temple.

Maggie risked a quick glance at Emma who nodded. "I'll see you guys tomorrow," she said and hugged the couple.

"We'll drive you to the inn," Owen said to Tracy and her friends were soon on their way, leaving her with Carlo.

"I'll take you home," he said and wrapped an arm around her waist.

"Thanks. I appreciate it," Emma said and leaned into him for support. Together they slogged through the snow that had started to accumulate in the hour or so while the guests had been partaking of the dessert table and hot beverages after Connie and Jonathan had left. More than once her shoes slipped on a wet patch, but luckily Carlo was there. He bundled her into his van and in no time they were on their way to her house which was only a few blocks away. In truth, had the weather been better, she might have walked the short distance to clear her head, but the quickly falling snow had made that impossible.

Carlo pulled his van into her driveway and she said, "Thank you. I appreciate you driving me back."

"I'll see you in," he said, but she waved off his offer.

"No need. I'm okay." Although she was a little woozy, the effects of the champagne had started to wear off.

"I'll see you in, Emma. Don't argue with me," he said and before she could protest again, he'd charged out of the car and walked around to open her door. He offered his assistance and seeing the glower on his face, she didn't argue.

She took hold of his hand and stepped out of the vehicle. The ground was slick beneath her feet and he once again provided stability until they were comfortably inside the warmth of her cottage. As she turned to face him, her wet soles slid awkwardly on her wooden floor, but his powerful arms were around her, keeping her upright.

"Let's get you settled," he said and once again she didn't fight with him maybe because a big part of her wanted him to stay, even if she was still unsure of whether it made sense to move their relationship to the next level. He walked her to her bedroom and over to the bed. Whirling on one foot, he presented his broad back to her to give her a chance at modesty, and said, "Get tucked in and I'll go."

She stared at him as he stood there, rocking back and forth on his heels, obviously uneasy. But was his unease about staying or going? she wondered because it mirrored her own emotions.

"What if I don't want you to go?" she said, her voice unsteady.

CARLO STOOD STOCK STILL, processing her words over and over. How many times had he wished for a moment quite like this and yet, not like this with her not really herself.

"I don't think that's such a good idea," he said as he heard the rustle of fabric that warned that she was getting undressed. To keep from turning to look at her, he focused on the wall in front of him with its feminine wallpaper of pink roses in a stripe pattern.

"You said to trust you. I do," she said, her words still a little slurry and accompanied by yet more rustling. The bedspread he hoped as he peered over his shoulder and found her with the covers tucked up to her chin, her arms and shoulders bare.

His cock twitched and tightened at the thought of her all bare beneath the bedspread.

"I should go," he said, but her words came again, blurred with sleep this time.

"Please stay."

"I warned you before, Emma. I'm not a saint," he replied and waited for her response, but all that followed was a long inhale and a soft snore.

He turned to find her fast asleep, one hand tucked up to her cheek and the other spread out on the empty space beside her, as if she was reaching for something. Someone. Him.

His brain told him to go. That nothing good could come of his staying.

But his heart . . . the heart that had longed for so long to be with her made up thousands of excuses for why he should remain in the blink of an eye. Everything from what could happen if she woke up ill to her falling out of bed and cracking her head open. And with all those dire scenarios running through his head, he gave in to his heart's desire.

He walked over to a wing chair placed invitingly before a gas fireplace in her bedroom. The remote for the fireplace was on a small table by the chair. There was a hint of damp and chill in the air thanks to the snowy night and since he planned on sleeping above the covers as a safety precaution, he snapped on the fireplace.

The warmth was instantaneous and welcome as he slipped off his shoes, socks, suit, and shirt. The heat warmed him as he stood there in his briefs and carefully folded his shirt and pants, and hung his suit jacket over the chair, delaying. Hesitating as he considered what might come of his decision not to leave.

But with the decision made, he returned to the bed and gently picked up the arm flung out over the empty space beside her, careful not to wake her. He slipped into that space and as soon as he did, she shifted closer and flung her arm back over him and nestled her head on his shoulder.

It was torture being so close to the person he wanted most and wasn't sure it made sense to have. But as the warmth of the fireplace and her body chased away the chill, he closed his eyes and let himself believe that it wasn't all a big mistake. That come the morning and the light of day, everything would be as it should and he and Emma . . .

He paused there, not wanting to jinx himself with the thought. Whatever was meant to be would be and with that he wrapped an arm around her to keep her close and let himself dream.

Chapter 15

Emma woke to tempting warmth and a teasing tickle against her cheek. Half asleep, she tried to smooth away whatever was causing it and encountered a wall of hard muscle and crisp chest hair. She groaned and screwed her eyes shut as memories of the night before pummeled her brain.

"You okay?" Carlo said and his deep voice rumbled through her, awakening other parts of her body.

"I am so so sorry," she said and met his amused gaze.

"I have to confess that in all the dreams I had about our first night together –"

"You dreamed about us being together?" she asked, and her heart pounded, rushing blood to all those already alert parts.

With a half grin that awakened that enticing dimple she had noticed the night before, he shifted so they were face-to-face on the pillow and covered the hand she had splayed on his chest. "I never imagined our first night together or the morning after would be quite like this."

There was no mistaking the look in his eyes and what he had expected, but that didn't keep her from saying, "What did you imagine?"

"Something more like this," he said, cradled her cheek, and whispered a soft kiss across her lips.

"And like this," he continued and shifted to the sensitive spot right below her ear where he dropped another kiss before leaving a trail down to where her neck met her shoulder. The lick of his tongue had her shuddering a second before his tender love bite rocked her world.

She moaned and arched up. The bedspread that had been separating them and covering her slipped down a dangerous inch. Enough that he bent and kissed his way across the swell of her breasts before returning to her lips.

Her nipples were tight, sensitive against the fabric, but she wanted to feel his skin against hers. She jerked the bedspread down as he hauled her close and skin met skin.

They both shook and broke away from the kiss, breathing heavily.

"Is this how you pictured it?" she asked and shifted even closer. The long hard ridge of his morning erection pressed against her belly and damp heat flooded between her legs at the thought of him making love to her. Filling her with his incredible length. Covering her with his big beautiful body.

"Maybe," he said softly earning her puzzlement as he gently drew up the bedspread to cover her breasts.

"Just maybe?" she asked and stroked her hand across the hard sweep of his collarbone.

"I always imagined I'd take you somewhere nice. Maybe the Lighthouse Inn. We'd have dinner. A little wine. Not too much because when I make love to you, I want to know it's you responding, and not the liquor."

Warmth bathed her cheeks at the recollection of the night before and how that hadn't been the case, but he was gentleman enough not to mention it as he continued.

"We'd walk back. Maybe stop for ice cream on the corner or some pastries at the bakery because we were going to have coffee and dessert back here."

"Just coffee and dessert?" she teased and reached up to smooth away a dark lock of hair that had fallen onto his forehead. His hair was silky and thick. Alive beneath her fingers as she tangled them into the ever-tousled waves of his hair.

With a shrug of broad powerful shoulders, he said, "Maybe more, but only if you wanted more."

He waited, obviously expectant. "Maybe I'd want more," she said, still caught in that seesaw of emotions that lately had her opening herself to more with him.

He smiled and cupped her cheek. "Do you realize we've never been on a real date?"

She hadn't realized because they had spent so much time together over the years. And then there had been all her friends' weddings where he'd been her plus one. Not really a date, but close to one considering she'd not had a date with anyone else in all that time.

At her silence, he said, "I'd like to go on a real date with you. I'd like to take you to dinner, walk you home, and see where it might go."

She wanted to say that they were exactly where it might go and that she wished he'd touch her. Kiss her again until she was breathless. Make love to her until she was writhing on the sheets beneath his hard, powerful body. Instead she let common sense reign and said, "I'd like that. Are you free tonight?"

He grinned and nodded. "For you I'd cancel any plans."

CARLO STOOD AT THE door as he had countless times before. Only this time he was as nervous as shit, all done up in the blue suit he'd worn just a couple of days earlier at the press event, holding a bouquet of pink carnations and a bottle of red wine which he'd spent more on than he'd ever had before in his entire life.

He wanted to make a good first impression for their first ever date. Silly considering he'd known Emma for over eight years, but it was their first date because he wasn't counting the night at his friend's restaurant as a date. He hadn't picked her up, paid for the meal or taken her home. That night didn't count, but tonight definitely did. Tonight was an official "maybe we should be more than just friends and business colleagues" date. He hoped it wouldn't be the last one.

The door popped open about five seconds after he knocked and he recalled Emma's mantras to brides who were too eager to rush down the aisle. *Count to five.*

Had she been waiting expectantly on the other side of the door and used her own suggestion to keep control? he wondered.

"Come on in," she said and he stepped into the warmth of her cottage. Warm not just because of the radiators with the slight hiss from their steam, but because of the bright colors and comfortable looking couches and chairs arranged before a fireplace with logs that looked ready to be lit.

Warm, dare he even say hot, because of the woman standing before him in an emerald green velvet dress that smoothed across her slender curves, making him itch to touch them. The color deepened the green of her eyes, reminding him of the most secret parts of a forest at night.

"You look beautiful," he said and thrust the flowers and bottle of wine at her.

She smiled hesitantly and skimmed her hand down her midsection. "Thank you. You look so handsome in your suit."

Trying to ease the tension vibrating between them, he mimicked her actions and ran his hand down the front of his suit jacket. "This old thing? I wanted to look nice for you."

She laughed as he intended, and the uneasiness evaporated like morning dew beneath the rising sun. "That's my line," she said and gestured toward the kitchen. "Let me get a vase for these and then we can go. Where are we going by the way?"

"The Dunes. Mac and Meghan do such a fabulous job with the menu and I wanted to support our locals," he said.

Emma nodded and walked toward the kitchen. He heard the clink of glassware and running water as she called out, "I love that place. It's so romantic."

He'd been going for romantic because he wanted to romance Emma like she'd hopefully never been romanced before. He only wished he could have seen her face as she said that to figure out if Emma thought romantic was a good thing. But as she strolled out of the kitchen smiling, the bright pink carnations tucked into a vase, he supposed that she thought romantic was a good thing.

"I love carnations. The scent is so spicy," she said and buried her face into the blooms to take a big sniff.

"I know. You have bunches of them in your garden every year."

She appeared a little taken aback by that and set the vase on the coffee table in front of the couch. "I didn't realize you'd noticed."

He stepped closer, took hold of her hand and said, "I've noticed a lot about you, Emma. Like how your hands get cold when you're nervous." Like they were now, and he rubbed them to bring them warmth.

"How your nose sometimes crinkles when you're really really thinking about something," he said and tapped the tip of her nose

He closed the last little distance between them and cradled her waist with his hand. Bending slightly, he whispered a kiss across her cheek. "And that your lips are so soft and sweet, it's all I can do not to kiss you senseless right now."

She turned her face just enough that her breath spilled across his lips as she said, "Sounds good to me."

He kissed her with all the pent up need he'd been holding back, the kiss hard and demanding. She answered back just as greedily, opening her mouth beneath his to accept the slide of his tongue. Grabbing hold of his lapels to hold him close, she pressed herself against him. Over and over they kissed until they were both shaking and breathless and finally broke apart.

"I think we better go eat," he said roughly, his body shaking with need. His brain sure of only one thing: if they didn't leave soon, he wouldn't be able to keep from making love to her right then and there.

She nodded and said, "I think that's a good idea."

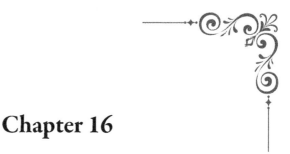

Chapter 16

Jonathan's Thunder SUV prototype sat at the curb outside her cottage. As Carlo clicked a button on the fob, the interior lights clicked to life. At her questioning glance as Carlo opened the door for her, he said, "Jonathan wanted someone to put it through everyday paces while he and Connie were away."

"Not quite sure I see you as a soccer mom," she teased and sat in the luxurious interior of the SUV. The seats were a buttery soft leather. The assorted gauges on the dash looked like what she imagined high tech rocket ship controls would appear, only wrapped in gleaming burlwood and charcoal gray polymer.

"Very nice," she said as Carlo slipped into the driver's seat.

He grinned and soothed his hands across the shiny wooden steering wheel. "Perfect for a soccer dad. You know us Portuguese love our soccer."

She rolled her eyes. "Don't I?" She glanced toward the back of the luxury SUV. "So how many soccer players do you think you could fit in here?"

He shot a quick glance back before starting the engine with the push of a button. "At least three or four kids. Perfect."

Just like it was funny that they'd never been on a date, they'd never talked about what either of them wanted in life. "You think you'd like three or four kids?" she asked.

He shrugged. "Never much thought about it. Two would be nice. Boy and a girl. And you?"

As he watched her from the corner of his eye, she said, "I never thought about it because . . ." She didn't know how to finish because in the space of a millisecond they'd stepped onto dangerous ground.

He shot her a quick look and apparently sensing her discomfort, he said, "I'm grateful Ricardo and Javier have so many kids. It takes the pressure off the rest of us, you know."

His words alleviated some of the pressure she had been feeling and luckily, they had reached the restaurant which was less than a mile from her home. As smoothly as he had pulled the car out of her driveway, Carlo parallel parked it a few spots away from their destination.

"You know it parks itself, right," she said and motioned to a button on the dash.

With a shrug, Carlo said, "Growing up in the Ironbound you had to know how to parallel park to survive. Don't want to lose the skill."

Emma laughed and held her hands up in surrender. "Us suburban girls don't do parallel park."

"And Jersey Girls don't pump gas," Carlo said with a chuckle and hurried out of the car.

She opened the door and he rushed over to help her out of the SUV. A sharp breeze blew off the river inlet, sending a chill through her and Carlo tucked her against his side and shielded her from the wind with his body. They picked up their pace and speedily reached the entrance of the Victorian-style building where the restaurant was located.

The restaurant had three stories and its location close to the mouth of the river gave it an unimpeded view of Sea Kiss Beach, the river inlet, and across the way, the piers and lights of the neighboring Jersey Shore towns to the south. On the ground floor a front porch wrapped around the entire building while the other stories had verandas that faced the beach and river. In warmer weather guests could sit and have drinks on the front porch or meals on the verandas.

Even though it was off season, the restaurant was fairly full, but since Mac and Meghan were friends, the hostess immediately had a table ready for them. After checking their coats, they were guided to a spot on the third floor. From that height, the views were spectacular and thanks to a clear night, dozens of stars were visible against the inky dark sky.

Fine linens and china graced the table. Crystal twinkled with the light cast from the votive candle in the table's center. A tussie mussie of bright colored flowers and herbs sat not far from the candle.

"This is lovely," she said as Carlo held out the chair for her.

He bent and whispered in her ear, "But not as lovely as you."

Heat raced across her cheeks and she hoped the intimate light would hide her telltale blush. "Thank you," she said and took an inordinate time to open her napkin in the hopes of letting the color fade.

The waiter arrived barely seconds later with the menus and quickly rattled off the specials.

"May I get you something to drink while you decide?" he asked.

"How about some wine?" Carlo asked and at her nod, he ordered a bottle of a vintage she recognized as being quite expensive.

As the waiter hurried away to place the order, she lowered her menu and whispered, "You don't need to impress me."

"But I *want* to impress you," he teased and grinned, his dark eyes bright with humor and a wink.

A wink? In all the times they'd been together, she'd never seen him wink. Ever.

She circled her index finger around in the general direction of his eye and said, "What was that?"

"This?" he said and winked again. "I thought it was pretty obvious what it was."

"A spasm? Maybe a twitch? Oh my god, are you having a stroke?" she teased.

"Come on, Em," he said just as the waiter came over with the wine. After showing Carlo the label, he expertly uncorked the bottle, poured a bit into a glass, and offered it up to Carlo, but Carlo gestured for the man to let Emma do the approving.

"She's the real expert," Carlo said in explanation.

With a nod, the waiter handed Emma the glass. She took it, swirled the wine around to check out the legs, and then took a sip, inhaling air with it to bring out the full flavor of the wine. "Excellent," she said and the waiter immediately poured her more and prepared a glass for Carlo.

They placed their orders and after the waiter walked away, Carlo lifted his glass and said, "To our first date. May it be the first of many."

"Only if you promise not to wink again," she said.

Carlo stifled a chuckled. "I promise," he said, but punctuated it with a playful wink.

"You're so bad," she replied with a laugh and shake of her head.

"You can't even begin to guess how bad. Just ask *mamãe*," he challenged.

"No way. I can't imagine you doing anything to upset your mom," she said, but he proceeded to tell her a story about how Tomás, Paolo, and him had terrorized their mom one day with a collection of frogs.

"She's afraid of frogs? I never pictured your mom being afraid of anything," she said.

The waiter came over that moment with their appetizers. Emma had ordered a roasted beet and goat cheese salad over arugula. Glazed pecans were scattered across the surface along with a duo of crostini fragrant with garlic.

Carlo had ordered lobster bisque, creamy and topped with a few pieces of lobster and the meat from one claw.

"It all looks delicious and not at all like the frogs legs my *mamãe* fed us," he said and picked up his spoon.

"She fed you the frogs?" Emma asked, grimacing at the thought. They might be a delicacy to some, but all she could picture was unappetizing slimy green skin on a plate.

"Well, she told us they were frog legs. Made us sit there and eat them." With a shake of his head and a lopsided grin, he added, "Tasted like chicken because it was chicken. We didn't know it at the time, so she got her revenge."

"Yes, she did," Emma said with a laugh and wondered what it must have been like to raise three – no make that five – such active boys. But as Carlo told her a story about another adventure, she realized it was one more tale about just the three youngest brothers.

"I guess you didn't hang out as much with Ricardo and Javier because they're so much older than the three of you," she said and was surprised by the hint of sadness that crept onto his features. She reached out and took hold of his hand when he reached out to pick up his wine glass. "I'm sorry. I didn't mean to upset you."

"It's just . . . Ricardo and Javier stuck together more because they were older, but also because I think it took them a little time to get used to having a new mom and then us."

Emma was taken aback by his comment. "New mom? I don't understand."

"*Mamãe* is my dad's second wife. Ricardo and Javier's mom died from cancer when they were very young. My dad, *their* dad, was single for about three years before he met and married my mom. I was born about three years later," he explained, squeezed her hand to reassure her that he was over any upset, and then went back to his bisque.

As she returned her attention to her salad, she wondered what else she didn't know about him despite the many years they'd spent together. Much like there was so much he didn't know about her. Since he'd shared a part of his past that obviously bothered him, she decided to share as well.

"My dad walked out on my mom and me when I was seventeen. As hard as it was because of the way he treated us, I was upset when he left," she said and didn't say more even though she could have. She could have told him about how that upset turned to hate when over the course of the next few days they'd discovered that he'd stolen every last penny from their bank accounts. Luckily, he hadn't been able to touch the house whose sale had given them a bit of a cushion, but only a little cushion.

"I guess there's a lot we have to learn about each other, but it can't be all bad, can it?" he asked as a busboy came by to whisk away their dirty plates.

"Not at all. I was lucky to meet Maggie, Connie, and Tracy while I was doing work study at Princeton. They're like my sisters. I wouldn't trade that for anything," she said.

"I'm happy to say that Ricardo and Javier finally decided it was good to have little brothers they could torture," he replied with a laugh and raised his glass. "To family."

She smiled and joined him in the toast. "To family and to us getting to learn more about one another."

As they sipped the wine, the waiter came over with their meals. Carlo had ordered a porterhouse steak with a porcini mushroom compound butter, scalloped potatoes, and broccolini sautéed in garlic. She had opted for something a little lighter. Perfectly seared scallops paired with lemony orzo and spinach.

Hunger for food replaced the hunger for more knowledge about him. Silence reigned for long moments until the edge was off that hunger and conversation resumed.

"Are you excited about becoming an aunt?" Ricardo asked while he was cutting a piece off his steak.

"Terrified. I'm not used to babies," she confessed.

"You and me both. The women in my family don't seem to think men can take care of babies so they tend to keep them away from us," he admitted.

"The da Costa family is old school, huh?" she said.

Carlo wagged a finger with indignation and shook his head. "Don't include me. I plan on being a hands-on kind of dad."

It was easy for Emma to picture Carlo that way. He was always so patient with his brothers and the staff that worked with him. It was so easy it was scary, but also comforting. She let herself focus on the positive picture of Carlo holding a little baby. Maybe even her little baby.

"Will he be born with soccer cleats?" she teased, wanting to keep the mood lighthearted.

"He or she," he said, smiling. "I'm an equal opportunity dad."

With a chuckle, she said, "I'm impressed, but I always suspected you weren't as chauvinist as your older brothers."

"I was trying to impress," he said, grinned, winked, and with another few forkfuls, he finished off his meal. "This was so good."

She nodded as she also took the last few bites of her meal. "Mac did an awesome job."

"Makes me a little jealous," Carlo admitted.

His comment caught her a little off guard. Carlo made meals this good but for sometimes hundreds of people. "You can rock a meal like this in your sleep."

He seemed a little chagrined and shrugged. "I wasn't fishing for a compliment."

Reaching across the table, she took hold of his hand. "I know, but I want you to understand how good you are. As a partner and a friend."

CARLO HEARD THE FRIEND word again. It was one Emma seemed to toss out a lot, but if it wasn't already clear to her, he wanted to make sure she understood. "I want to be more than just friends, Emma. As for being partners, we haven't talked about it in a while, but that would be nice as well."

A splash of color painted her cheeks and her green eyes darkened to emerald. "It would be nice, Carlo." She hesitated, but then forged ahead. "I want to be more than friends too, I think."

He'd take that . . . for now. "Would you like some dessert?"

A sexy smile came to her lips. "I thought we might go back to my place. I made a cheesecake and I have some fresh berries for it too."

"My favorite. Thank you," he said and hoped that her desire to be alone with him would be another step to a change in their relationship.

He signaled the waiter for the check and in no time they were out of the restaurant and in the SUV, heading back to Emma's cottage. He pulled into the driveway and hurried around to help Emma out of the car, but she was already stepping out. He held out his arm for her and helped her avoid an icy patch. Together they hurried to her front door, chased by an arctic blast of wind.

Once inside, Emma gestured to the couch. "Make yourself at home."

He rubbed his hands together against the chill that had followed them from outside. "Mind if I get the fire going?"

She ran her hands across her arms. "Please and may I say you get brownie points for not assuming."

"That's me, sensitive guy," he said, but in his mind he could hear his brothers kidding him about checking to see if he still had his balls.

Unlike the gas fireplace in her bedroom, the one in the living room was wood burning. She'd already laid out the logs and paper to get a fire started. He struck the match and lit the newspaper. The flames spread greedily and in seconds the first pop from the wood told him the fire had caught. He held his hands out to the flames as they grew, savoring the warmth.

The clatter of plates and cutlery from behind him alerted him to Emma's return. She had placed thick slices of cheesecake on two plates and topped them with assorted berries in a fruity sauce. She set the plates on the coffee table in front of the couch next to empty glasses and the uncorked bottle of wine he had brought.

"That looks great," he said, sat on the couch and poured them each a glass of wine.

She handed him one of the plates as she said, "I used your recipe, so I hope it came out as good as when you make it."

He cut off a big piece and popped it into his mouth. Murmured an appreciative, "Better."

She smiled and picked up her own plate. Forked a piece of the cheesecake and ate it. "Mmm. Maybe I should bake from now on and let you handle the planning."

He shook his head vehemently. "No way I am dealing with those bridezillas any more than I have to."

Laughing, she cut off another piece and chewed on it thoughtfully. Eyeing him intently, she said, "I've seen you charm the worst of them. You just give them that melty chocolate look-"

"Like this," he said and forced himself to look intense.

"God no," she said with a laugh. "That's you're scary pissed off look. Usually one you shoot at Paolo when he's not listening."

As much as he loved his brother, Paolo could be a handful at times. Restless much like he'd been at his youngest brother's age. Finishing the slice of cheesecake, he laid his empty plate on the table and snared his glass of wine. He leaned back into the cushions of the sofa, sipped the fine cabernet, and said, "Don't you ever get tired of dealing with the crazy ones?"

With a sigh, she raised her own glass and tasted it before replying. "Sometimes, but it's good business. Some of them even end up being repeat business," she said with a grimace.

"Second marriages –"

"And third or fourth," she jumped in with a harsh chuckle.

"Not for you, I guess?" he asked and hoped that her answer wouldn't be one about never getting married. Peering at her intensely, he waited for her response, but instead she half-smiled and did a little circle around his face.

"That's the look that melts those women," she said, obviously in avoidance mode. He wasn't about to let her off so easily.

He shifted closer on the couch, until his knee brushed her thigh and when she looked away, he cradled her cheek and urged her to face him once again. Apparently realizing he wouldn't give up until he had an answer, she licked her lips nervously and said, "If I marry someone, it will be forever."

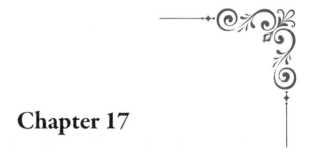

Chapter 17

F*orever.*
The word lingered between them, rousing more emotion than Emma had thought possible.

Carlo shifted his thumb up to trail it across her lips and gazed at her with those dark intense eyes that could make a nun waver from her sacred vows. That look kindled need inside her that only he could quench. He leaned close until the warmth of his breath spilled across her lips, fragrant with the scent of wine, and he nuzzled her nose with his.

"I wish I had the right words to say, Emma. I wish . . ." He took her lips in a kiss that said more than any words.

She could love this man forever, she thought as she opened her mouth to his kiss and took him in. His breath, his taste, his sweetness. He made her feel cherished and for that moment, she let herself believe she could be a woman he would want in his life. Forever.

He tunneled his fingers through her hair, his touch gentle, almost a massage against her scalp. His kiss went on and on, but he banked the passion rising between them, keeping his touch more reverent than enticing.

She eased away and searched his features, wondering at his restraint and he once again ran his thumb across her lips, almost as if kissing her goodbye. "It isn't easy not to take more from you tonight, Em. But when I do, I want it to be forever just like you do. I want you to believe that too and I'm not sure you do. At least not yet."

She sat back, pulling away from him and not just physically, but he kept up his gentle touch as if to reassure her.

"It isn't easy for me to believe, Carlo. I saw what happened with my parents –"

"I know, but if you hold on to that and to the way your dad treated you, who loses?" he said and while her brain acknowledged he was right, her heart still didn't dare believe.

He obviously sensed her conflict since he didn't push. "How about we sit and enjoy the fire, the wine, and the company?" he said.

"I'd like that." She didn't want to end the night so soon, especially when it had been so nice up until she'd messed things up again. But then the little voice in her head said, That's just what your dad would say. She couldn't argue with that. She still carried the emotional scars from years of being told nothing she did was ever good enough. That if something went wrong it was because she had screwed up.

Carlo had been right when he said that if she held on to the way her dad had treated her she'd be the one who'd lose. And she didn't want to lose the amazing man beside her and the promise of the life they could have together. Armed with that, she decided to prolong the night and said, "What do you plan to do with your week off?"

He grinned and winked at her, his brown eyes glittering with amusement. "I plan on wooing a very special lady. Do you have a problem with that?"

Caught up in his playful mood, she said, "Depends on who that lady is."

Laughing, he wrapped his arm around her neck and hauled her close. "I guess if you don't know, I have to show you again," he said and kissed her, all traces of gentleness and restraint gone until she was clinging to him and breathless.

"I guess it would be me," she said when she finally shifted away again, slightly dazed.

"You guessed right."

A WEEK WITH BARELY anything to do was a rare thing in his business, but with Connie and Jonathan's rush wedding and the press conference, he hadn't dared accept work for anything the following week, especially since they had a schedule crammed with assorted holiday parties in the two weeks prior to Christmas. Except for checking in to make sure their supplies were ordered and would be in on time for next week's rush, he really had nothing to do. Well, nothing to do except court Emma and as he'd discovered over their last few encounters, that was going to take a great deal of patience and restraint.

He had wanted to do nothing more than to make love to her last night. As he thought of how she'd responded and remembered the feel of her lips and her body pressed to his, he grew hard with need. But as he had told her and everyone else who'd been pushing him, he was a patient man. He didn't want to be proved a liar.

Trying to shake off his need, he forced himself from bed and into his morning routine. Some quick strength exercises while he watched the financial news. Satisfied with what he saw on the tube, he checked the weather on his phone before dressing for his run. Unlike last night's chill and wind, today was promising to be a balmy 50 degrees by mid-day and it was already well on its way to that number.

He dressed lightly and headed east through town, passing Emma's house on the way. Although it was early, the lights were on inside and cast a welcoming glow in the rosy dawn, but he pushed on. One did not woo in sweaty running clothes.

As he continued down Main Street there were more lights on in a few households. When he reached the end of the residential section and the first businesses, a colorful illuminated banner across the street welcomed people to Sea Kiss. In the business section, festive wreaths and garlands of twinkling bulbs wrapped around streetlamps added to that feeling of welcome. On the doors and windows of the various shops and offices were holiday decorations and more cheerful lights. In front of the small food market and further down by the cheese shop, surf and skate shop, and hardware store, delivery trucks were unloading supplies and the drivers waved at him as he ran by.

He waved back and smiled, loving the small town feel and the peace it brought him. In some ways the street reminded him of Ferry Street in Newark's Ironbound with its strip of stores, restaurants, and his family's bakery. Everyone knew everyone else and what was going on with them. Everyone watched out for each other.

Another couple of blocks up and the street became residential again, with larger seaside homes and inns. When he hit the boardwalk there were other runners already there, taking advantage of the early morning and the warmer weather. He pushed southward and at the end of Sea Kiss he went up and over the inlet bridge to the next town. Known for its party atmosphere, the heart of its boardwalk had a more commercial vibe than its northern neighbor. Unlike Sea Kiss which was mostly residences along the beachfront and boardwalk, assorted businesses and restaurants lined the western part of the street for a few miles before he crossed over into the next town. Upscale and all residential along the waterfront, that town was more like Sea Kiss, but not as welcoming. Maybe because he always felt a little out of place with the wealthier citizens. Some of those residents had been Emma's customers at the trendy bridal salon just blocks away in the center of town.

Emma, he thought and his heart raced a little faster, but not from the run.

Unlike him, she had work today even if she had no weddings scheduled until after the New Year. She still had to plan for those events and assist any new customers who might come into the bridal salon.

They'd made plans to have dinner tomorrow night, but he intended to surprise her today with a picnic lunch to hopefully break up her day and give her a little time to rest. Maybe even continue with their getting to know you plan so they could move on to the next phase of their relationship. As he daydreamed about what that might be, he caught sight of the lighthouse up ahead and realized he'd reached the halfway point in his run.

Turning, he raced northward, eager to get home and put his plans for the day into place. His pace was quick, far quicker than how he normally ran so he was winded and dripping sweat by the time he got home. Steam came off him as he bent over in front of his house, gulping in cold air until his breath was somewhat under control. He entered, stripping off his clothing as he did so. He was eager for a shower to wash away his grime so he could head out for the day.

He savored the streams of hot water easing the slight soreness in his muscles and driving away the damp chill of the morning. As the water cooled, he hurriedly washed and vowed that when he finally replaced the mobile home with his dream house, he'd have a hot water tank big enough for the world's longest shower. Or maybe for a two-person whirlpool tub where he and Emma could soak. Maybe even enjoy a little intimacy in the steaming bubbly waters.

As arousal rose up again at the thought, he twisted the tap for a blast of cold to tamp his desire and rushed from the shower. He might not have a lot to do today, but he wanted to get it done quickly and hurry over to visit Emma.

Emma, Emma, Emma, the little voice in his head mocked as if to warn that he was placing too much hope in the thaw in her demeanor. Just like he'd lingered too long in the relationship with Sasha, yearning for a change that had never come.

He swiped away those thoughts the way he might an app on his phone and rushed out the door to the SUV sitting in his driveway. So far it had performed like a dream, although he was still getting used to the lack of engine noise and worried that he might run out of juice. Jonathan had assured him that the car was smart enough to let him know well in advance when to plug in. Plus Jonathan had already installed a charging station at his new research and development center which was only a few blocks from Carlo's warehouse.

To be on the safe side, he drove to the charging station at the Pierce company parking lot and plugged the SUV in. Did the quick walk over to his warehouse. As he entered, the place hummed with activity like a hive of worker bees and the queen bee at the center of it all was Paolo. He stood back and watched with pride as his youngest brother directed the staff to organize their assorted linens, china, glassware, and cutlery which sometimes got in disarray when they'd been as busy as they had been the last few weeks. The slow week would let them get things ship shape and that would make things easier for their future gigs.

As Paolo took one last look at the clipboard in his hand and turned to walk to their offices, he finally noticed Carlo leaning on the door jamb.

Paolo ambled over, slapped the clipboard against Carlo's chest, and with a teasing smile said, "It's about time you got here. I hope you have a good excuse for not being here at the crack of dawn like you usually are."

With a shrug, Carlo said, "Decided to stay in bed this morning."

Paolo's brown eyes, so much like his own, widened in surprise. "Don't tell me you melted the Ice Queen that quickly?"

Carlo shook his head. "Actually, no. But even if I had, I'm a gentleman. I don't kiss and tell."

Paolo arched a dark brow. "Really? Did you get to first base? Second?" his brother pressed, but Carlo ignored him, went into his office, and sat at his desk to shuffle the papers on his desk. Paolo followed him in and plopped into the chair before Carlo's desk.

"We all good on the deliveries for the next few days?" Carlo asked after he skimmed through the paperwork.

"Yeah and Tomás is personally checking with Jesse about the cheese she ordered for us," Paolo said and rolled his eyes.

"Personally, huh? You think the two of them –"

Paolo raised both hands to direct him to stop. "I'm a gentleman too, *mano*. But there's definitely something there if you ask me."

Which both pleased and worried Carlo. He liked Jesse a lot which was why he helped her out by placing orders through her and letting her work for them. He also wanted his brother to be happy and maybe decide to stay in Sea Kiss instead of re-enlisting. But if his brother left, Jesse would have to deal with losing a man she cared about all over again.

"I think I'll go check on that order myself," he said and shot out of his chair.

Paolo waved a finger in his face. "Don't get involved. Tomás hates it when you go all control freak."

Carlo jerked as if struck and pointed a finger at his chest. "Me? Control freak?"

His brother elbowed him playfully. "Why do you think you and Emma get along so well? You're made for each other."

Carlo wished that was true which had him wondering about Paolo as he returned to his desk and sat. "I haven't heard you mention anyone lately. Someone warn all the ladies in town about you?"

With a sheepish look and a shrug of broad powerful shoulders, his brother took the seat in front of the desk and said, "I've had my eye on someone only she's older. Still married."

Carlo had definitely not seen that coming. He steepled his hands before him and examined his brother closely. "Married? Do you think that makes sense, *mano*?"

"She's separated and getting divorced from what I hear," Paolo said and as he did so, a surprise thought came to Carlo.

"*Caralho*, not Tracy. Please tell me it's not Drama Queen Tracy," he said, recalling everything that had happened at her wedding just over a year earlier.

Spots of color dotted his brother's cheeks before Paolo decided to busy himself by grabbing the papers on Carlo's desk and rifling through them as if he was checking the orders.

"Come on, Paolo. Spill," Carlo insisted and yanked the papers from his brother's hands.

"She's not that same person anymore. I guess she learned a painful lesson. It happens to a lot of people," Paolo said and shot his head up to glare at Carlo with a laser sharp gaze.

"Water under the bridge and the only reason I'm worried is that Tracy's just not our kind," Carlo said.

"Just like *mamãe* wasn't *papai's* kind? A poor little girl trying to strike it rich. Isn't that what *avô* used to say about her behind her back?" Paolo challenged.

And to her face, Carlo thought. "It's not the same."

"Then what is it? Is she too fancy and too rich? Like Owen and Jon, your two new best buds? Are you saying the da Costa brothers aren't good enough for the likes of people like them? Like Emma?" his brother retorted, his growing anger apparent.

Damn if his brother hadn't just out argued him. With a wry smile, he handed the papers back to Paolo and said, "You should have been a lawyer, you know. I hardly ever win an argument with you."

Paolo jabbed a finger at him. "Just remember that, *cabrão*. And I'll promise not to mention your past love life again if you promise to keep an open mind about Tracy."

A hard promise to keep, but he trusted Paolo's judgment, as surprising as it was in this instance. "Deal," he said and offered his hand to seal the bargain.

Paolo shook it and then with a solid tug, urged Carlo to his feet. "Now go check on Tomás and make sure he's staying out of trouble."

"Done," he said and jerked his jacket off the back of his chair and slipped it on for the short walk to where he'd parked the SUV. But as he arrived at his destination, the day had already warmed considerably, the sun was out, and a soft almost spring-like breeze blew off the ocean, calling him to skip the car and stroll the half a dozen or so blocks to the center of the business district where Jesse had her cheese shop.

Barely fifteen minutes later, he walked into the store and the bell above the door chimed to announce his entry. He always loved the feel of this shop with its wrought iron baker's racks holding collections of crackers, nuts, jellies, jams, oils, vinegars, and assorted treats to pair with the cheeses Jesse sold. There was an Old World feel to the shop, as if you'd just stepped back to the 1800s when Sea Kiss had been formally founded. For the nearly two centuries before that, the town had just been a collection of buildings and tents used by Methodists for summer revival meetings.

As he walked toward the display counter, muffled voices came from a hidden spot behind and off to the right of the counter. A second later Tomás strolled out carrying a big wheel of cheese with Jesse trailing behind him hugging a medium-sized cardboard box. Their slightly mussed looks, pinkened cheeks, and shamefaced expressions said they'd been playing around with something other than the inventory in the storage area.

"Is this a bad time?" he asked to which Jesse and Tomás replied, "No" and "Yes" simultaneously.

Jesse jabbed Tomás in the ribs before opening the glass door of the refrigerator where she kept the larger wheels and inventory of cheeses within easy reach for customers. Tomás feigned injury, placed the wheel on a shelf, and took the box from her to empty the contents into the refrigerator.

Jesse wiped her hands on a towel tucked into her apron and said, "What can I help you with today, Carlo?"

"I wanted to surprise Emma with a picnic lunch. Do you think you could put one together with some cheeses, meats, and other goodies?"

Jesse smiled. "I'd love to. I know most of Emma's favorites," she said and bent to remove several items from the counter display. "Let me get the basket from the back and I'll load it up for you with some crackers, lemonade, and other treats."

She rushed toward the small storage area tucked into one corner of the narrow space. The rasp of things being moved about on shelves filled the silence as Tomás finished his chore and Carlo waited, but not just for the picnic basket. He wanted an explanation from his brother as well as a promise he'd be mindful of Jesse's situation.

When Jesse returned, she worked to assemble the lunch items and Tomás ambled out from behind the counter to wait, arms across his chest as he leaned against the wall. His head was downturned as he was clearly in avoidance mode.

A few minutes later, Jesse passed the small picnic basket over the counter to Carlo. "I packed some plates, cutlery, and glasses in there as well."

"That's great. What's the damage?" he asked, but Jesse held her hand up to wave him off.

"My treat. You and Emma do so much for me. And a big thank you for the orders for next week that Tomás brought over. I'll have everything ready for you in the next few days," she said and glanced at Tomás nervously.

"I'll swing by to pick it up," Tomás said and straightened from the wall. "I'll see you later," he added, but made no effort for a more personal goodbye with the shop owner.

Jesse didn't seem to take offense, possibly understanding that Tomás was uneasy with any public displays of affection.

"How about you give me a lift back to my car?" Carlo said, tucked the basket under one arm, and wrapped the other around his brother's shoulders.

"Sure thing, *mano*. I have to get back and help Paolo anyway," Tomás replied and walked with him to the door, where they broke apart since there was no way two men as big as them were going to exit side-by-side.

On the sidewalk, Tomás peered back into the store for a second before motioning his brother in the direction of the da Costa delivery van parked at the end of the block. As they walked toward the vehicle, Carlo noted the slight hitch in his brother's stride.

"Knee giving you trouble today?" he asked, concerned for his brother in a number of ways.

With a chagrined smirk, Tomás shook his head. "Nope. Banged the good one on a shelf when you made your very inopportune entry."

"It could have been a customer, *mano*," Carlo chided.

Tomás looked around and held his hands out as if to say, "Where?"

Carlo tracked his brother's gaze and realized he was right. It was late morning, but in the off season the locals and what few visitors were in Sea Kiss midweek didn't seem to venture out until after twelve.

"She's not the kind of woman you play around with," Carlo warned, not that Tomás was normally the kind to mess around with a woman.

With a reluctant shrug, Tomás nodded. "*Eu sei*. Believe me. And I tell myself it doesn't make any sense to get more involved with her when I'm not sure what I'm doing."

Carlo understood, but that didn't change the hurt that could happen. "She's already lost one man in her life, *mano*."

"Don't you think I worry about that? About hurting her?" Tomás said and ran his fingers through the longish strands of his hair in frustration. It had grown out from his buzz cut in the weeks he'd been home.

Carlo wrapped an arm around his brother's shoulder again. "I trust you to do the right thing. Never doubt that."

Tomás nodded and peered at Carlo from the corner of his eye. "And what about you? Are you going to do right by Emma?"

Carlo jiggled the basket under his arm. "I'm trying. It's just hard to get past all the walls she's put up."

Tomás considered him thoughtfully for a long second. "Keep trying. And when the walls come tumbling down –"

"I'll be the happiest man alive," Carlo said with a smile.

Chapter 18

With a day free of appointments, Emma decided to straighten up the gowns in their stockroom, putting them back in order by color, style, and in some cases, designers for those brides who were dead set on having a gown by a "big name."

She had just finished moving all the gowns by one of the designers into their own area along a far wall when a pale peach dress in the adjacent row caught her eye. She recalled ordering the sample on a whim since the color limited not only the season when it might be worn, but who might wear it. Dragging the gown off the rack, she removed the protective cover and walked with the dress to the full-length mirror at the far end of the stockroom. She held the gown against her body and pictured herself wearing it. Did a fanciful little swing of the skirts that sent them swaying back and forth.

The pale peach was perfect with her fair skin and strawberry blonde hair. It also deepened the color of her eyes, making them look as rich as a precious gem. The style was simple, but elegant with a strapless sweetheart neckline and a bodice that nipped in at the waist before flaring in waves of silk with an overlay of delicate tulle. A thick belt with intricate beadwork smoothed the transition from bodice to skirt.

So beautiful, she thought with a sigh and didn't realize she'd said the words out loud until a very male voice repeated the sentiment.

"Very beautiful," Carlo said as he walked into the room, his gaze loving and intense.

She whipped the gown behind her to hide it from his gaze. If she should ever be a bride in that gown, she didn't want bad luck. "I wasn't expecting you."

He held out a picnic basket. "I wanted to surprise you."

138

"Well you did," she said more curtly than she intended. "I'm sorry. You just caught me by surprise." And in a moment that might reveal way too much that she wasn't ready to admit to yet.

"Is it a bad time? I could go," he said and gestured to the door with his head.

Wanting to make up for her earlier abruptness, she stepped close to him, rose on tiptoes and kissed him. "I'm happy to see you," she said as she moved away, the gown still hidden behind her back.

"Wait for me in the showroom while I put this away and we can have lunch in my office. I don't have any appointments this afternoon."

Carlo nodded and sauntered out, leaving Emma to take one last glimpse at the dress before she hung it with the other gowns in vaguely similar hues, but even tucked in amongst them, it stood out beautifully. She hurried out to the showroom where Carlo stood patiently in the hall, the picnic basket tucked under one muscled arm.

She slipped her hand into his free one and playfully tugged it. "This was so nice of you. I needed a break from the stockroom."

He bent, kissed her temple, and said, "And I needed to see you."

"We were at the wedding on Saturday and went out last night," she reminded, discreetly skipping over the Sunday morning after the wedding. But she was secretly pleased by his words.

"And that's way not enough time together," he said.

Warmth flooded her, but the fear that seemed to always be with her rose up as well. "You're going to get bored of me," she said, turned and walked toward her office. Just like her father had grown tired of them, she thought.

As they entered her office and she closed the door, he trapped her against the wall, cradled her cheek and said, "Never. I will never get bored of you." And to prove it, he dipped his head down to take her lips in a searing kiss that soon had her holding on to him as her head whirled from its potency.

As he broke the kiss, he met her gaze, his dark and intense. "I know you think there's something inside you here that's broken," he said and tenderly tapped a spot over her heart. "That makes you feel as if you're not good enough for anyone, but that's not true. It's just not true," he repeated for emphasis.

A hint of pain, his not hers, colored his words. "Why does it sound like you're not talking just about me?" she said, slipped past him, and to the chairs in front of her desk.

Carlo followed and placed the picnic basket on her desktop. He urged her to sit and took hold of her hands. "Since our dating is all about learning about each other, I guess it's about time I told you a little more about me. I was engaged once before. Her name was Alexandra, but we called her Sasha."

"We?" she questioned with an arch of her brow.

"All of the family. She was one of the girls in the neighborhood and everyone always thought we'd end up together. We did, only Sasha had her own ideas about what our life should be like."

"I guess you had different plans?" Emma asked, but couldn't sit still to listen to his story. Nervous energy pumped through her at the thought there had been someone else. Someone with whom he'd been involved seriously enough to ask her to marry him. She rose and busied herself by opening the picnic basket and removing the contents as Carlo continued his story.

"I told you before that Ricardo and Javier are my half-brothers. Their mother's family were the owners of the bakery and my *avô* –" He paused at her questioning look. "My grandfather, actually my half-brothers' grandfather. *Avô* never let the three of us forget that or that my *mamãe* wasn't the right woman for his son-in-law. He was the exact opposite of my *mamãe*'s father who loved us to death."

Emma set the bottle of lemonade from the basket onto her desk and leaned against the edge, bracing her hands on it to keep from reaching for him. "Is that why you started your own business?"

He nodded and his broad shoulders rose up and down in a nonchalant manner. "It was one of the reasons. Sasha thought I should join my half-brothers at the bakery and she never let up about it. I worked two jobs to help me raise the money to buy my first food truck and get it going, but that wasn't good enough. Nothing I did was good enough because I could never be one of the owners of the bakery. That family was like Portuguese royalty on our stretch of Ferry Street. The epitome of the American Dream."

She remembered him telling her that his family's business was virtually an institution in the Ironbound and more than once she'd seen it picked as one of the top bakeries in New Jersey. Making the decision to leave that legacy . . .

She sat in the chair opposite him and this time she reached for his hands and held them, reassuring him with her touch and her words. "It takes a brave man to walk away from an easy life. You've built a wonderful business for yourself and your younger brothers. You should be so proud. *I'm* so proud."

A half smile quirked up one side of his lips and awakened that tempting dimple. "It means a lot to me that you think that. Sasha didn't hang around long once I stuck to my guns. As far as she was concerned, I wasn't good enough. Her rejection stuck with me for a while, but in the end, I realized it was her loss that she couldn't see the kind of person I really am."

Just like you shouldn't believe all the crap your father dumped on you, the little voice in her head chimed in.

If his passion had broken open a crack in the wall she'd built around herself, his honesty snapped the chains she hadn't even known were around her heart. Even though she was still wounded by that imprisonment, suddenly things didn't seem so impossible.

She leaned forward and whispered against his lips, "Sasha is an idiot."

It was impossible to miss the smile on his lips for a second before he kissed her. It was a kiss filled with comfort and promise, absent the passion of their earlier kisses. But it helped salve the wounds they had both suffered in their earlier lives, beginning the path to true healing.

As they drifted apart, they were both still smiling. At the noisy growl of her stomach, Carlo said, "I guess you're hungry."

"I am. Let's eat," she said.

CARLO LAY IN BED, HIS body sore in spots from his exertions of the day before. Despite supposedly having a week off, he'd been too restless to do nothing after his lunch with Emma.

Considering the emotional way lunch had started off for both of them, it had ended nicely thanks to the marvelous food Jesse had selected and packed for him. Both Emma and he finished with full bellies, laughter, and the promise to see each other again mid-week for dinner.

He'd returned to the warehouse and helped Paolo and some of his crew in organizing and inventorying the assorted items they used for their events and for preparing their food. That meant lots of lifting and carrying, but by the end of the day, they'd finished with the plates and glassware. A good thing since in the rush of all the events of the last month or so they were down a number of items due to breakage or loss. The kitchen utensils and pots were in pretty good shape, but a few new baking trays would be a big help since they'd been doing more and more wedding cakes lately also. By the end of the shift, he'd had a list of items to buy and would visit the restaurant supply place later to pick them up.

Even with his assorted aches, he got up and did his regular routine. Light workout and television news shows. Jog. Long hot shower that helped loosen the kinks and relieved some of the pain. In no time he was dressed and rushing out the door to get to the supply house, a large rambling one story building filled floor to ceiling with all kinds of restaurant items.

With no real schedule, he ambled up and down the aisles, picking out a tool or pan here or there that they might need. Then he headed to the china section where he loaded up on the replacement pieces before moving to the glassware section for the remainder of the items on his list. When he arrived at the register, he realized the cashier was a friend who had used to work at a restaurant in the next town over.

"Hey, Carlo. It's good to see you," the young man said and welcomed him with a bro hug and hand clasp.

"Good to see you too, Shaun. What are you doing here? Making some extra bank?" he said and piled his merchandise on the counter for Shaun to ring up.

Shaun grimaced and picked up the first item to ring up. "Making *all* my bank, dude. *Jersey Jose* closed. They couldn't cut it anymore."

Carlo had eaten a few times at the restaurant that had offered a mix of Coastal Cuisine and Tex-Mex. The food and service hadn't been bad, but then again, it hadn't been fabulous and there was a lot of competition in the area from similar eateries and real Mexican restaurants. "Sorry to hear that. If you ever want work during your off hours, we sometimes need experienced wait staff for an event."

"Thanks, dude. Hey, did you hear that the old Sea Kiss Convention Center is for sale? They finally got the insurance money after Sandy and started repairs but couldn't finish and decided to sell it off. You always wanted to have a place where you could do your own thing."

Carlo was surprised Shaun remembered. Emma and he had talked about it a number of times, but with as busy as they had both been, they hadn't really given it much serious thought in ages. Not to mention that since he wanted to have a different relationship with Emma, he hesitated to raise the idea of a partnership again, fearing it would give Emma too easy an excuse to push him away if she was getting cold feet.

"I hadn't heard. Thanks for the news," he said and intended to check it out with the local real estate agent. The place was probably well out of his price range, but it never hurt to ask. After all, if he didn't ask the answer would always be "No."

Just like with Emma, the little voice in his head reminded.

He finished checking out and loaded up the Thunder SUV, appreciating the roominess of the rear storage area. Jonathan had seemed to think of everything, but the real test now was going to be how the car performed with the added weight of everything he'd just bought. He pulled out onto the street and hit the accelerator. The car took off without any hesitation or strain. It was enough to convince him that maybe electric cars weren't just for people who didn't really have to work.

Barely minutes later he was pulling into the loading dock at his warehouse. Paolo and Tomás were standing by the one bay, looking over some papers. Dozens of boxes sat behind them on the dock waiting to be unpacked thanks to a recent delivery. He got out and walked up to them.

"Everything okay?" he asked, wondering if there was an issue with the delivery.

"Fine. Just checking to make sure we got everything. Last thing we want is to find out next week that we're missing something important," Tomás said.

Carlo nodded and tossed the key fob to Paolo. "Stuff is in the back of the Thunder."

"Where are you going?" Paolo groused as he walked away.

"I've got a call to make," he said, thinking of the convention center and what he could do with a place like that. Besides lose his shirt. And possibly Emma if he rushed her into it.

He entered the office and closed the door, not sure that he was ready to share the news with his brothers or anyone else just yet. At his desk he shifted to his computer and pulled up the name of the realtor who he had first spoken to about a location for his business. *Mary Sanders*. She had helped him find and get a deal on their current warehouse. She was also the realtor who had assisted Jonathan in finding the location for his new research and development center.

Leaning back in his chair, he dialed Mary and she answered by the second ring. "Carlo! So nice to hear from you. How are things going?"

"Things are good, Mary. Thanks for asking," he answered, but hesitated, wondering if he was crazy for even making the call.

"What can I help you with today?" Mary asked in her usual all business tone.

He took a breath and pushed ahead. "Rumor has it that the convention center is for sale," he said, trying to keep his voice neutral although the call alone was enough to tell the shrewd real estate agent that he had an interest in the place.

"Rumor is right for a change, but I have to tell you that the price is on the high side if you ask me. The place isn't finished inside and there's a lot of work left to be done. It seems that they blew through their Sandy insurance money and then some. But it's a prime location and with Jonathan Pierce hopefully bringing new blood into the area, it's bound to see a lot of traffic. In fact, I'd be surprised if Jonathan doesn't jump on this for his company to use as a meeting center."

Carlo wouldn't be surprised either. The location was great. Right at the westernmost edge of town but facing the inlet and the river. From the upper story there was a picturesque view of all the waterside Victorian buildings in Sea Kiss as well as the ocean and the neighboring towns to the south. From what he remembered, there were two nice-sized ballrooms with river views and then a few smaller ballrooms which faced the town and another section of river. He'd worked in the kitchens one summer and they had been immense with lots of stockrooms and walk-in refrigerators. He wouldn't doubt that he could probably put everything in his warehouse into the areas and still have room left over.

"How much are they asking?" he said while tallying in his own mind what he had in his operating and savings accounts and what monies he might be able to put together from other sources like his retirement fund and the sale of the warehouse building.

"Four million. Like I said, on the high side considering the shape it's in."

A huge number. One that might be out of my reach, he thought. "How much do you think I could get for the warehouse?"

There was a long pause before Mary said, "Based on recent sales, I'm going to say a million and a half at least. If we could get the town to rezone it for multi-purpose including residential, at least two million if not more."

With the money he had in the various bank accounts, that still left him short well over a million dollars. Before he could say anything else, Mary jumped back in. "You know your house is on land that could easily fetch a million. Maybe more."

"That's not something I want to consider right now," he said, not yet ready to trade his dream home for the business of his dreams. His dreams and Emma's. When they had been talking about an event planning business together, they had tossed around the idea of buying a building where they could host the events in order to increase their profits.

"Just saying," Mary said in a sing song. She had been jonesing for the property his home sat on for years, but his answer had always been the same: No.

He shifted forward in his seat and drummed the fingers of one hand on the surface of his desk, considering whether to even look at the place. But he knew that if he didn't, he would never forgive himself. "I've got a light week. When do you think we could go see the property?"

"I'll make some calls and let you know."

Chapter 19

Emma had been to Carlo's home a number of times, but usually for outdoor events in the garden that he'd taken such care to landscape into a veritable oasis. She hadn't really been inside the mobile home that many times. Not that at a first glance you could tell it was a mobile home since it looked like a large ranch thanks to the landscaping and care he'd taken to give it curb appeal.

The home was located just half a block from the beach and was a wonderful location which at one time had been occupied by a big old Victorian. Carlo's neighbors, an older couple whose family had been in Sea Kiss for generations, had told her during a summer barbecue party that the original building had burned almost to the ground one winter night due to a problem with a furnace. Fire was the one thing many people in town feared thanks to the old Victorians. Behind the lathe and plaster there were no stops to prevent fire from shooting up inside the walls. Due to its age, the wood in the old buildings was so dry that it was like kindling, adding to the fire risk.

Luckily the family living in the home at the time had survived, but they'd decided to sell the property and a structure that was beyond repair. According to the neighbors, Carlo had gotten a deal on the land in exchange for having to clear it since the owners hadn't wanted to do that. They also hadn't wanted to sell the property to one of the developers in the area. They'd wanted someone who planned on living in Sea Kiss full time and not just rich summer people who would build a fancy home that stood empty for most of the year.

Like Carlo had lived there for close to a decade and planned to do for quite some time. She knew he wanted to eventually build a Victorian style home for the family he hoped to have one day. A family with a child like the one she'd pictured during her daydreams, with reddish brown hair and hazel-green eyes. Blush-free olive skin. Her heart hurt with the idea of that child. With the promise of what could be if she dared to believe she was good enough for a wonderful man like Carlo.

She raised her hand and held it up an inch from the door, hesitating because she knew once she stepped inside, there was no going back on this journey. But before she could knock, the door flew open and Carlo stood there, his big shoulders nearly filling the doorway and an expectant little boy grin on his face.

"Come on in. It's cold out there," he said and as if to prove it, a biting wind swept up the block from the ocean and swirled around them, causing her to shiver.

She stepped into house and for the first time the home had a chance to really speak about the person who lived there. It was meticulously neat, not unlike how Carlo insisted his business be kept. At one end of the open space was a living room set up with a large screen television on the far wall. The windows in the room faced the street and Carlo's lovely gardens. Curtains in deep navy bracketed the windows and contrasted with the pale yellow of the walls. A large ornately carved wooden cross was hung between two of the windows. On the opposite wall, the space between the windows had a collection of frames with family photos and one of the two of them. Even in the dark of a winter night the space created a feeling of welcome.

On the opposite side of the room was a kitchen with lovely cherry cabinets and a multi-burner range perfect for a chef like Carlo. A trio of pots sat on the stove, low flames beneath keeping the contents warm. Enticing smells wafted from there to where she stood. Beyond the kitchen was a hallway that she assumed led to his bedroom.

Between the kitchen and living room was a small dining table that had been set with fine china, crystal, silver, and a delicate centerpiece of roses, miniature carnations, and lisianthus in various shades of pink and purple. At one side of the centerpiece was a pink taper candle waiting to be lit.

"It's beautiful," she said and he gestured toward the living room. She slipped out of her coat as she walked there and handed it to him.

"Thank you. It's home," he said, almost apologetically and took her coat from her.

"It's lovely," she said to reassure him, sensing that he really needed her approval.

He smiled and dipped his head to acknowledge her comment. "Thanks again. Can I get you something to drink? Wine? I just opened a bottle of cab franc."

"I'd like that," she said as she sat on the couch.

He walked back past the kitchen and to a hall closet where he hung her coat before returning to the narrow breakfast bar in the kitchen. He poured two glasses of wine and as he sauntered back to the living room, she took a moment to appreciate that he'd dressed up for their dinner date. He wore a blue striped button-down shirt that hugged the powerful lines of his shoulders and chest but hung loose around his lean midsection. Faded jeans lovingly embraced his muscled legs.

He handed her the wine and took a seat beside her on the couch. Raising the glass, he said, "To a lovely night."

She met his gaze over the rim of her glass. His gaze was intense, but hesitant, as if he was unsure of just what tonight would be about. But she wanted him to know she was ready to take the next step with him. "To a lovely night," she said with a welcoming smile, clinked her glass against his, and took a sip.

"Delicious," she said. "I'm looking forward to what you've got cooking. It smells wonderful."

"I slaved all day on it," he said in a teasing tone, but she sensed that he had spent considerable time in preparing the meal. It was just the way he was. Thoughtful. Hard-working. Caring. Responsible. Loving, she thought as she glanced at him again and noted the way he was looking at her.

"I know it's going to be wonderful," she said because well, it was Carlo making it and he never did anything halfway. Which made her wonder whether he'd make love the same way, with such caring, loving, and thoughtfulness. Determination. Warmth built inside her at the thought and she took another sip of the wine, but her hand trembled as she did so.

"I hope so, Emma," he said and she realized he was as nervous as she. Bolstered by that, she laid a hand on his knee and said, "Relax, Carlo. I'm sure everything is going to be perfect."

He covered her hand with his and squeezed it. "It's nice to have you here for more than just a quick visit. It's weird that's never happened before."

"It is, but we're both work-a-holics remember? I'm glad we're here now and changing what happened before. Maybe even for the future." And because she needed not only to make it clear to him that she was ready to move on, but reinforce that decision for herself, she leaned forward and brushed a kiss across his lips. As she went to move away, he cradled her cheek and kept her near, deepening the kiss with a swipe of his tongue along her lower lip and a gentle bite that urged her to open for him.

She moaned as he tasted her. Moved his mouth against hers, his kiss rousing and yet gentle. Enticing the way good food made you take a taste and then want more.

She was breathless, almost lightheaded, when he moved, barely an inch away. His warm breath bathed her lips as he said, "Maybe we should get started on dinner."

"Definitely," she said because if they kept on kissing, she was sure the meal he'd spent so much time on might not ever get eaten.

He slowly rose from the couch and held out his hand to her. She slipped it into his and stood. She followed him to the dining room table that she no longer thought of as small, but as intimate. There was no way she could sit there and not be aware of him.

He pulled out the chair for her, ever the gentleman, and she sat. Laid her glass on the table and focused on him as he ambled to the stove and checked the heat on the pots. He pulled off the lids to check them, letting the fragrances of their contents scent the air. Her mouth watered at the deliciousness of the aromas wafting from the kitchen.

Bending, he yanked open the oven and pulled out a tray. It clattered on the granite as he laid it there and then scooped off something onto waiting plates. After he moved a sauté pan off the stove, lifted it, and drizzled something onto the dishes.

He hurried over and placed one serving before her and another before himself. Asparagus wrapped in Serrano ham was grilled and drizzled with a balsamic reduction and roasted figs.

"This looks amazing," she said.

He picked up his knife and fork and said, "*Bon appetit*."

Her stomach did a little rumble and she dug into the appetizer. The asparagus was earthy, but a perfect foil to the saltiness of the cured ham and sweetness of the balsamic vinegar and figs. She laid a hand against her mouth and said, "OMG, this is fabulous."

A wry smile quirked his lips. "I'm glad you like it. I have to confess I love any excuse to use figs and Serrano ham together."

"Well, it works," she said and polished off the rest of the dish so fast, she was embarrassed at her gluttony. "I'm sorry, but this was so good."

"*No problema*. Excuse me while I finish up the *paella*." He rose, cleared off the plates, and walked back to the range. In seconds he was taking something else from the stove and dishing assorted things from the pots.

"Can I help with anything?" she said, feeling a little guilty to just be sitting there.

"Nope. It's all good," he said and in no time he was returning to the table with the dinner plates.

Her mouth watered again at the fragrant aromas and the sight of the wonderfully elegant presentation. A beautiful heap of rice with the crusty crispy *socarrat* bottom off to one side. Perfectly grilled scallops, shrimp, and half a lobster tail were nestled on top of the rice along with bits of browned chicken, colorful chorizo sausage, roasted peppers, and peas.

"It definitely looks all good," she said. She forked up some scallop, chorizo, and rice first and the flavors exploded in her mouth. The chorizo was smoky sweet and the rice had the earthiness of the saffron, but it was balanced enough not to overwhelm the delicate flavor of the scallops. A moan of satisfaction escaped her and she covered her mouth with her hand and heat burst across her face.

"I'm so sorry, it's just amazingly delicious."

CARLO NEARLY CHOKED on his food at the sound of her moan because all he could imagine was her making that sexy sound as he made love to her. Coughing to clear his throat, he said, "Glad you like it."

"I love it," she said and buried her face in her meal, but it wasn't enough to hide the flush of color on her cheeks. Once again, his mind went to sex and how that delightful flush would paint her beautiful body with color.

He hardened and forced himself to focus on dinner. He even reconsidered that maybe he shouldn't have chosen foods that included some known aphrodisiacs because he clearly didn't need any help to get hot and needy. Trying to distract himself from what might have been ill-advised menu choices, he said, "Have you heard from Connie at all?"

Emma grinned and chuckled. "She's on her honeymoon, Carlo. I think she's probably got better things to do than to text me," she said, and more color flooded across her cheeks, probably at the thought of what her friend might be doing. What he hoped they might be doing later.

"Yeah, probably. Maggie and Tracy doing okay?" He knew how important her friends were to her.

Emma was mid-chew, but after she swallowed, she said, "Maggie's busy with all the last-minute holiday events at her store and prepping for spring. Tracy . . ." She paused and sighed. "I worry about Tracy."

And he worried about Paolo being interested in Tracy. "What's up with her?"

"She's moving to Sea Kiss," she said and forked up a bit of the lobster tail.

Great, he thought. Not. "I guess you're happy about that," he said, but it was unfortunately obvious he wasn't.

Emma stopped eating and peered at him. "She's not a bad person, just a little . . . confused. She was always in love with being in love and because of that she made a big mistake."

"I'll say. It didn't take a genius to see he was a shit," Carlo said and regretted it again immediately. "Sorry. I didn't mean to judge."

"It's okay. Just promise me you'll try to give her a chance. See the real Tracy we all love," she said and laid a hand across her heart to emphasize it.

"For you I'd do anything," he said and meant it without hesitation despite his concerns with Paolo's interest in the older woman.

Emma glanced at him, her gaze thoughtful, as if considering if he was truly serious. Seeming to realize that he was, she nodded and said, "I appreciate that."

He'd wanted to change the topic, but not go to such a negative place. This was supposed to be the night where things might move forward. Since they'd almost finished their meals, he said, "I'm glad you could come tonight."

"I'm glad too. It's nice to finally get to spend some time with you in your home," she said and forked up the last little bit of her rice. "This was delicious. Was there something besides saffron in the rice?"

He nodded. "A little bit of chili and paprika to add more pop to the flavor."

"It totally worked." Then, as if a light bulb went off in her head, she added, "Those are all aphrodisiacs, aren't they? So's the seafood."

"A guy has to do what a guy has to do," he said with a shrug and an unrepentant smile.

She laughed and with the sexy smile of a temptress, replied, "Totally not necessary."

The words exploded from his mouth, "*Caralho*, Emma." But he was determined not to rush the seduction he'd planned so carefully. Shooting for a more lighthearted tone, he said, "I wish I'd known before I worked so hard on dessert."

She chuckled again and shook her head. "I can't wait to taste it. I'm sure it will be . . . tantalizing." She lifted her glass, her hand slightly unsteady and he picked up his glass and tapped it to hers.

"I hope not to disappoint," he said. "Why don't we have dessert over on the couch?"

Glancing back toward the sofa, and maybe thinking about where it might lead, she nevertheless said, "I like that idea."

"Go get comfortable and I'll bring the dessert over in a minute."

"I can't wait to see what it will be," she said.

Chapter 20

Emma finished off the last of her wine, stood, and hurried to the couch while Carlo cleared off the table and returned to the kitchen. He loaded their plates into the sink and in no time, he was walking toward her. He placed the two plates, linen napkins, and spoons on the coffee table and sat next to her.

A perfectly molded flan was topped with a rich caramel sauce. A trio of chocolate covered strawberries rested beside it.

"Looks delicious and tantalizing as promised," she said. She plucked one of the strawberries off the plate and offered it up to him to eat like Eve offering Adam the proverbial apple.

With his perfect white teeth he took the strawberry between his teeth and stared at her as he bit down through the chocolate. A bit of strawberry juice squirted onto his lips and it was just too much for her to resist. She negligently dropped the remainder of the strawberry on the plate, shifted close, and licked away the sweetness from his lips.

His gaze locked with hers, questioning, as he sat, his body visible vibrating as he struggled for control. "Are you sure, Emma?" he said, the tones of his voice low. Strumming alive something dangerous inside her.

Her voice wavering, unlike her determination, she said, "I'm sure, Carlo."

He wrapped an arm around her waist and pulled her close, kissing her with restraint until she bit his lower lip playfully and said, "I promise I won't break."

"*Meu deus*," he said and unleashed his control.

He hauled her tight to his chest and deepened the kiss, thrusting his tongue past the seam of her lips to dance it with hers. Retreating to explore the edges of her lips, he cupped her breast and her hard nipple pressed into the palm of his hand beneath the fine cashmere of her sweater. He swept his thumb across the tip and tempered his kiss, beginning a gentle exploration of her mouth that had her straining against him until it just wasn't enough.

She slipped into his lap, her thighs cradling his body. Her center pressed intimately to the long ridge of his erection with only the denim of their jeans separating him. As she moved her hips back and forth across that hardness, he groaned and grasped her waist, his hands so big they almost spanned her waist.

"Please, Carlo. Please don't stop," she said as she shifted across him, passion building inside her.

A muttered curse burst from his lips and he bent his head to the crook of her neck to place a gentle kiss there. His breath was hot and unsteady as he slipped his hands beneath the hem of her sweater and slowly drew it upward to reveal the black lace demi bra she had worn in anticipation of a moment just like this.

He roamed his gaze all over her body and lightly skimmed his hands across her shoulders and down her arms. "You are so beautiful, *meu amor.*"

My love, she translated and shook with the pleasure of it and the need as he slowly trailed his hands upward to cup her breasts through the thin lace. His gaze fixed on her face as he teased the hard nubs between his fingers and she grabbed hold of his shoulders to steady herself. The heat of desire and sudden shyness sent warmth through her body and up to her face.

"I've dreamed of this. Of seeing this beautiful blush paint your body," he said, and stroked his thumbs across her taut nipples. "Of tasting you," he said and peeled down the lace to suck the tight tip into his mouth.

She moaned and closed her eyes against the sight of him suckling her. He rubbed her other nipple with this thumb and forefinger, every tug and pull of his mouth sending bursts of need to her center. Desire building until it wasn't enough and she started to move against him again, seeking release. Urged onward by his soft entreaties as he loved her with his mouth and he tightened his hand at her waist to guide her movements.

Arousal built at her center, growing with each stroke of her hips. With each lick and suck of his mouth at her sensitive breasts until with a gentle bite, he sent her over the edge. She shuddered violently and called out his name and he wrapped his arms around her. Gentled her with tender kisses and the stroke of his hand across his hair.

"You are so beautiful. So special," he said as he calmed her as her climax ebbed.

But as it did, embarrassment set in. "I'm so sorry. You didn't –"

"I loved giving you pleasure, *meu amor*. It gave me pleasure," he said and brushed back a lock of hair that had come free of her french braid, his gaze fixed on her face.

She licked her lips, suddenly shy again. "I . . . I want to give you pleasure, too. I want . . . Tell me what you want."

CARLO SUCKED IN A BREATH and tightened his gut, fighting the desire to rip off all her clothes and take her right there on the couch. Holding his breath, he mustered the barest self-control and slowly exhaled. "I want you in my life, Emma. I've wanted you in my life since the moment I laid eyes on you."

Surprise flitted across Emma's face. "Does that mean . . ." Her voice trailed off, confusion replacing surprise.

"I want you in my bed, too, *meu amor*. I really do, but I also want you to know it's not just about sex, even though all I can think about right now is what it would feel like to be inside you."

A faint half smile came to her lips. "Really? Because that's what I'm thinking about as well."

Carlo closed his eyes and lifted his face upward. "Emma, I'm barely hanging in here, trying to be a gentleman."

"Again, really?" The rustle of clothing was followed a second later by the brush of lace across his nose and then his hands.

"*Caralho*, Emma. Please don't tell me –"

"Open your eyes, because as much as I adore your restraint, that's not what I want from you right now. Or tomorrow. Or the next day."

He tightened his hands on her waist to keep from touching her, dipped his head down and did as she asked and nearly lost it. She had removed that tempting black lace bra and was now naked from the waist up. A flush of delicate color deepened the peaches and cream of her complexion and the dusky deep rose of her tight nipples.

"Emma –"

"Touch me, Carlo. Make love to me because that's what we both want," she said, her voice filled with determination.

No saint could resist, and he was no saint. He surged to his feet, his arms bracketing her back, and she wrapped her legs around his waist. His long strides ate up the short distance to his bedroom. At the side of his bed he urged her to slip down his body, but kept his hands at her waist, keeping her close. "Are you sure, *meu amor*?"

"I'm sure you've got too many clothes on." Emma chuckled, grabbed hold of the edges of his collar and with a sharp jerk, sent buttons scattering across his hardwood floor as she yanked open his shirt. She soothed her hands along his midsection, tracing the ridges there before moving upward. Cupping the thick muscles of his chest, she ran her hands across his nipples which were already tight with desire. He trembled from the need racing across his body, barely keeping his passion in check.

Emma slipped her hands onto his shoulders and eased off the shirt. She leaned forward and kissed the underside of his jaw. Shifted to the crook of his neck and then down to suck his nipple into her mouth and his knees weakened from the force of his need.

"Emma," he said and cradled the back of her head to him.

She bit him gently and he groaned and reached for the button on her jeans. "I want you, Emma. I need you."

She dropped her hands to her jeans, undid the zipper. The rasp of it was loud in the room, but not as loud as their rushed breaths. She quickly shimmied out of her jeans and after she did so, she sat on the edge of his bed, leaned back on her elbows and spread her legs slightly apart. With a sexy smile, she said, "What are you waiting for?"

His own hands shook as he popped the button on his jeans, carefully undid the zipper past his straining erection, and then kicked off his deck shoes as he stepped out of his pants.

At Emma's sharp intake of breath, he walked to between her legs and she sat up, skimmed the back of her hand across him.

"You remember when the guys teased you about the size of your feet?" she said and encircled him in her hand. As she stroked downward, he closed his eyes with pleasure and groaned.

"They were just jealous," she said and kissed him before taking him into her mouth.

He held her to him, but then quickly pulled away. "I'll lose it if you keep that up."

A siren's smile played across Emma's lips as she stroked him yet again. "That's the idea, Carlo. I want you to lose that control you're so famous for."

He loved her sexiness and didn't want to disappoint. Reaching out, he took hold of her lace panties and dragged them down her long shapely legs. Braced himself at the sight of the darker reddish curls at her center as he imagined parting her and driving in. Because he was already at the edge, he hurriedly yanked a condom from his nightstand and opened the packet. When he went to sheathe himself, she took over the task, leisurely rolling the condom into place.

"That feels so good, Emma. So good, *meu amor*," he said and cupped her breasts. Caressed her nipples as she ran her hands up his shoulders and urged him close until his erection brushed her center. Even through the condom the heat of her bathed him. He trailed his hand down her body and parted her to find the swollen nub. Circling it with his finger, he slipped another finger into her wet and stroked her, building her passion until she was shifting anxiously on the bed and grabbing at him to get closer.

The flush of passion stained her skin which was hot beneath his hands as he grasped her buttocks and urged her forward until he was poised at her center.

He locked his gaze with hers as he entered slowly, fighting not to plunge into her like a savage. He was feeling savage. Possessive. Wanting her like nothing else he'd ever wanted in his life.

"You're so tight, Emma. So hot," he said and held his breath as she fisted around him and the first waves of her release built inside her.

"Carlo," she said and arched her back, deepening his penetration. "So big, Carlo. So full. You make me feel so full."

He pushed forward, burying himself deep and held still, nearly unmanned by the feel of her around him. But as she moved beneath him and moaned, it was impossible to hold back any longer.

Chapter 21

Carlo drove into her and Emma cried out as a wave of pleasure nearly swamped her over the edge. She hadn't wanted to fall over so quickly. Not when she'd waited so long for this. Not when the feel of him, inside her, above her as he shifted his big body, was more than she ever could have imagined.

She moved her hips in rhythm with his, making love with him. Savoring the spill of his breath against her body as he bent to kiss her. Accepting the slide of his tongue that mimicked the thrust of hips until she started to shake as she neared the edge.

"Carlo," she called out and tangled her hands in the thick, tousled strands of his hair. Urged him to her breasts because she wanted his mouth on her. Wanted his hot lips and gentle teeth coaxing her ever higher.

"You taste so sweet," he said as he suckled her and ground into her, driving her closer to a climax.

Inside her the wave built ever higher. Grew ever more powerful until it crashed over her like a tsunami. She called out his name and threw her head back, shaking and grasping Carlo to her as he continued to pump into her, seeking his own release. Driving her into the mattress with the force of his thrusts until he came and stilled, his big body trembling as he held his weight off her. His skin damp as she ran her hands across his shoulders and urged him down onto her.

"I want to feel you against me," she said and gentled him with long strokes across his skin.

"I'm heavy," he said, but didn't move, keeping them joined until long moments passed and he finally had no choice but to leave her side.

As he walked away, Emma watched, enjoying the sight of his powerful body and how his muscles shifted with each step, but without the weight of him, a chill settled over her. She shivered and climbed into the bed and under the covers as she waited for his return. Barely minutes later he strolled in, his smile bright. His face and body so beautiful it took her breath away and made her heart ache with what she felt for him.

He slipped into bed beside her and drew her into his arms. She pillowed her head on his shoulder and stroked her hand across his chest, needing to touch him almost as if to reassure herself that he was really there. That they'd really just made love.

CARLO SMOOTHED A HAND up and down her back, sensing she needed the connection. Maybe even something more, but somehow he couldn't find the words to say. He'd waited so long for this and now that it had finally happened . . .

He wanted to say that he loved her because he did. But he worried he'd scare her off. And so they lay there in silence for long moments until Emma said, "I'm not sorry we did this, Carlo."

Not quite what he'd been hoping to hear. "I'm not either, Emma. I want you," he said and turned so that they were facing each other. "I want you in my bed. In my life."

She cradled his cheek and traced her thumb along the edges of his lips, her gaze serious, almost worried. "I know you want that now –"

"I want you forever, remember? *Forever.* That won't change," he said and to prove his point, he kissed her and drew her close. Touched her as he'd dreamed of doing for so long. Caught her up in the undeniable passion that existed between them because she couldn't reject that. Couldn't refuse to accept what was so right between them. He hoped that in time she would finally admit to what was in her heart.

Afterward they lay together, limbs entwined. Hearts pounding against each other and breaths slowly returning to a calm and measured rhythm. Silence grew between them again until he said the words he should have said earlier, "I love you, Emma. I've loved you for a long time. For as long as I can remember."

A long hesitant moment followed until she said, "I care for you, Carlo. More than you can imagine. More than I ever thought I'd care for any man."

Weeks earlier he'd worried he'd be friend-zoned. It was nothing compared to what he was feeling now with her admission because it was impossible not to hear the "but" she was about to drop on him. So he beat her to it.

"I understand, Emma. I won't push you for anything you're not ready to give." Even if that meant she'd never give him the one thing he wanted more than her body. Her love.

EMMA HEFTED ONE OF Tracy's suitcases from the trunk of her car and followed Tracy as she rolled an even bigger suitcase up the sidewalk and to the front door of the Lighthouse Inn. Tracy planned to stay at the inn until she was able to locate a home in the area. Emma was happy her friend was moving on with her life and even better, that she would be nearby. With Connie coming back any day from her honeymoon and Maggie being able to take a break over the holidays, they would all be together again for Christmas and the New Year.

Emma needed her friends now more than ever. The other night with Carlo had been . . . amazing. Earth-shattering. Scary. Giving herself to him physically had been satisfying, but she had totally risked her heart. Something she hadn't been prepared to give just yet. Maybe never and she knew just how unfair that was to him. As unfair as Sasha had been to him so many years earlier.

She dashed that thought from her brain. She wasn't this Sasha whoever she was who didn't think Carlo wasn't good enough. If anything, he was way too good, especially for someone like her.

"Emma. Earth to Emma," Tracy said as Emma almost ran into her at the front door to the inn.

"Sorry. My mind was elsewhere," she offered in apology.

"That's obvious, Em. How about we do lunch and talk about it after I get all checked in?" Tracy said.

"I'm game, Tracy. I've missed our talks," she said and her friend held the door open so Emma could walk through with the suitcase.

The young woman at the front desk checked her in quickly and in no time the innkeeper helped them trudge up the stairs to the second-floor room, a spacious suite with views of the river inlet and reproductions of period antiques. Beautiful watercolor seascapes decorated the walls while a vase of fresh flowers sat on the dresser beside a small wrapped plate of assorted biscuits and candies.

"This is lovely," Emma said as she looked around the space.

"It's a nice first step to my new life," Tracy said with a smile. Her friend looked happier than she had in a long time and Emma was glad for that.

She walked over to Tracy and slipped an arm around hers. "Let's start this new life with a nice lunch. Maybe even some champagne to celebrate? What do you say?"

"I say that sounds wonderful. Any idea where to go?"

Normally Emma would say the Dunes, but that would bring way too many memories of Carlo and their first real date. As wonderful as the other night had been and as much as she wanted a repeat, she didn't need a reminder of her fear that she wasn't being fair to him so soon.

"How about the Pavilion? It's in the next town over and right on the beachfront."

Tracy nodded. "I love the beach, especially in winter. There's something pure about it without all the crowds and noise."

Emma couldn't argue with her. Even though the Benny tourists were the lifeblood of the area, their absence in the winter brought calm. "I agree. It's peaceful in the winter. Good for sorting out what's on your mind."

Tracy peered at her intently from her slightly greater height and said, "I can see you need to do a lot of sorting out, my friend."

With a shrug, Emma said, "I do, but so do you which is why I'm glad you're here."

Tracy smiled and gave her a one-armed hug. "Then let's get going. I'm hungry and haven't been in a while."

Now that Tracy mentioned it, Emma noticed her friend had lost some weight which wasn't good since Tracy had always been slender. The fine wool of her friend's sweater hung loosely on her body as did the pants she wore.

"That's good to hear. You need a little more meat on your bones," she said, which reminded her of a comment Carlo's older brother had said about her a month earlier.

Carlo, Carlo, Carlo. It was like she couldn't get him out of her brain, but she had to so she could decide where she wanted their relationship to go next.

They headed back to Tracy's new Jaguar which was sitting in the parking lot of the inn and it took only a few minutes to drive through Sea Kiss and over to the next town and the beachfront. Unlike Sea Kiss, the boardwalk here had a number of stores and restaurants along both the boardwalk and across the way on Ocean Avenue. Since it was winter it was easy for them to find a place not far from the restaurant. In the summer months you might have to drive around for some time to find a spot. Most people gave up and parked many blocks away and did the long trudge to the beach, often laden with beach chairs, coolers, and kids too young to do the walk balanced awkwardly on mom's hip.

The breeze that had kicked up the night before had blown itself out and the temperature had warmed, making it a pleasant walk to the restaurant. As they entered, the hostess smiled and called out a greeting to Emma who had arranged a number of events at the restaurant for assorted bridal showers and rehearsal dinners.

"So good to see you, Emma," Sarah said and hugged her.

"Good to see you too. This is my friend, Tracy," she said and introduced the two women.

"I've got the perfect table for you. We just finished bussing it," Sarah said and gestured to a waitress who hurried over. Sarah handed the young woman the menus and they followed her to a table right against the windows and facing the ocean.

"Lovely, thank you," Tracy said and took a seat across from Emma.

"Yes, lovely. Could you please bring us a bottle of the Dom Perignon?" Emma said before she even looked at the menu.

"My pleasure. My name is Mia by the way. Would you like to hear today's lunch specials?" the waitress asked.

"We'd love to, Mia," Emma said and the young woman expertly rattled off a number of specials, from a roasted beet salad to a chef-suggested lobster roll.

"Thank you," Tracy said and perused the menu and Emma did the same, finally deciding on a lobster mac and cheese which never failed to be good at the restaurant.

Tracy ordered the same thing which prompted Emma to say, "Comfort food since we both need comforting?"

Tracy rolled her eyes and nodded in agreement. "For sure. Am I to assume you've had a falling out with Carlo?"

An assumption that was so wrong Emma couldn't contain a chuckle. "Surprisingly, not. In fact, Carlo and I . . ." The words to describe that wonderful night failed her, but it seemed Tracy didn't need to hear the words to know what had happened.

"Oh . . .my . . . God. You and Carlo. Finally," she said just as Mia returned with the bottle of champagne and glasses as well as a busboy with a standing ice bucket for it. Tracy said nothing else as the waitress expertly opened the bottle with a small pop and poured the champagne into crystal flutes that she set on the table before them.

"Your meals will be out shortly," Mia said and hurried away with the bus boy.

Tracy picked up her glass and said, "To new beginnings for both of us."

Emma raised her flute and clinked it against Tracy's. "To new beginnings."

After they each took a sip, Tracy said, "I sense a lot of hesitation there. You still dealing with daddy issues?"

Leave it to Tracy to cut to the heart of the matter in no time. "Maybe," she replied, her feelings still too new and uncertain.

Her friend peered at her over the rim of her glass before taking a big slug from the drink. She set the glass on the table and said, "Do you love him?"

Of all the questions she'd asked herself since last night, that wasn't one of them. "I love him, but I couldn't say it. After . . ."

"Please tell me you told him after," Tracy pleaded, leaning closer to Emma across the narrow width of the table. "Please, Emma."

Her hand shook as she picked up her glass and took a sip, avoiding her friend's gaze.

"Please please, please, Emma," Tracy repeated in challenge.

Emma drained her glass and set it back on the table. "I wish I had, but I couldn't, Trace. The words wouldn't come out of my mouth even though it was so amazing. So wonderful. *He* was so wonderful, and he said it. He said he loves me," she said, the words tumbling out of her mouth faster than she wanted. Revealing way too much, but then again, Tracy was one of her best friends and if anyone would understand and respect that revelation, Tracy would.

The busboy arrived with their meals and Mia followed, refilled their glasses and said, "Can I get you anything else, ladies?"

"We're all good, thanks," Tracy replied.

"Yes, thanks, Mia," Emma echoed as the buttery and cheesy smells of the mac and cheese and lobster filled her senses and made her stomach rumble noisily.

Hunger for food apparently replaced Tracy's hunger for more information for several minutes, but then her friend picked up the discussion again. "Carlo and his brothers strike me as good and honorable men."

"Because your choices in men have been so on the money," Emma said and instantly regretted it. "I'm sorry, Trace. That was a low blow."

"But accurate, Em. I'd like to think I'm wiser now and dealing with why I made those horrible mistakes. I let my need for the love I wasn't getting from my parents drive me to love the wrong man. I'm working to let go of that past. Can you get over your past to make the right choices for the future?"

"I'm trying, but it's not easy. There's still so much hurt there. So much fear," Emma confessed.

Tracy nodded. "That you're trying is a good first step at least. And it won't be easy, but nothing worthwhile is ever easy, is it?"

"It isn't, but I'm going to try, Trace. I don't want to lose him," she said, finally voicing what was in her heart.

Tracy raised her glass for another toast. "Here's to trying."

Emma tapped her glass to Tracy's. "To trying."

Chapter 22

Carlo followed Mary Sanders around as she showed him the convention center.

It was easy to understand how the owners had blown through all their Hurricane Sandy insurance payout and more. The monies had all been plowed into brand new walk-in freezers and refrigerators as well as a state-of-the-art kitchen that he itched to try out. But as the real estate agent continued the tour it was clear that there was still a lot more work to do to make the building usable. The storerooms, ball rooms, and bathrooms all had exposed studs, but luckily brand new electrical and plumbing.

He turned to Mary and asked, "They've passed all the inspections so far?"

Mary pulled out her folder with the information for the property, reviewed it, and nodded. "All the finished areas have complied with code requirements and are ready to use. Roof, framing, plumbing, and electrical have all passed the inspections. Now it's just the sheet rock and the final touches to do."

"Rooms and rooms of sheet rock and paint. Lighting fixtures. Landscaping," he said dejectedly. Even if he managed to scrape up the money to make an offer the owners might consider, he wouldn't have enough to do all that other work. He was short by quite a lot.

"You say they're pretty firm on the price?" he said as they continued their stroll through the building before stepping out onto the veranda that wrapped entirely around the structure. He stood there, arms akimbo, and surveyed the views. The veranda provided access to the street and parking lot, but more importantly, there was also a nice-sized garden on one side and stunning visuals of the river from two different sides of the building.

"Firm, but no takers so far and to be honest, with as much as needs to be done I think they need to come down on their price. On top of that, the building is landmarked so they can't take it down for more profitable housing. There are not that many locals who can swing what they're asking. Except of course for maybe –"

"Jonathan Pierce. I know he's one of the few who can afford it," he said. If Jonathan got involved in any kind of bidding war, there was no way he'd be able to compete and buy the building.

With a resigned sigh, he held his hand out to Mary. "Thanks so much for taking the time to show me the place."

The real estate agent nodded and glanced back toward the building. "She used to be a grand old dame. It would be nice to see her beautiful and full of life again."

"It would," he said and strolled down the steps and as Mary had done, peered at the elegant Victorian structure. In his mind's eye he pictured people strolling up the walk and into the building while others milled about the gardens and lawn.

"Are you still interested?" Mary asked, head tilted at an inquiring angle to emphasize her question.

Despite all his misgivings about what it might cost, he nodded. "I am. I'll get back to you in a few days."

"I look forward to hearing from you," she said and they both returned to their cars.

It was a short ride back to his warehouse. Sea Kiss was not only quaint, but small. Barely a square mile sandwiched in between two larger, more commercial towns. In his parking lot, he stopped to look at the warehouse that was currently home to the company he'd built with his blood and sweat. It had taken a lot of hard work and sacrifice, but it had paid off. His business was thriving, but he was sure it could be bigger and better and guarantee the future of the da Costa brothers. And Emma if she'd have him.

The loading dock was quiet today, but inside there was a hub of activity as Tomás and Paolo directed their crew to finish the restocking of all the inventory he'd ordered as replacements and the food and other supplies for the next two weeks of holiday parties before Christmas and the New Year. Christmas Eve.

Véspera de Natal was the big night for his family and would soon be here. He pictured Emma at his side as she'd been so many times before. Maybe this year he'd go with Emma on Christmas Day to see her mother or spend time with her friends who would certainly be celebrating their first holidays together as husband and wife.

Buoyed by that possibility which shook off a little of the disappointment about the costs of the convention center, he waved a greeting at his brothers and went into his office. He pulled up his accounts again and reviewed them. After, he considered how much he could get for the sale of the warehouse, but it still wasn't enough to cover the purchase and work needed on the convention center.

"Why the long face, *mano*?" Tomás asked as Paolo and he strolled into his office.

"Don't tell me she blew you off," Paolo said and plopped into a chair. Tomás dropped into the chair next to him and arched a brow. "Did she?"

Carlo shook his head and blew out a harsh laugh. "Emma and I had a very nice dinner, not that it's any of your business." To keep them from continuing to pry about his love life, he said, "What is your business is *this* business. I just came back from seeing the convention center. It's for sale."

Both brothers sat up straighter in their chairs, their interest piqued. "You want to buy it?" Paolo asked, excitement making him bounce up and down in his chair.

"It's a great opportunity," Tomás added and shot a quick look at Paolo as if to gauge his interest.

"Even though you might not be around come February?" Carlo challenged since as far as he knew, his brother had not yet made up his mind about re-enlisting.

Tomás shrugged. "A man can't stay in the Army forever, *mano*. Even if I go back this time, these old bones won't hold out for many more deployments."

Carlo was happy to hear that since he always worried about his brother's safety whenever he was on a mission. Continuing, he said, "There's just one problem. Or maybe two. The cost of the property and Emma. This is just the kind of opportunity we talked about, only . . ."

"You had more than dinner and now you're not sure you want to mix business with pleasure. There was pleasure, right?" Paolo teased and leaned closer to scrutinize Carlo's face.

Carlo felt the heat rise to his cheeks and ignored his brother. Hesitating because he didn't want to violate the trust Emma had placed in him, he said, "Emma is right to worry about mixing a personal relationship with a business one."

But he knew it was also more about the number her father had done on her with his emotional abuse. Plus, he suspected there was more to the story that she still hadn't told him.

His two brothers shared a look and he had no doubt what they were thinking.

"I'll speak to her when the time is right, but it isn't. I'm way short of what I'd need for a bid. On top of that, the building still needs a ton of work which means I need even more cash to get it ready for customers," he explained.

"I don't have much, but you've paid me well. I can kick in whatever I have," Paolo said with a nonchalant shrug.

"I haven't had many needs in the Army so I've stashed away a nice nest egg for civilian life. I'm in," Tomás said, adding his support.

Carlo held his hands up in disbelief. "Just like that. Without even taking a look at the place?"

His two brothers glanced at each other again and just shrugged as if they didn't have a care in the world. Paolo dipped his head in Tomás's direction, and his middle brother looked at him and said, "We trust you, Carlo. Whatever you want to do, we're here for you like you've always been there for us."

Carlo's throat choked up with emotion at the trust his brothers were placing in him. With a nod, he managed to choke out, "*Obrigado.* I won't let you down."

"We know," they said in unison and rose to get back to work. As they left the office, Carlo hoped their trust in him wouldn't be misplaced. He likewise hoped that Emma could get over her issues and learn to trust him as well.

EMMA PLACED THE PLATE with the flan and chocolate covered strawberries on the coffee table in front of Carlo. "We never did get to eat that delicious dessert you made, so I thought I'd give it a try."

She sat cross-legged on the couch beside him, plucked a strawberry off the plate, and held it up to him.

"You remember what happened the last time you offered me this treat?" he said with an arch of his dark brow and a playfully dangerous glitter in his gaze.

But she was feeling just as deliciously sexy. Bringing the strawberry to his lips, she said, "Why do you think I made this dessert?"

He took hold of her hand and bit off most of the berry. He chewed it slowly and made a point of licking his lips, daring her to taste him.

She did, but just a fleeting kiss meant to tease and entice him.

He reached for a berry and held it up to her lips. She bit into the berry and juices exploded all over her mouth, but she had barely swallowed when Carlo had his mouth on hers, kissing and tasting her. He urged her into his lap, but she slapped his hands away with a laugh and stood.

"I've got a much more comfortable place for us," she said, tugging him out of her living room and into her bedroom. On the way in, she snagged the remote and flipped on the gas fireplace. It cast warm intimate light in the otherwise dark room.

At the edge of the bed, she paused in her headlong rush and faced him. "I want you, Carlo, but not just physically."

With a wry grin and a sweep of his gaze around the room, he teased, "Color me confused, because this sure seems like a seduction to me."

"Shut up," she said and urged him to sit on the edge of her bed.

"Domineering too? I think I may like this," he said, barely containing a laugh.

"You're not taking this seriously," she said with a pout, reached down and yanked the black sweater he wore up and over his head, baring his upper body.

"But I am, Emma," he said and eased his hands to the tiny buttons on the V-neck cardigan she wore, undoing them quickly. He groaned as the fabric parted to reveal she had nothing on underneath. Quickly he covered her with his hands, jerking a rough sigh from her as he caressed her breasts.

"I can't think when you do that," she said and swayed toward him.

I It grinned and replaced his hands with his mouth, causing her to wrap her arms around his head and hold him to her. She dropped kisses on his temple and forehead and moaned as he gave a rough tug at her nipple with his mouth.

"Carlo, please. Stop," she said and eased her hands between them to urge him away.

"Emma, is something wrong?" he asked, leaning back onto the bed.

"Nothing's wrong, Carlo, but I want tonight to be about you. I want you to know just how much I care for you."

Carlo shook his head. "*Meu amor*, I know. Trust me –"

"I do, Carlo. I really do only . . ." she said, hating that what should have been a special night might suddenly go south.

"*Meu amor*, we have all night, don't we?" he said and reached up to cradle her breast again. He bent his head to kiss the tip of her breast while he whispered, "Don't over think this. Just enjoy."

She couldn't think with his mouth moving on her, making her insides clench with need and her center grow damp. She laid her hands on his shoulder and urged him to lie down on the bed. As he did so, she hurriedly yanked off her own pants and then undid his jeans and stripped them off his body, exposing him to her gaze. He was so beautiful. So lethally masculine. The firelight cast its light on his skin, painting him golden in spots, but casting shadows also. She traced her finger along those lines across his abdomen, then skipped her finger down to his navel and lower until she encircled him.

He groaned as she ran her hand up his erection and it jerked and trembled beneath her palm. She stroked him and his big body shuddered. His voice was tight as he held out his hand and said, "Come here, Emma. Please."

She had wanted to pleasure him but couldn't resist his plea.

She took hold of his hand and with a surge of power, he had them in the center of the bed with his big body trapping her beneath him. She loved the weight of him. The feel of his hard body against hers and the press of his erection at her center, so hot and thick. Lord, she wanted to love him, be one with him as settled himself at her center, slowly parting her.

"Carlo, protection," she said, fearing they'd both lose their heads and do something foolish. Although a picture of a baby that was a mix of both of them flashed through her mind for a hot instant.

He muttered a curse, reached for his pants from the floor, and jerked a packet from his back pocket. There was a rip of foil and suddenly he was back over her, but trailing kisses down her body until he reached her center.

"Carlo," she protested, halfheartedly she had to admit, but that plea became a moan as he parted her and sucked at the sensitive nub with his mouth. He eased one finger and then a second into her to stroke her until she was wet and arching her hips to him, seeking satisfaction.

EMMA KEENED WITH PLEASURE and her nails bit into his shoulders as he tasted her. Beneath his lips and hands, her body vibrated with the first tremors of her approaching climax. As she called out his name again and his erection jerked at the sound, Carlo couldn't wait any more.

He danced kisses up her body until he reached her breasts again. Suckling her, he poised at her entrance and with a subtle move of her hips, Emma took him inside inch-by-pleasurable-inch. He stilled, awed by the feel of her around him. Beneath him. By her pale beauty in the firelight and the pleasant heat from the fireplace that couldn't compare to the warmth of her body.

"You take my breath away, *meu amor*. You are so beautiful," he said as he rose up on his arm to look at her. Wanting to see her as passion rose, rousing the blush on her skin and deepening her amazing eyes to a green as deep as the most precious emerald.

Emma ran her hands across his shoulder and down to cup his chest. She skimmed her thumbs across his nipples and his gut tightened with the caress.

"You like that," she said and rose up to suckle him, causing him to groan and close his eyes against the pleasure.

She bit the tip gently and he had to move as desire pummeled him.

He shifted in and out, driving passion ever higher in both of them. Straining not to lose control as her climax approached and the waves of her release rolled over him. Over and over he stroked until with a sharp thrust, she arched upward with her climax and he couldn't hold on anymore and fell over with her.

Chapter 23

Emma was cradled between his legs as they finally ate the flan and finished off the strawberries covered in chocolate. As he set aside their plates on her nightstand, he wrapped his arms around her and drew her back against his chest.

"Delicious. As good as mine," he said and kissed her temple.

"Liar. There's no way it was as good as yours," she said and rubbed his forearms with her hands.

"Way better since we actually ate it, Em," he teased.

She laughed and shook her head. "You're incorrigible," she teased.

But a second later he had his hand between her legs, touching her intimately and rousing need again.

"No, that's incorrigible, *meu amor*," he whispered in her ear and proceeded to show her just how good it was to be bad.

CONNIE RETURNED THAT weekend from her honeymoon and brought with her a couple of unseasonably warm December days. With the temperature hovering in the mid-fifties, Emma and her friends had grabbed a couple of big blankets and laid them out behind the Pierce and Sinclair beach houses to enjoy the weather, sun, and a picnic lunch that Emma had picked up earlier from Jesse's shop.

Connie had finished eating and was lying on the blanket, wearing a lightweight jacket. Unbuttoned, it fell open to reveal a very pronounced baby bump.

"OMG, Con. Did you swallow a coconut or something on your honeymoon?" Emma kidded and gently ran her hand over Connie's newly burgeoning belly.

Connie leaned up enough to see it and smiled, happiness radiating from her like summer sunshine. She skimmed her hand across the growing mound and said, "It's like the baby was waiting until after the wedding and then said, 'Bam it's time to show me around.'"

Tracy laughed and said, "You tell that little girl she's got to wait. It's not time for her to come out yet."

Connie glanced at her friend, a slight scrunch to her brows. "You think it's a girl? That's the way I've been feeling too."

"I hope it is so she can have wonderful friends like all of you," Tracy said and hugged Emma, who was sitting beside her on the blanket.

Cross-legged, Maggie was opposite Connie on another blanket. She turned to take a look at Connie's protruding belly and with a laugh, she said, "Are you sure there aren't twins in there?"

"No, twins, thankfully. We have enough going on with the new building, the house renovations, and my new job," Connie said.

Maggie swiveled and laid shoulder-to-shoulder beside Connie. Maggie spread her hands across her own belly and said, "Good thing since Owen and I are having twins and may need some help."

Connie shot up to stare at her friend while Tracy squealed and leaned over to hug both of them.

In shock, Emma covered her mouth with her hands as tears came to her eyes. "Twins?" she said shakily.

Maggie nodded and grinned. "I guess all that trying worked for us," she said with a laugh. "The doctor said twins. I'm almost at the start of the third month and we heard the two heartbeats at our last visit."

"Wow, Maggie. That's amazing," Emma said and reached out to grasp her friend's hand.

"Amazing and scary, but it's nice to think that Connie's baby won't have to wait too long to have friends around," Maggie said and hugged Emma.

Tracy clapped joyfully and said, "And the babies will have Aunt Tracy and Auntie Em –"

"Sweet lord, how many times do I have to tell you not to call me that," Emma said with a heavy sigh and a roll of her eyes.

"But you're going to be a fabulous aunt, Emma. So am I," Tracy said and hugged her hard, sensing that she needed the support.

Emma could picture it. Tracy and her, the favorite old maiden aunts, taking their friends' trio of babies for ice cream or to the amusement park on the boardwalk a few towns over. But then the image in her mind morphed and that reddish-haired, hazel-eyed baby came into the picture again as it had the other night and joined her friends' babies. She embraced that image and found the courage to say, "Carlo and I . . . we've been seeing each other. Seriously."

The squeals that followed that announcement were as loud as those for Maggie's news.

"That's epic, Em," Connie said, earning a groan from Maggie.

"That's so Jon of you, but it is epic," Maggie teased, mimicking the surfer lingo Connie's husband was so fond of using.

"It is," Emma said, but her friends knew her too well not to see she was still reluctant.

"It's going to work out, Emma. He loves you," Maggie said and leaned forward to squeeze Emma's hand to emphasize the point.

Connie added her support by moving across the blanket to hug her. "When Jon and I first got together, I was worried too, but Jon said to take it organically. I laughed and thought he was crazy, but look," she said and gestured to her belly.

"Organically, huh?" Emma said with a shake of her head. "I'll try, Con. I'll try not to over think it," she said, recalling the words Carlo had said to her just the night before.

"Try, Emma. Try to set aside all the hurt your dad did to you. Trust Carlo," Connie said.

Tracy emphasized it with a hug. "Carlo is a good man. He'll make a good father."

"I hadn't thought that far ahead," she said although she had. Not that she could admit it yet or even truly believe it.

"Liar, but we'll let it go for now, Emma. We can all tell it's too soon," Maggie said.

"It is and all I want to think about right now is enjoying this gorgeous day with my best friends forever," she said and to prove her point, she joined them all together in a group hug.

Their laughter and smiles filled Emma with joy and comfort. She knew that no matter what, they'd be there for her through good times and bad. Her one hope was that the times to follow would only be good for all of them.

CARLO SCROLLED THROUGH his electronic ledger one last time and then his 401K summary. Not that he wanted to tap into that, but he would if it would secure the future for him and his brothers. And Emma. For the last several years his dreams had always included Emma both in his personal life and his business one. But he still hadn't had the courage to talk to her about the convention center and as much as he dared hope, he feared Emma remained unsure about their personal relationship. Flipping to the spreadsheet he'd created to keep track of the funds he'd been able to put together for the bid on the convention center, he sighed with regret. With what Paolo and Tomás could contribute they only had enough for a substantial portion of the purchase price, but nowhere near what they'd need to finish the renovations to the building.

He could reach out to Emma, but his gut tightened with concern. He wanted her to be a part of it so much. But how would it affect their too new relationship? he wondered and settled more deeply into the cushions of his chair. He steepled his hands before his mouth and rested his head on the back of his chair, considering what to do. How to do it.

A sharp series of knocks on the frame of his door yanked him from his thoughts.

Jonathan Pierce stood there, looking tanned, relaxed, and incredibly happy. "Dude, why do you look so down?"

Carlo hopped to his feet and hurried to bro hug his friend, clap his back, and clasp his hand. "*Mano*, you look great. Marriage obviously agrees with you."

"I feel great, Carlo. I never thought I'd say this, but married life is awesome," Jonathan said with a huge smile. His sea blue eyes gleamed like sunlight on the ocean.

"I can tell. You really do look happy," he said and motioned him in the direction of a chair in front of his desk. "What brings you here today?"

"I just got back and found out the convention center is for sale. You know me. I wanted to jump on that, but when I called Mary Sanders, she said she couldn't help me. That she already had another client interested in the property."

Carlo nodded and shoved his hands in his pockets as he sat on the edge of his desk. "I guess you're here because you figured out who it was."

"I did and it makes a lot of sense. I know Emma and you have talked about starting an event planning business together and that's a perfect location. Lots of opportunities for holding events," Jonathan said, the surfer dude replaced with the businessman who had turned the energy and vehicle industries on their heads.

"A good place for you to have conferences as well. The ballrooms seat a nice number of people," Carlos said.

"According to the specifications on the main ballrooms, they're approved for five hundred people each. Perfect for the kinds of conferences I wanted to have. I've got some ideas on the first one I'd like to hold there, but I want no part of dealing with the food, planning, and everything else it takes," Jonathan admitted with smile as he tacked on, "I'd rather be surfing."

"Or inventing another fabulous new car." Carlo reached across his desk to grab the fob sitting there. "It worked like a dream," he said as he returned the key to Jonathan.

"Glad to hear that, Carlo. We have high hopes for the Thunder. Are you game?" Jonathan asked and pocketed the fob.

"Game? Does that mean you want to be like an Angel Investor?" Carlo said, wanting to make sure that he understood just what Jonathan was proposing.

Jonathan laughed. "An Angel Investor, huh? Haven't been called that before, but I like the sound of it." His friend eyed him thoughtfully and plowed on. "I have total faith in you, your brothers, and Emma. Partners, Carlo."

"Partners, huh?" Carlo asked, liking the idea of working with a man like Jonathan. An honorable, smart, and loyal man. A true friend as unexpected as it was considering how different their backgrounds were.

"In exchange for my contributing a share of the funds, I expect to have use of the spaces for conferences and meetings. We'll coordinate to avoid conflicts. You and Emma can use the property for events," Jonathan clarified.

"And a restaurant. My brothers and I would like to have a restaurant in one of the smaller ballroom spaces so that there's regular income for our workers. Also help employ more people in the area," Carlo said, holding his breath and hoping Jonathan wouldn't be opposed to that part of the bargain.

Jonathan held out his hand to seal the deal. "I like that idea, Carlo. There's always room for another restaurant and more jobs in the area."

Carlo wrapped his hand around Jonathan's. The other man's hand was calloused and strong. The hand of a man who had worked hard for everything he had, just like Carlo had labored to build his life so in some ways they maybe weren't all that different. "Deal, Jon."

"Good. I'm going to reach out to my corporate counsel about setting up a new LLC for this project. We'll need the names of all the partners from you and then we can sit down and discuss the finances. I'd like to get moving on this quickly."

Quickly, Carlo thought and a scintilla of fear curled through his gut. Quick was not what he had in mind when it came to Emma and the business they had talked about so many times. But they also couldn't risk losing a once in a lifetime opportunity.

"I'll talk to my brothers and Emma and give you a rundown on what we can contribute to the purchase," he said, burying his worry about Emma's reaction.

"Awesome. This is going to be an epic project," Jonathan said and enthusiastically shook his hand, his blue eyes bright with excitement which alleviated some of Carlo's misgivings.

"Epic," Carlo repeated, praying that Emma would think so as well.

Chapter 24

Emma ran her finger down the list of appointments scheduled at the bridal salon for the upcoming two weeks before Christmas and the two weeks after that. They only had a last-minute appointment in a week for a couple who had decided to celebrate the New Year with a party where they would also renew their vows after fifty years of marriage.

Fifty years! Emma thought. While there were still people who made it that long, she'd also seen more and more people who after many years of marriage decided to part and go their separate ways. On the bright side, the bridal salon had planned many a marriage for baby boomers willing to give it a second chance.

Brave people, she thought, considering she was afraid to even give it a first chance. Hell, she was even afraid of being able to commit to a relationship with a man with whom she'd just spent the most marvelous week. Well, not quite a week. Three dinners, two nights, two breakfasts, and a lunch, but who was counting?

You are, the little voice in her head chastised. Love is not a formula based on the right amount of dates or lunches, it tacked on with an annoyed huff.

Or nights of mind-blowing sex, she shot back, silencing it. She jotted down the date and time for the meeting with the older couple and walked to the cabinet to pull out the folder with the interview one of the bridal salon owners had done when the couple had come in earlier that week. Emma had been too busy with Connie's wedding and her boss had helped her out by doing the initial legwork.

She stopped at the coffee machine to make herself a cup before heading to her office to review the interview and other papers her boss Lucy had assembled. Lucy had done a great job in jotting down the couple's preferences for their dream New Year's Eve party and renewal of their vows.

Emma's mind flooded with ideas on how she could bring their dreams to life. She started with a list of viable places where the event could be held based on the number of guests the couple had estimated. Next came photos of possible decorations, centerpieces, and flowers that would bring back the flavor of the Sixties beach wedding the couple had celebrated fifty years earlier. Which had her recalling a wedding dress in the stockroom that would be just perfect.

She rushed out of her office and into the stockroom where Lucy was finishing up the organizing of the dresses that Emma had started last week.

"How's it going?" she asked her boss as she hurried to the row where she had last seen the gown she had in mind.

"Thankful for at least one wedding over the holidays. It's always such a tough time of year financially and mentally. I mean, how many times can you redo the stockroom?" Lucy said with a laugh as she moved a dress from one rack to another.

"I totally get it," Emma said, likewise thankful for the job. It would help take her mind off some things. Hangers skittered across the metal rack as Emma flipped through the wedding dresses until she caught sight of the gown that she thought would be perfect for the vows renewal. She hoped the "bride" would feel the same way.

She pulled it out, draped it over her body, and called out to Lucy. "What do you think?"

Lucy stepped out from between two rows of gowns, peered at her and wrinkled her nose in a way that Emma had learned meant she was either undecided or unconvinced. "What do I think?" her boss repeated and scrutinized the gown again.

"Wedding. Beach. Sixties feel. Floral wreath with just the barest hint of veil trailing down," she said, hoping to bring to life the idea she'd had after reading the couple's interview.

The nose wrinkle went away and was replaced by emphatic nodding. Lucy circled a finger around the outfit and said, "I can totally picture that, but just in case . . ."

Emma knew what that meant as well. "I'll have a number of other gowns available for Mrs. Adler. Have I ever failed you before, Lucy?"

There was no hesitation in her boss now as she shook her head. "Never."

"Good. Then I'll get back to work. I'll have the full proposal ready for the meeting next week and since we won't have that much time to prepare, I'll call around and make sure the venues I'm suggesting are available."

She started to walk away, but Lucy called her name. She stopped and faced her boss. "We don't say it often enough, but we really appreciate the work you do for us. Evelyn and I have talked about the possibility of you joining us here in a more long-term position. Maybe even a partnership," Lucy said.

A partnership? Emma mulled. Considering she'd already been there for close to nine years she had thought about the possibility of becoming a partner more than once, except of course if she left for the event planning business that Carlo and she had discussed so many times. Confused, she narrowed her gaze and examined her boss. "I appreciate that, but if you don't mind me asking, why has this come up all of a sudden?"

Lucy stiffened, pulled her shoulders back, and lifted her chin an inch. "I know you and Carlo are close and with him interested in the convention center . . ."

Emma shook her head and frowned. "I don't have a clue what you're talking about, Lucy."

Lucy did a nervous little shuffle and said, "I had brunch with Mary Sanders on Sunday."

"The real estate agent?" Emma asked, still puzzled.

"She mentioned the building was for sale and I'd seen Carlo with her last week and so I asked her about it. Mary wouldn't confirm it, but she didn't deny it either. I'm so sorry. I thought you knew," Lucy said apologetically.

She wanted to believe there was a valid reason why Carlo hadn't told her if in fact he was interested in the property. After all, the convention center would be an ideal place for the business they had talked about so often in the past. But they hadn't discussed it at all in several months. There had been so much going on with their friends that had spilled over into their lives and made talk of anything like that virtually impossible.

And there had been that kiss that had forever changed the relationship between them and made it awkward to discuss certain things. And last week of course. An amazing and marvelous week on a personal level. One which had made her think forever was maybe possible for them.

There had to be a valid reason why he hadn't told her, she urged herself as a cold knot of dread formed in her gut much like the one when she'd realized the extent of her father's duplicity. She didn't want to think that Carlo hadn't mentioned it to her because he didn't want her involved.

"I appreciate that you and Evelyn think of me that highly, Lucy. I'll certainly consider it and let you know," Emma replied, her tone calm in a dead sort of way.

A flicker of surprise flitted across Lucy's face. "Yes, please consider it, Emma. We'd love to have you here as a partner. I feel bad that we haven't discussed it before now."

She nodded. "Thanks. If you don't mind, I have an errand to run this afternoon. I'll be back tomorrow," she said, but didn't wait for her boss to reply.

She intended to get to Carlo and find out just what was up. If what Lucy had said was true, she wanted to know why he hadn't seen fit to tell her.

THE TEXT FROM EMMA had been cryptic and troubling.

Please come as soon as you can. I'm home.

He worried that something bad had happened to either one of her friends or her mother and prayed that it was nothing serious. His van screeched to a halt at an awkward angle in front of her house since her Sebring was already in the driveway.

Racing up the walk, he noticed several lights were on in the house, but as he peered through the front window, he couldn't see anyone inside. He knocked, but no one answered. Worry increasing, he made a fist and pounded on the door, striking it so hard it rattled in its frame.

"Emma. Open up," he said roughly and was about to strike the door again when it flew open.

She stood there, arms wrapped herself in a gesture that was achingly defensive. Her skin was pale, almost bloodless. Her eyes were as hard and sharp as the thin slash of her lips.

"Is something wrong? Is someone hurt?" he said and went to cradle her cheek, but she jerked away from his touch.

"You might say that," she said and walked into her living room, leaving him to follow, not that he sensed he was welcome. Everything about her was stiff and unyielding, from the tight set of her shoulders to her stone face.

She sat in the middle of the couch and he understood he was not invited to sit beside her. Instead, he took a spot on the coffee table in front of her and she looked away, either unwilling or unable to meet his gaze.

"I don't understand, Emma. What's wrong?" he said and cradled her cheek which was ice cold despite the warmth in the room from the fire she had started in the fireplace. He applied gentle pressure and urged her to face him, but even then, her gaze was downcast.

"When were you going to tell me that you planned on buying the convention center with Jonathan Pierce and your brothers?"

"How did you find out?" he said, which he realized was not the answer she wanted to hear as her head snapped up and green fire blazed from her gaze.

"How? My boss Lucy saw you with the real estate agent. She also heard the property was for sale and put two and two together. Decided to offer me a partnership in the bridal salon because she was afraid I was jumping ship and joining you," she said, her voice trembling with anger and pain. She forged on, silencing him with a slash of her hand when he would have spoken. "But then she realized I knew absolutely nothing about it. I was confused. Hurt. Angry. I went to see my best friend Connie. To my surprise, she knew as well. Seems I'm the only one in the dark about your new venture."

"It's not what you think, Emma," he pleaded and reached for her again, but she pulled away from him.

Her words dripped ice as she said, "Then please tell me what to think. I wouldn't want to over think this after all."

She was more pissed off than he'd ever seen her, and he understood. He should have told her right away, but he'd been afraid of what that would do to their newfound relationship. He laid his hands on his knees to keep from touching her until he could fully explain. "I heard the property was for sale over a week ago. I didn't dare dream, but it's perfect, Emma. Except for the price of course and I didn't want to say anything until I could figure out if I could buy it. If *we* could buy it," he said, gesturing between the two of them.

"But you figured it out apparently. You talked to your brothers. Talked to Jon. Were you ever going to talk to me?" she said, clearly hurt by his failure to reach out to her.

"Of course. I was going to, Emma. We always talked about going into business together and buying the convention center would let us do that. We could use it for weddings and other events. Have a full-time restaurant that my brothers could manage. Jon wants to have conferences at the location. He wants us to plan and run them," he said.

"You had time to discuss all this with your brothers and Jon, but not me? You made all these plans without even once asking me if I was interested?" she asked, her voice rising with each word.

"I get it, Emma. I was wrong not to talk to your first, but I wasn't even sure it was possible. My brothers came in when I was reviewing my finances and they were totally in to help me, but I was still short. By a lot. I was going to talk to you then, but . . ." He stopped cold, afraid of where this conversation was going, but knowing it had to go there to clear the air with her.

"I was worried that this thing between us –"

"Thing?" she said with an imperial arch of her brow and ice dripping from her words.

"This relationship. It's all so new, Emma. And we both always worried that mixing business with the personal would be a problem."

"It *is* a problem if my partner doesn't bother to involve me in discussions," she said with such determination it chilled him to the bone.

He held his hands up in pleading. "You don't mean that, Emma. It's just that you're upset right now."

"You think?" she said sarcastically which was totally unlike her.

"Please, Emma. Give me a break. I made a mistake. Please forgive me," he said.

Chapter 25

Forgive him? Emma thought and dragged a hand through her hair, pulling the strands away from her face. She stared at him and tried not to see the caring on his face. The upset that she was upset. His confusion at her response which she was finding impossible to control.

"You should have told me, Carlo. I shouldn't have heard it from other people. You can't imagine what that was like for me." *Like finding out from others that all her family's money was gone.*

"I'm trying to understand, Emma. I can see how upset you are, but I had my reasons," he said.

"My father had his reasons for keeping things from my mother and me as well," she said and the color fled from Carlo's face.

"I'm not your father. I could never do to you –"

"He stole my college fund. And all the money that my parents had in the business they used to own together. And everything single penny in their personal accounts as well," she said and shock registered on his face.

"I didn't know," he said, his voice soft and filled with concern.

She tightened her arms around herself and rocked back and forth. "It's not the kind of thing you tell people, Carlo. Shit, it was hard enough to tell you about everything else."

"I'm not your dad, Emma. You can trust me," he urged and laid his hands on her knees, trying to reassure her.

"It's not easy for me to trust," she said and the hurt was apparent on his face.

"If you can't believe in me after everything we've been to each other . . ." He shook his head, slapped his hands on his thighs and rose. He stared at her, his eyes blazing fire. His face as hard as granite. "I think I should go and I think you're right. You can't mix business and pleasure. If you decide you want in on the convention center, reach out to Jon. He's the one who's going to handle the legal end of things."

He didn't wait to hear what else she might have to say. With only a few long strides he ate up the ground to the door and slammed it behind him so hard it rattled the windows and some trinkets on a nearby bookcase. One that had been close to the edge fell off and shattered on the hardwood floor, just like her heart was breaking into thousands of pieces.

Worse yet, she only had herself to blame. She could have set aside her fear and listened to what he'd said. Forgiven him for putting things in the wrong order in his eagerness to start the business they'd both wanted for so long. It had been easy to imagine that business years earlier when it had only been a dream. When she hadn't become involved with him as she had and it had become so much more than she could have imagined. Become so much more for her to risk and maybe lose.

He'd hurt her, but she suddenly realized she'd hurt him also. Badly. The pain had been etched on his face as he'd stood and stormed out the door. Much like Sasha hadn't believed in him years earlier, she'd failed to believe him as well. Her heart ached that she'd done that, but it was better to end it all now before they hurt each other even more.

As she settled into the soft cushions of her couch, it was impossible not to remember the kisses they had shared there and the man who had been so important in her life for so long. The man she'd just let walk out the door maybe to never return.

It was for the better, she told herself. That didn't help the chill in her heart that not even the heat from the fireplace could dispel. Or the overwhelming sense of emptiness that settled inside her, making her feel more alone than she ever had in her entire life.

"THIS IS BAD," PAOLO muttered beneath his breath as Tomás placed a glass with whiskey in front of Carlo. It was the third one he'd had but so far it hadn't dulled the pain in his heart.

Tomás sat next to him on the sofa and laid a hand across his shoulders. Gave him a reassuring squeeze. "She'll get over it. Just give her time."

Carlo shook his head, picked up the glass, and downed the whiskey in one swallow. "You didn't see her, *mano*. I'm not sure she'll ever forgive me."

"Then who's the bigger fool?" Paolo said and refilled his glass. Jabbing at the air with one finger, he said, "I warned you she was just like –"

"*Cabrão*, if you fucking say Sasha, I will hurt you," Carlo said, raised the glass, and sipped it more slowly.

Paolo started to speak, but Tomás jabbed him in the ribs, causing Paolo to grunt and rub his side.

"I wasn't going to say Sasha, *cabrão*," Paolo said which this time earned him a shot upside the head from Tomás.

"What did he say about saying her name," his middle brother warned the youngest.

"I appreciate you coming over –" Carlo began, but Paolo cut him off.

"What else could we do when you don't show up for work on one of the busiest weeks we have?"

"*Caralho, mano*. How can you be so dense?" Tomás chided and squeezed Carlo's shoulder again. "You take whatever time you need, Carlo. We can handle all the parties this week."

"It's not like someone died, Tomás," Paolo said, even though it felt that way to Carlo. He hadn't hurt this much since his *avô*, his mother's father, had passed. He took another sip of the whiskey and said, "I'll be in tomorrow. Early. I'll make up for the time we lost today."

His brothers shared a look of concern but seemed to understand that he didn't want to discuss it any further. He'd deal with it in his own way and on his own time.

As for Emma, he'd give her the time she needed to deal with what had happened between them. But he wasn't going to give up on her no matter how much it hurt right now. No matter how hopeless it seemed at the moment.

"I'll be there tomorrow," he repeated, certain that getting back to work was the first step in returning to normal.

EMMA STARED AT HER reflection in the window in her office. Outside a light snow was starting to cover the ground and dusting the trees with white. The sky was a dull grey but had more color than her skin which was as pale as the snow falling outside.

She practiced a smile, trying to appear cheery since the older couple who wanted to renew their vows was arriving in just a few minutes to discuss the event with her. She had laid out the materials with her suggestions on the salon's conference room table and she hoped the couple would like what she proposed.

Her phone rang and as she returned to her desk, she saw the receptionist's number on the caller id. She picked up the phone and the young woman said, "Mr. and Mrs. Adler are here."

"I'll be up in a second," she said cheerily. Maybe too cheerily. She didn't think she had fooled anyone around the office this week. Or her friends for that matter. They'd each made a point of coming by to see her and try to cheer her spirits.

Mr. and Mrs. Adler were sitting in the bridal salon's reception area and for a couple who had been married for fifty years, they looked remarkably young and still in love judging from the way they held hands and gazed at each other. She plastered the smile on her face, walked over, and introduced herself.

In no time she had ushered them into the conference room where she had prepared the materials and to her surprise, Lucy joined them a few seconds later. At Emma's questioning glance, her boss said, "The Adlers are my parents' neighbors and I just wanted to see what fabulous ideas you have for them."

And while that might be true, Emma also suspected that Lucy wanted to be around just in case she had a meltdown in the midst of all the happily-ever-after celebrations since Emma was not feeling anyone's happiness at the moment. As Emma placed the copy of the couple's wedding photo before them, she also spread out the various ideas she had for the decorations and flowers.

"You didn't mention that you need invitations, but if you do we can arrange for those as well," she said and the couple glanced at each other and smiled.

"We hold a big New Year's Eve bash every year so everyone knows it's happening. We never tell them where it is to keep it a surprise until the last minute, so we plan on doing the same thing this year," Mrs. Adler said. She was a trim woman with short cropped blonde hair that had just the first touches of grey around her face. She had to be approaching seventy but didn't look a day over fifty.

"That sounds like a lot of fun and it will truly be a big surprise for them when you renew your vows, but why New Year's Eve? I see from the picture and interview that you got married in June," Emma asked.

Mr. Adler, a polished and bespectacled man who reminded her of a 1920s banker and not the Sixties hippie in the wedding photo, finally took his eyes off his wife. He gestured to the photo and said, "Marie and I met on New Year's Eve in New York City. Turned out we were both going to school there. I was at Columbia."

"And I was at Barnard. It was quite a time in our lives, wasn't it, Simon?" Marie said wistfully.

"That it was. Fate always has surprises for you and that was our surprise – finding each other on New Year's Eve."

"So that's why you always do the surprise party?" Lucy asked.

Marie and Simon looked at each other again lovingly, but then grew more serious and Simon continued their story. "We never suspected that night how tough things would get. I'm a practicing Jew and Marie is a devout Methodist. Neither of our parents was very happy that we were dating, much less marrying."

"They made our lives very difficult, but that didn't stop us, did it?" Marie said and cupped Simon's cheek.

"No, it didn't. When neither family would accept the relationship, we decided to elope. Got married by one of Marie's minister friends right there on Sea Kiss beach. Spent the summer traveling around in that beat-up old Volkswagen van," Simon said.

"Needed new shocks by the time we were done with it," Marie added with a wink at her husband and a wave of color washed across both their cheeks.

It was impossible not to get caught up in their romantic story and the obvious love and affection they still had for one another. Battling back tears, her voice husky as she suppressed the emotion threatening to overwhelm her, Emma said, "Well we're going to help you surprise your friends with the best New Year's Eve ever and the most romantic vow renewals you can imagine."

She reached for one folder and hauled out a photo of the lovingly restored 1960s Volkswagen van that a friend of Jonathan's was willing to let them use. "How about we start with you arriving in this beauty?" she said as she placed the picture in front of them.

The couple gave an appreciative chuckle and nodded. "We think that would be perfect." Marie said and Simon quickly added, "As long as the shocks are in good shape."

Emma laughed and shook her head. "Wonderful. I'll make sure the van is up for it," she said in a more serious tone and proceeded to show them her other suggestions. The rest of the meeting went smoothly and after they had set up a meeting for Marie to try on some gowns and Simon to pick out his suit, the Adlers left with beaming smiles.

"That went well," Lucy said as Emma collected her materials from the conference room.

It was impossible to miss the relief in her boss's voice. "Did you think it wouldn't?" she asked, slightly miffed by Lucy's lack of confidence in her.

Her boss realized her gaffe and quickly apologized. "I know you're a professional, Emma. You've handled bridezillas I wouldn't have gotten close to without a chair and a whip. But the Adlers are special people and it's a rush job and . . . You haven't been yourself the last few days."

She hadn't although she'd tried hard to hide it. Obviously, she'd failed at it miserably much like she'd failed with Carlo.

"I haven't been myself. Carlo and I . . . It's a complicated situation."

Lucy nodded and peered at her thoughtfully. She motioned Emma to a chair and she sat, not sure what to expect. Lucy was a good boss and never did the lecture thing and it felt like that's where they were headed.

"You heard what Marie and Simon told you about their parents being displeased, but that's not even half the story. Since I know you won't talk about anything I tell you in confidence –"

"I won't. You know that. It's part of the wedding planner code," she said with a smile, trying to lighten the mood.

Lucy chuckled and grinned. "Yes, it is," she said and continued. "Their parents *really* didn't want them to marry. Both sets of parents threatened to cut off their money for school and when Marie and Simon eloped, they did just that. The young couple spent the summer in that van because they were basically homeless and working any jobs they could to raise the money to pay for college."

Having worked her way through Princeton as well, Emma understood how difficult that would have been for them. Especially at colleges as pricey as Barnard and Columbia.

"Somehow they did it and Simon became a successful investment banker. Marie went on to medical school and is still practicing," Lucy advised.

"That's quite a story," Emma said with an appreciative dip of her head.

Lucy surprised her then by laying a hand on hers and leaning close. "It's a story that says anything is possible if you love each other enough."

"I care for him," she said, echoing what she'd told Carlo weeks earlier.

Lucy shook her head and blew out a frustrated sigh. "You *love* him, Emma. Trust me. If you didn't, it wouldn't hurt so much."

After an unexpected hug from her boss, Lucy stood and walked out of the room, leaving Emma to stare at table with the Adlers' wedding photo and the plans for their big event. An event to commemorate fifty years of love, but also the sacrifices they'd made to be together.

The ache that had been inside her since the day Carlo had left became almost unbearable. She wrapped her arms around herself and bent, wanting to curl up and cry it felt so bad. If love was about that kind of hurt, she didn't think she needed love in her life.

Armed with that conviction, she sucked in a rough breath and drove away the pain. But as she did so, the emptiness returned and she wasn't sure she could live like that either.

Roughly tossing together the materials on the table, she hugged them to her chest and headed to her office. She had work to do planning someone else's happily-ever-after and once she was done and somehow got through the Christmas holidays, she'd plan a getaway for herself. A week or two away from Sea Kiss and everything familiar would be just the thing she needed to get back to normal.

Only now normal didn't seem as inviting as it once had.

Chapter 26

"Did she call you?" Carlo asked as Jonathan sat down across from him in the conference room of Connie's new law office on Sea Kiss's Main Street. Jonathan and Connie had bought the building and renovated it at the same time that Jonathan's contractors had been working on restoring the old guitar building for Jonathan's new research and development center.

A grim smile darkened Jonathan's normally happy face. "I'm sorry, dude. I never expected this whole thing would get this gnarly."

"It's not your fault, Jon. I knew Emma came with a whole mountain of issues. I just didn't realize the mountain was called Everest," he said, trying to put the other man at ease over the situation.

Jonathan chuckled as Carlo had intended and then shook his head. "Women. Connie had her share of daddy issues too, so I get it. Emma will come around, Carlo."

He wished he could be as certain as his friend, but every attempt he'd made to contact Emma in the past week had been rebuffed. She hadn't answered his texts or phone calls. Since they hadn't had any events to work together for the two weeks before Christmas, which was only days away, there had been no business reason to see her either and he was missing her. Badly. She was all he thought about day and night and everything was suffering for it. Luckily his brothers had picked up the slack for him, but with Tomás possibly returning to the Army in another month or so, he had to get his head back in the game. Especially if they were going to go through with the purchase of the convention center. That was what he had to focus on for the moment and so he said, "What did your guys say about the condition of the building?"

Jonathan stared at him hard, but then relented and changed the topic. "It's in good shape. Whatever damage Sandy did has been repaired. Walls, roof, general structure, electrical. I don't have to tell you the new equipment is top notch. You saw it for yourself, but even with all that, the three million they're asking for is on the high side since there's still a shitload of work to do before the building can be occupied."

"I agree, but I'm not sure we should low ball them," Carlo said.

Jonathan nodded, but then yanked out some papers for Carlo to view. Comparables for other properties that had recently sold, including the old guitar building Jonathan had bought only months before. As Jonathan fanned the papers across the conference room table, it was obvious that none of the properties had sold for over two and a half million.

"I see the numbers, Jon. But none of these are prime locations on the water. Those always cost way more," he argued, playing devil's advocate.

"They do, but I think it's going to cost another million to get that building ready to open. We're talking major investments in sheet rock, paint, lighting, landscaping, and more, especially since it's landmarked. That limits what anyone can do with the property," Jonathan pointed out and Carlo couldn't argue with that.

"We offer two to start?" he said and waited for Jonathan as his friend looked over the comparables again.

"Two to start. We shoot for two and a half as the max otherwise we walk away. Do we agree?" Jonathan asked.

It would break his heart to walk away from such an opportunity, but his friend was right about the price and the work it would take before they could use the building.

"I agree," he said.

Jonathan hesitated for a moment before he asked, "What about your brothers?"

"They trust my judgment. Besides, I'm putting up the bulk of the money for our share and Emma's."

"What if Emma's not interested?" Jonathan asked making Carlo wonder if Jonathan knew more than he was saying on account of his wife's friendship with Emma.

"Then I'll cover her share somehow."

"No way," Jonathan began with an emphatic slash of his hand. "I don't expect you to tap into your 401K or sell your house to cover anyone else's share of this partnership."

"I don't need your charity, Jon," he said. He wasn't about to take advantage of a friend's generosity to expand his business.

"And I'm not offering a handout, Carlo. That's not the way I work. We can structure the partnership where I get an insider price for event space and first crack on dates to offset my initial investment. Take it from me, I'm the winner there because once people see what an amazing venue it is, you'd probably be able to charge way more for the space than what I intend to pay you."

He searched Jonathan's face for any sign of duplicity, but his friend was as open as he'd ever been. "Done. You'll call Mary?" he asked as Jonathan gathered up the papers on the table.

"I will once Connie finishes setting up our LLC. Rumors are flying already, and I'd hate for the asking price to go up just because they think I'm involved. Any thoughts for the name of the partnership?" Jonathan asked.

With a laugh, Carlo said, "Four Guys and a Girl?"

Jonathan joined him with a hearty chuckle. "I think Emma would prefer 'lady.'"

With a shrug, Carlo said, "Definitely a lady. A very pissed off one. I leave you to choose a name."

"Great. We don't have to name the partners to form the LLC so we won't need Emma for that, but the lawyers are going to want some kind of partnership agreement eventually. You'll talk to her?" Jonathan asked and tucked the papers into a well-worn leather knapsack.

"I've been trying, *mano*. She won't answer," he admitted in frustration.

"She'll be at our house for Christmas Eve. You're invited to come. Lots of family and friends will be there."

With a heavy sigh, Carlo shook his head. "That's my family's big night so I'm normally in Newark with them. Besides, the last thing you want is an arctic chill descending on your festivities."

Jonathan clapped him on the back. "Yeah, you're probably right. It's gnarly enough without adding fuel to the fire. I'll hold off the attorneys as long as I can."

"I appreciate that," Carlo said and the two men stepped out into the reception area where Connie was busy unpacking law books from a box.

"Shit, babe. You shouldn't be lifting anything heavy," Jonathan said and rushed over to help his wife.

"I'm pregnant, not an invalid. Besides, they're not that heavy," she said as she grabbed a few and plopped them on a shelf in one of the bookcases that lined one wall of the reception area.

"I can't believe you even use these anymore. That's so 18th century," Jonathan groused as he helped her with another stack of books.

"I don't, but they make people think you're a real lawyer," she said with a roll of her eyes as Jonathan took yet another pile from her hands.

As Carlo grabbed yet more books, she directed him to another bookcase where she had some official looking plaques and awards.

"How are you doing?" she asked and gestured to where he should place the legal tomes.

"I could be better," he confessed and after, endured her prolonged scrutiny.

"I don't know who looks worse. You or Emma," she said and instructed him and Jonathan on where to place the next round of books. He was grateful that after her comment, all the attention was on emptying the boxes sitting in the reception area. Once the cartons had been broken down, tied up for recycling, and placed at the curb, the three of them stood in the room, inspecting their work.

As Connie had said, the books, awards, and photos grouped on the shelves were not only pleasant to look at but screamed "Lawyer." Successful lawyer at that, he thought, proud of his friend for what she had accomplished.

There were more boxes inside her office. Jon and he helped her unpack those as well as hang her various diplomas and proofs of her admissions to the New York and New Jersey bars and various courts in the area. Carlo rested his hands on his hips as he viewed the documents and with a low whistle said, "Very impressive, counselor. I'm glad I have you on my side."

Connie stepped over and laced her arm through his. "You do have me on your side and in more ways than one, Carlo. Give her a little more space.

She's confused and hurt and even if the latter might be unreasonable, to her it's completely understandable."

Carlo glanced at Connie out of the corner of his eye. She was a beautiful woman and pregnancy had only seemed to make her prettier. Or maybe it was the glow of happiness as Jonathan walked over, slid an arm around her waist, and dropped a kiss on her forehead.

"Get your own girl," Jonathan teased.

Carlo smiled and put his hands up as if in surrender. "Believe me, I'm trying to."

Connie jabbed him in the ribs. "Try harder."

Chapter 27

Everything was moving along perfectly for the Adler's New Year's Eve vow renewal. Marie Adler had come in right after their meeting and immediately fallen in love with the dress Emma had picked out. Emma had met Simon the next day in New York City at his own tailor and they had selected his suit and exacted a promise that it would be available the week after Christmas. Since she was in Manhattan already and not far from Maggie's office in the Chrysler Building, she decided to pop in and visit her friend.

As Maggie rose from behind her desk and walked over, Emma couldn't help but see the very noticeable baby bump that stretched the fabric of Maggie's dress. Maggie realized where Emma's attention had been drawn and smoothed the wool across her belly, making it even more pronounced. "Crazy isn't it? I just passed three months and I look almost as big as Connie."

"And the doctor's sure it's twins?" Emma asked, but how else was it possible for her friend to be so big so fast.

"For sure," Maggie said and took a seat on the sofa beside Emma. The antique piece, as well as most things in the office, had belonged to Maggie's mother who had died in childbirth along with her baby son when Maggie had been a young child.

"How have you been feeling? No morning sickness like Connie?" Emma had worried about Connie's illness which had lasted up until her fourth month, disappearing just in time for her wedding.

"Healthy as a horse," Maggie replied with a broad smile that lit up eyes as blue as a Sea Kiss ocean. "How are you doing?"

"Not preggers, thankfully," Emma replied with a laugh which earned a raised brow from her friend.

"Which implies that maybe you and . . . I hope it was Carlo . . . finally, you know," Maggie finished awkwardly.

She had avoided giving her friends any real details about what was happening with Carlo because she knew they'd never leave it alone if she did. But her friends weren't stupid, and it was obvious something had gone south after they had finally become involved.

"We did and . . ." She hesitated, unsure of what to say, but this was Maggie. Mama Maggie. The one person everyone in the group knew they could go to for understanding and comfort. She inhaled deeply and held it. Rushed on with her confession of sorts.

"We did and he was amazing. Caring. Sexy. Gorgeous," she said and the heat of a blush blasted up her neck to her face.

Maggie examined her for long moments. Finally, hesitantly, she said, "And so you decided to ditch this caring, sexy, gorgeous man because?"

With a slash of her hand, Emma said, "I know you know everything the Pierce brothers do, so I don't have to tell you that Carlo and Jon are buying the convention center."

Nodding, Maggie sat back onto the cushions of the sofa and urged Emma to face her. "From what I understand, it's Carlo, his brothers, Jon, and *you* who are buying the place."

Shaking her head vehemently, Emma quickly countered Maggie. "He didn't tell me about it. I had to find out from my boss when she offered me a partnership in the business because she was afraid of losing me."

Maggie tsked and said, "Evelyn and Lucy should have offered that to you a long time ago. How many times did you complain to us about that?"

Emma couldn't argue with her friend. She'd been working nearly nine years at the salon from when she'd started part time during college to when she'd become a regular and really expanded their wedding planning business to what it was today.

"I complained about it a lot," she admitted.

"And now you have a chance to do what you've wanted to do for a long time. What you talked about doing with Carlo for years, right?"

"Right, but you of all people know the problems you can have with mixing business with your personal stuff. It caused you and Owen a shitload of problems. And Carlo didn't even mention it to me until I called him on it. How was I supposed to react?" she shot back.

Maggie peered at her intently, obviously considering how to respond. With a dip of her head, she said, "You've known Carlo over eight years. Worked with him. Spent time with him and his family. In all that time did he ever do anything that would make you think that he wasn't a good man?"

The little voice in her head was swift with a reply, but Emma hesitated until she reluctantly said, "No, but we all thought my father was a good man."

Maggie laughed harshly. "No, you didn't. You always told us what a bastard he was to you and your mom. And we could all see how he had beat you down, but you found the strength to pick up the pieces of your life and move on."

Emma smiled sadly and stared at Maggie through the haze of tears. She took hold of her friend's hand and said, "What I found were the best friends a girl could ask for. You guys gave me the strength to move on."

Maggie shifted on the couch and hugged Emma hard. With a playful shake and a kiss on the cheek, Maggie said, "Now it's time to move on to the next level."

The next level was way higher than she'd ever pictured herself. It was almost like being at the edge of cliff, with uncertain ground beneath her feet. Her friends would always provide safe and steady terrain, but with Carlo she felt as if the ground was crumbling beneath her feet. But if she didn't take a leap of faith and believe that the fall would take her to a better place, she'd never be able to move on with her life. A life which included one smart, honorable, and very sexy man.

I SHOULD HAVE STAYED home, Carlo thought as he glanced around the Christmas Eve table to find everyone paired off like the animals on Noah's Ark, even his two youngest brothers. Paolo had brought a long-time female friend from the neighborhood while Tomás had invited Jesse and her six-year-old son Brandon to their family's Christmas Eve gathering. Tomás was currently goofing off for the young child by eating some "gross" squid legs, earning loud complaints from Brandon and an admonishment from Carlo's mother for Tomás to behave.

With a big chew and swallow, the calamari disappeared, prompting an even louder "Ewww" from Jesse's son. Tomás ruffled Brandon's wheat-colored hair and the boy teased his brother with, "You're just jealous 'cuz you got no hair."

"You're right," Tomás said and ran his hand across the fresh buzz cut. The motion drew Jesse's immediate attention and the smile that had been there before at their good-humored kidding faded. Possibly because she knew the main reason for the hair cut would be that Tomás had decided to re-enlist again once the doctors approved him for active duty.

She put on a brave face, though, much as he had for most of the afternoon and night as his mother and his older brothers and their wives had set out one dish after another for family and the friends who had popped in and out during the course of the day. It had been busier in the afternoon hours which had saved him from the scrutiny of his parents and older brothers. But now that it was just close family sitting down for the meal, it was impossible to avoid the inevitable inquisition.

"Is Emma coming by later?" his eldest brother Ricardo asked as he placed a roasted stuffed turkey in front of their father so he could commence carving it.

Javier and his wife popped into the dining room barely seconds later, laden with a plate brimming with cod and greens drizzled with fragrant olive oil and another dish with deep fried marinade pork chunks which they set on the table. Much as Ricardo had done, Javier asked, "Is she going to be here tonight?"

Paolo jumped in to try and save him by making light of the situation. "*Mano*, he scared her off with his ugly mug because he's not as handsome as the rest of us."

All the men around the table laughed, while the women paused to stare at him as if he was the prize bull at the fair. Finally, Ricardo's wife said, "You're all just jealous because he's the handsomest da Costa brother."

"Thank you, Sofia," Carlo said.

Ricardo walked over and laid his meaty hands on Carlo's shoulders and squeezed affectionately, if not a little too hard as well. "Sofia, *meu amor*! He's scrawny like that chicken you brought home the other day from the butcher. Since we can't take him back, we'll have to make sure he eats enough tonight to fatten him up!"

Relieved to be the brunt of their jokes instead of continuing the discussion about Emma, he joined in to goad his oldest brother. "Well then you better bring in what I cooked because I know that will be everyone's favorite dish tonight."

Javier strolled by and teasingly cuffed Carlo on the back of the head. "*Cabrão*, I bet it's some *nouvelle* thing he thinks is food. Are you going to get out a tweezer to serve it to us?"

"Please watch your mouth, Javi. It is *véspera de Natal* you know," Carlo's mother Rosa chastised at his brother's use of the cuss word.

Suitably reprimanded, Javier made a face, walked over to their mother, and hugged her. "Sorry, *mamãe*, but you know how hard-headed Carlo can be."

His mother eyed him a little too seriously, warning him that trouble would soon follow. "I do. You'd think he'd either do something about that Emma or find someone else to give me some grandbabies."

Carlo closed his eyes and lifted them heavenward. "*Deus,* give me strength," he thought and muttered a curse beneath his breath, but obviously not low enough for his mother not to hear.

"Carlo! That's enough. Now get up and help me bring out the rest of the food," Rosa commanded, but as he got up from the table slowly, like a tired old man, he suspected his mother had a different reason for wanting to get him alone.

Like a school child headed to detention, he trudged to the kitchen where his brothers were already grabbing dishes to take out and their wives were busy pulling other items out of the oven, including the offering he had brought for the meal. As he headed to the counter, his mother in tow, the two other women looked their way, shared a glance, and immediately excused themselves.

The stuffed chickens he had made for their Christmas Eve meal sat in the roasting pan on the counter, one of the items his sisters-in-law had just removed from the oven. He had modified the traditional dish by deboning the birds and wrapping that meat around stuffing made from bread, eggs, spices, chicken livers and olives. It would make for easier slicing as well as more convenient leftovers for Christmas day.

"They look good," his mother said as she came to stand before him as he lifted one of the chickens with perfectly golden and crisp skin from the pan and placed it on a cutting board.

"Thank you, *mamãe*, but we both know you didn't ask me out here to talk about chickens," he said and peered at her from the corner of his eye.

She wiped her hands on a nearby towel and said, "What's going on with you, *meu filho*? Why isn't Emma here with us like she's been for the last what is it? Almost eight years?"

He shrugged as he started slicing the chicken and placing it on a serving platter. "We have some issues that we need to work out."

A harsh laugh exploded from his mom. "Issues? You know what are issues?" Rosa said and jabbed her meaty finger in his direction. "Marrying a man with another woman's children and having her family hate you for taking her place. Them never letting you forget that you're not as good as she was. Those are issues, *meu filho*!" She finished that statement with a sniffle and a swipe of her eye.

He laid down the carving fork and knife and dragged his mother into his arms. He and his brothers had suffered their *avo*'s bite, but it had never occurred to him that his mother had been suffering even more. Hugging her hard, he said, "You're the best mother any man, including Ricardo and Javier, could ever ask for."

With another sniffle, his mom reached up and brushed back a lock of his hair from his forehead. "We all have issues, *meu filho*. Life isn't perfect. But we find ways to deal with them so we can be with the people we love. You love her, right?"

He nodded. "I love her, *mamãe*. She's smart and beautiful."

His mother poked him in the ribs and teased, "She is and even with your ugly face, you'll make nice grandbabies."

"Don't rush it. First, I have to get her to see me again," he said and returned to carving the dish he had prepared.

His mother stepped back and cupped his face. "It's a season of miracles, Carlo. Believe and it will happen and if it doesn't, she's a fool. Who couldn't love my handsome and wonderful son?"

Teary-eyed and sniffling again, she shoved away from him to return to work and he couldn't resist kidding her. "I always knew I was your favorite."

"Bah," she said with a wave of her hand "Hurry up and get those *nouvelle* chickens of yours out there. We've got a family to feed."

Chapter 28

Emma's stomach groaned in protest after the long afternoon of appetizers and an evening of a multi-course dinner that the combined Pierce, Reyes, and Sinclair families had prepared at the Sinclair family beach home since the renovations to Connie and Jonathan's kitchen were still being worked on. The day had been spent pleasurably with the families who had so much good news to celebrate with not only each other, but with Tracy and Emma and her mother, who had been invited to join them.

As Mrs. Patrick, Maggie's housekeeper and their surrogate grandmother, rose to start clearing the dinner dishes, the four friends all jumped to their feet and urged the older woman to sit. She half-heartedly protested and said, "You girls spoil me."

As Connie's mom and Emma's likewise rose, they once again waved off any help and began to bring all the plates into the kitchen to load. They had no sooner placed them on the counter to rinse when Jonathan and Owen came in with assorted plates precariously balanced on their arms.

Disbelief in her tones, Tracy said, "You ladies have taught them well."

The two brothers laughed, unloaded the plates, and then went over to hug their wives.

Jonathan reached around and laid his hands on Connie's baby belly and said, "Can't take any chances with this precious bundle."

"Glad to hear that. Now get your ass out there and finish bringing in the dishes so we can have dessert."

"Dessert! I should have worn pants with an elastic waist," Emma complained and rubbed her hands across her bloated midsection.

"You can't disappoint my grandmother by not having dessert. She made your favorite flan," Connie said and started rinsing and loading the dishwasher.

Connie's grandmother's flan was legendary and second only to Carlo who did a fantastic tropical version with mango in the flan and a to-die-for passion fruit glaze. Last Christmas Eve he'd brought it to Connie's house in Union City and everyone had delighted in having a flan taste-off. She smiled as she recalled how Carlo had graciously given in and declared that the older woman's flan was the hands down winner.

Carlo, she thought with a sigh as she spent the next few minutes helping to clear away what was left of the main courses and packed up doggie bags for everyone to take home. Even Robert Pierce, Jonathan and Owen's father, who she had always pegged as kind of stuck-up and elitist, had insisted that someone make sure he got some of the roast pork, black beans, and rice to take home.

She did just that, making sure enough for another dinner was packed in a plastic container that would let the meal travel well. She made up several other containers with similar servings as well as others with the delicious roast turkey and stuffing that Maggie and Mrs. Patrick had prepared.

Before long everyone was back at the dining room table, sampling the many sweets that friends and family had brought. Italian pastries from Del Ponte's in Sea Kiss courtesy of Tracy. The famous Reyes flan. A fruit cake that Mrs. Patrick had baked, carefully soaked with rum syrup, and tended to for months. Cuban pastries that Connie's mom had ordered from her favorite bakery in Union City.

Since sweet treats demanded coffee, Jonathan and Owen took care of that for everyone, prepping all kinds of fancy coffees with the machine Owen had bought for Maggie, who was a coffee addict and was currently suffering caffeine withdrawal thanks to her pregnancy. Not long after that, an assortment of after-dinner drinks emerged, including a bottle of a very special Irish whiskey courtesy of Mrs. Patrick.

Emma sat back and took it all in, savoring the easy rapport of everyone around the table. Her mother must have felt the same since she leaned close and whispered, "This is a nice family you've made for yourself, Emma."

Taken aback, she peered at her mother intently to see if she was upset, but there was no hint of it on her mother's calm beautiful features. She was happy, something Emma hadn't seen in a long time and she wondered if her mother's new beau had something to do with it. "Are you seeing Bill tomorrow?"

Her mother nodded and scooped up a bit of the flan on her plate. "I am. Would you like to come with me? I'm sure he'd be pleased to have you join us."

She looked away and around the table. It had been easier than she had thought to come tonight, mostly because she hadn't been the only single person there. She wasn't quite sure she was ready to be a third wheel at her mother's and Bill's Christmas celebration. "I appreciate the invite, but maybe some other time. It's been really hectic at work and I'd love nothing better than a quiet day at home," she lied.

Her mother arched a brow, obviously aware of the fib. Not that she called Emma on it thankfully.

The rest of the night passed in a blur and it wasn't long before Emma was hugging everyone and saying her goodbyes at the front door. Connie's family and Robert Pierce would be staying at the Pierce beach house while Bryce Sinclair, Maggie's dad, would be staying with Maggie and Owen.

Tracy and she looped their arms around each other and trudged through an inch of freshly fallen snow as yet more flakes fell gently. Big fat flakes that stuck to their coats and lashes, making them smile and laugh at the sight they made in the short distance to their cars.

"Merry Christmas, Emma," Tracy said and hugged her. "Are you doing anything special tomorrow?"

Normally Emma would spend it with her mom, but not this year. "Just going to Mass and to relax after that. Maybe hit my treadmill to work off some of the calories from that spread we just had. How about you?"

Tracy chuckled and rubbed her too lean midsection. "Definitely treadmill or a run if this lets up. My parents . . ." She hesitated and a hint of sadness crept onto her friend's features. "They're off skiing somewhere. Aspen, I think. Or maybe Switzerland. Don't know and don't care."

But Emma knew her friend did and was about to offer to join her on Christmas day when Tracy said, "I'm going to pick up every real estate flier I can find to look for my new place. Hop on the Internet and look some more. Something nice and welcoming, like your cottage."

Emma nodded, reached up, and smoothed her hand across Tracy's hair to brush away some of the snow, but also offer comfort. "I told you that you were welcome to stay with me as long as you'd like. I have a spare bedroom."

The sheen of tears filled Tracy's eyes, but didn't spill over. With a brittle smile, she said, "I appreciate that. I may take you up on that offer."

"Good," Emma said and hugged her friend hard once again before heading to her own car just a few steps away.

The snow was still light enough to just brush away with a quick swipe of the wipers and she quickly pulled out and with a few quick turns was driving through the heart of Sea Kiss. Much as it had been the day of Connie's wedding, the snow combined with all the happy holiday lights and decorations gave the town an almost magical feel and she savored it since they normally didn't get much snow along the Shore although this year was proving to be different. If they did get snow, it didn't last for long unless it was a major blizzard thanks to the buffering effects of the ocean.

Mindful of the snow falling, but even more mindful of the love and magic that had enveloped her that night, she drove slowly, appreciating the sights of all the businesses and homes done up for the Christmas season. As she pulled into her driveway, she smiled at the dancing colors of the twinkling lights in her bushes and along the gutters and windows of her cottage. A big evergreen wreath gaily decorated with brightly hued glass balls hung at her door, greeting you, but somehow she couldn't find the will to leave her car.

It had taken her years to save the money to buy the quaint cottage in need of repair. She'd spent many a free day or weekend steaming off 1950s wallpaper, repairing and painting walls and cabinets, and pulling up matted pile carpets to reveal gorgeous parquet floors. But she hadn't done it alone. Her friends and Carlo had helped her transform the cottage into her home.

Tonight, after spending Christmas Eve with her mom, friends and their families, her home seemed suddenly empty to her much like she had felt the extreme emptiness within her at not having Carlo at her side the last two weeks the way he'd been there for so many years.

She wondered if he'd stayed up in his parents' Ironbound home for the night or come back to Sea Kiss. And she wondered if he could ever forgive her for the way she'd treated him or if he'd be willing to give her another chance because sitting there in her car, staring at the home she'd put together with such care, she realized that it would never be complete without love. Love like she had found with Carlo.

She put the car in gear and rushed back out of the driveway.

CARLO'S HOME WAS AT the most northern end of Sea Kiss, not far from the Pierce and Sinclair beachfront mansions. She turned onto his street and slowed the car to a crawl. Her heart raced in her chest as she saw his van was parked in front of his house and the glow of a light from within indicated he might still be awake despite the almost midnight hour. With a quick K turn, she pulled up behind his van and parked. Taking a deep breath, she mustered her courage and hurried to his front door.

Her heart was thudding in her chest, so loudly she thought she might not need to knock for him to know she was there. Dragging in a deep breath of fresh snow-kissed air, she raised her hand to the fanciful brass seashell door knocker, lifted it, and then rapped it quickly. Decisively. The sound seemed to carry in the still of the night and from beyond the wooden door came footsteps and then the snick of the lock.

The door opened and suddenly he was there, looking more handsome than ever, but there was a downward set to his normally smiling mouth and sadness in the dark cocoa of his eyes. He jerked back for a moment, obviously surprised to see her there, before recovering. In the blink of an eye, the first hint of a smile came to his lips and his eyes lost some of the dullness she'd noticed a second earlier.

With a quirk of his lips, he said, "I didn't know Frosty the Snowman made house calls."

Emma glanced down at herself and realized that in the short time she'd been standing there the snow had gotten heavier and now covered her black pea jacket. She raised a hand to her head and encountered the hard crust of partially melting snow covering her hat and hair.

"I must look like what the cat dragged in," she said and shifted on her heels back and forth, expectant. Anxious. Grateful he hadn't slammed the door in her face right away.

"Maybe I should drag you in so you can defrost. Is that okay with you?" he said, obviously just as unsure of what was happening at that moment and what would follow.

"I'd like that," she said and stepped over his threshold.

Chapter 29

When he'd told Jonathan the other day that Emma was lugging a mountain called Everest, he'd never expected that mountain to come to him, but he wasn't about to pass up the opportunity to try and make things right between them.

Once she was inside, he gently brushed the snow off her hat, hair, and then off her coat. It settled on the hardwood floor by his entry and immediately melted thanks to the warmth of his house.

"I'm so sorry. I'm making a mess," she said as she slipped off her jacket.

He took her coat and gestured with his head toward the living room. "Make yourself at home. I was just making myself some hot chocolate."

"Your famous hot chocolate with Bailey's and whipped cream?" she said and rubbed her hands together to warm them.

"The same. Sit down while I whip some up for us," he said and couldn't believe that after over a week apart and all that had happened, they were calmly standing there basically talking about nothing. It wasn't how he'd pictured it, but it was better than nothing since he'd been missing her terribly. Christmas Eve without her beside him had only reinforced that it was time to find a way to have her in his life in a forever kind of way.

With a dip of her head, she did as he asked and sat, pulled a throw from the arm of the sofa, and wrapped it around herself to get warm. That combined with the snow made him question just how long she'd been standing on his doorstep deciding whether to knock or not.

Determined to settle any uneasiness she might still be feeling, he chatted her up as he heated the milk and Baileys before adding sugar and the cubes he snapped off a bar of Mexican chocolate. "Did you spend Christmas Eve with your friends?" he asked.

She nodded and added, "And with my mom. Connie had all her family down too and so did Jon, Owen, and Maggie."

He stirred the liquid as the chocolate began to melt and turned down the heat, not wanting to scorch the mixture. "That must have been quite a lot of people and a lot of fun."

"It was really nice and the food was great. A mix of American and Cuban. Did you have a nice time with your family?" she asked.

He wanted to be honest and admit that he hadn't had a nice time without her but thought it too soon to move onto that dangerous ground. "It was okay," he said as with another few stirs the chocolate, milk, and Bailey's blended into a creamy smooth liquid.

Lowering the heat to a slow simmer, he quickly pulled down two large mugs from the cabinet and whipped cream from the fridge. He finished prepping the hot chocolates and strode to the sofa, where Emma was sitting cross-legged on the comfy cushions. She had slipped off her shoes and made herself at home which gave him hope.

He handed her the mug and sat beside her. Silence reigned for long moments as they both sipped their drinks and Emma murmured an appreciative, "Delicious."

"Thanks." He faltered, unsure of what to say next and glanced at Emma. She held the mug with both hands as she sipped. Bright pink color from the cold still painted her cheeks but slowly faded from the warmth in the house and the drink. A bit of cream clung to her upper lip until she licked it off. The action had his gut clenching with need and he couldn't just keep on sitting there, politely waiting for whatever she had to say.

"Don't get me wrong. I'm glad we can act like two civilized human beings around each other, but the last thing I feel around you is civilized," he said, wanting her to understand just how much she affected him.

Her hands shook as she set her mug down on the coffee table and then twined her fingers together tightly in her lap. She looked down at her hands and did a little shrug before risking a quick glance at him. "I . . . I wanted to say that I'm sorry. I know I haven't been fair to you and I hope you can forgive me."

His own hands were unsteady as he laid his drink down, turned, and cupped her cheeks. "Of course I forgive you, Emma," he said and laid his forehead against hers. "This past week . . . Christmas Eve without you. I want you in my life, Emma, and I hope you want to be there. I love you, Emma."

She cradled his head in her hands and met his gaze directly. Her eyes shimmered with tears as she said, "I didn't dare hope you'd still want that because . . . it's what I want, Carlo. My life without you has been empty and I can't imagine not having you in my life."

Joy filled his heart and he grabbed her hands in his. "Marry me, Emma. Be my partner in life."

"And in business, Carlo. I trust you and I love you," she said and kissed him, her mouth mobile on his. Demanding and he answered the demand, opening his mouth to hers. He pressed her down onto the sofa and hugged her body to his, loving the feel of her softness against him.

He broke apart from her only long enough to ask, "Say it again, Emma. Please, *meu amor*."

She smiled and her green eyes glittered with happiness. "I love you, Carlo Aleixo da Costa. Love, love, love you!"

"Oh, God, Emma. I couldn't have asked for a better Christmas gift than to hear that," he said and kissed her again. But soon, kissing alone wasn't enough and he had to touch her. Smooth his hand across her breast where the hard tip pressed into his palm and he took it between thumb and forefinger to caress it.

She moaned into his mouth as he did so and she broke away and breathlessly said, "I think I know what I want from you for Christmas."

He propped one arm on the sofa to rake his gaze across her flushed face with her kiss-plumped lips and eyes blazing emerald fire. "Really? And what would that be?" he said, his tone teasing but with barely contained need.

"Make love with me, Carlo. I want to be with you tonight. Every night," she said and threaded her fingers through his hair to urge him back down so she could kiss him again. Take hold of his hand and lay it against her heart so he could feel the heavy uneven thud of hers beneath his palm.

IN A POWERFUL SURGE, Carlo wrapped her up in his arms and cradled her against his chest.

She grabbed hold of his shoulders and kept on kissing him as he marched across the space and down the hall to his bedroom where they fell onto the bed together, laughing and kissing. Jerking and yanking at their clothes in their haste to be together.

They scrambled into the center of his huge bed and he was on her, caressing and tasting her breasts with his mouth and hands. Dipping one hand down to find her center, kindling her passion until her body was shaking and on the edge. But as much as she wanted him inside her, stretching and filling her, she needed to pleasure him also.

With a forceful shove on his shoulder and a roll, she had him on his back and straddled him. At his questioning glance, she smiled and cupped his pecs. Brushed her thumbs across his hard nipples and then bent and tongued them. Beneath her center, his erection jerked and he groaned and held her head to him.

"You like?" she whispered.

"Yes, a lot," he answered and she kissed her way down his center to take him into her mouth, loving and sucking on him until he was trembling and tangled his fingers through her hair to urge her up. She met his gaze which was so dark it was almost black.

He laid his hands on her hips and shifted her over him. She raised her hips and guided him to her center, slowly sank down onto him until he filled her so snugly she almost came from the pressure of him inside her.

She bit back her moan of pleasure, but he said, "I love to hear you when we make love. To watch the color sweep over your body." As if to prove it, he drew the back of his hand up her body to run it across her breasts. Her nipples tightened into even harder nubs with the tender caress and a flush of color stained her skin.

"You are so beautiful, Emma. I'll never get tired of looking at you. Being inside you," he said with a subtle shift of his hips that dragged her eyes closed with the need it built.

"Open your eyes, Emma. I want to see you go over with me. I want you to see me lose myself in you," he said and brought his hands back to her hips.

She did as he asked, opening her eyes to lock her gaze on his. Watch his face as she rode him, rocking her hips and meeting the thrust of his hips driving her ever closer to the edge until with one final push, her climax exploded across her body.

She called out his name and ground down onto him, wanting him so deep she wouldn't know where either of them began or ended. "I love you, Carlo," she whispered.

"I love you, Emma. Forever," he said and cradled her to him, his erection still deep and hard inside her as her climax ebbed. But then he was rolling her beneath him and awakening need again. His strong powerful thrusts driving her toward another release that washed over them as they gazed at one another.

He dropped onto her, his big beautiful body pressing her into the mattress. His weight comforting and filling her with peace and contentment such as she'd never known. When he shifted to lie on his side with her tucked against him, his thigh across hers, she stroked her hand along the thick muscle there. Her touch tender and soothing. Her heart filled with so many emotions, expectant as she said, "Will you marry me?"

His body did a little jump, as if he was in disbelief, but then he said, "On one condition."

She sat up and propped her head on her hand so she could see his face to hear his one condition. "Which is?"

"You plan the most epic wedding for us at the Sea Kiss Convention Center."

She grinned and ran her hand across his chest to lay it over his heart. "*Meu amor*, I think that's technically two conditions. But yes, I will."

He covered her body with his again and playfully teased, "Will what?"

"Will love you and marry you. Will plan an epic wedding at *our* place," she said and gave herself over to his loving again.

Epilogue

The May day was a harbinger of the summer season that would soon be there, bringing hordes of tourists to Sea Kiss. Bright sun flooded through the windows of the ballroom where Emma and her friends where getting ready to walk out to the lovely riverside garden behind the convention center. The landscapers had managed to get in an assortment of bushes thanks to an early March thaw and April showers had welcomed home the foliage. With early May warmth, the pink and red azaleas that had been planted were in full bloom along with dozens of spring bulbs in a riot of color. The lawn was the bright green of new life and set off the blazing white covers on the chairs where guests were gathering for the ceremony. At the farthest end of the lawn, Carlo waited with the priest from a local Roman Catholic church by a floral arbor resplendent with spring blooms and peach-colored ribbons.

Her heart ached at the sight of him looking so handsome in a new bespoke suit in deep blue. He wore a peach-colored tie that matched the color of her dress. *The* dress that had called out to her so many times over the years. The dress and she had been meant to be together just as Carlo and she had been destined to be together.

"Stop pecking out there. Everything is going fine. Lucy, Evelyn, and I have it under control," Tracy said and rubbed her hand across Emma's back.

"Are you sure?" she said, worried since it was the first time she'd ever planned a wedding, but had then been forbidden from running any part of it on the day of her big event.

Emma's mother came to her side, hugged her and said, "It will be fine. More than fine actually since you planned it, my beautiful girl."

Tracy motioned to the ear bud she wore. "For sure, Em. It's under control. No worries," she said, but then a hint of concern flitted across her friend's face as she glanced toward where Maggie and Connie sat in chairs, waiting for the walk down the aisle. Jesse stood beside them, holding Emma's bouquet, a troubled look on her face.

Emma examined Maggie and Connie, her two very pregnant friends. Maggie had her hand on Connie's shoulder and Connie looked a little flushed, raising alarm. They had picked the early May date so that Connie would still be a couple of weeks away from her due date and Maggie's a month after that. Although with first babies and twins, you could never be certain of what would happen.

She hurried over and kneeled before her friends. "You feeling okay?"

Connie smiled easily, but then grimaced. "Okay. Just a little backache. It'll pass."

Emma glanced at Maggie, whose face reflected the worry on Jesse's. Maggie peered at Tracy and Emma's mom and said, "Maybe we should get this show on the road."

Tracy's gaze skipped over all the women and she nodded. "I'll let Lucy and Evelyn know we're ready."

Her friend stepped away to talk to Emma's former bosses and Emma laid a hand on Connie's knee and again asked, "Are you sure you're okay? We can change things if you're not."

Connie nodded, but her lips compressed with a tight twist and she rubbed her hand across her belly, contrary to her answer. "I'm okay, but we should get moving," Connie said, confirming that maybe not all was right with her friend.

A second later a knock came at the door. Tracy opened it and Jonathan, Owen, and Paolo walked in first followed by Tomás and Jesse's son Brandon, who was the ring bearer.

Jonathan immediately rushed to Connie's side, obviously sensing something was wrong, but she waved him off and beamed him a smile. "Don't worry, Jon. I would not miss seeing my best friend get married to the man of her dreams for all the money in the world."

Emma knew her friend was lying through her teeth, but she also knew that once Connie set her mind on something, there was no shaking her loose.

"Let's go. I'm ready to get married," she said and there was no doubt there. No hesitation. She was going to marry a wonderful and amazing man and she didn't want to wait a second longer to do it.

A HUSHED SILENCE FILLED with anticipation settled across the guests as the small chamber music orchestra wound down the piece they'd been playing. Carlo sucked in a breath as his stomach did a nervous flip flop and he laid a hand there to calm the flutter.

At a small wave of Lucy's hand, the orchestra began to play and two of the wedding salon's staff positioned by the doors to the building opened them to reveal Brandon holding a pillow with the rings and behind him the rest of the wedding party. He rose on tiptoes and searched for Emma but couldn't see her past the groomsmen and bridesmaids.

"Patience, my son," the priest said and laid a reassuring hand on his shoulder.

"I'm trying, Father. I'm trying," Carlo said and contained himself from bouncing on his heels to dispel some of the nervous energy pumping through his body.

Connie and Jonathan rushed their pace a little as they came up the aisle and it was impossible to miss that Connie's smile was a little forced. Maggie and Owen came next, likewise moving quickly and before they were even at the altar, Jesse and Tomás came next, followed by Paolo and Tracy barely five seconds later. His brother Paolo was beaming as Tracy smiled at him. Carlo forced back that worry because today was all about him and Emma and their happily-ever-after.

As the women filed into a line on one side of the altar, the men took their spots beside him, Tomás at his side next to Paolo with the Pierce brothers after.

Another excited silence filled the air as Lucy and Evelyn directed their people to roll out the white carpet down the middle of the aisle. As soon as it was in place, the orchestra struck up the first notes of a Vivaldi concerto which echoed through the sunny spring day.

Emma and her mother Juliana stepped out onto white carpet and did a measured pace down the aisle, but as his gaze connected with Emma's he saw the impatience and eagerness there, which relieved a little of his nervousness. When the two women reached the arbor, Juliana turned and lifted the delicate lace veil from Emma's face and kissed her. Juliana then took hold of Emma's hand and guided it into his as he reached for her.

What followed next was a blur until he heard the priest asking him, "Do you Carlo Aleixo da Costa take this woman, Emma Anne Grant, to be your lawfully wedded wife, to have and to hold, from this day forward, for better, for worse, for richer, for poorer, in sickness and in health, until death do you part?"

He smiled and nodded, his eyes never leaving Emma's face as he held her hand, slipped on the ring, and said, "I do, I will keep you Emma in my heart and soul *forever*."

The priest had to hide his grin as he continued. "Do you Emma Anne Grant take this man, Carlo Aleixo da Costa, to be your lawfully wedded husband, to have and to hold, from this day forward, for better, for worse, for richer, for poorer, in sickness and in health, until death do you part?"

Her hands shook as she eased the ring past his knuckle, settled it on his finger, and raised his hand to kiss the ring. "I take you Carlo *forever*. You are my partner in every possible way and the love of my life. I love you."

The priest continued. "By the power vested in me –" he began, but Carlo couldn't wait. He hauled Emma into his arms and was kissing her as the priest finished. "I now pronounce you man and wife and not too soon, may I add," he said with a laugh as they continued kissing.

The laughter and clapping of the audience as well as the music from the chamber orchestra forced them apart, but there was no denying the joy on Emma's face which mirrored what he felt inside. He held his arm out to her and said, "Are you ready Mrs. da Costa?"

She beamed a smile at him and said, "I've never been more ready. Forever and always, remember?"

"As if I could forget," he said, tucked her close against his side and together they took the first step into the rest of their lives.

Coming in June 2020 from Hallmark Publishing and Caridad Pineiro

SOUTH BEACH LOVE

Head to Miami for a Hallmark summer romance celebrating family and tradition,

from New York Times bestselling author Caridad Pineiro.

Tony Sanchez, a celebrity chef, comes home to help with his niece's *quinceañera*—a traditional big celebration for her fifteenth birthday. He meets up with Sara Kelly, an old friend's baby sister, who's now running a restaurant in South Beach. Attraction flares between them.

But Sara is enlisted to cater another *quinceañera*—for the girl who's his niece's rival. Many prominent families will attend, and Sara sees it as an opportunity to get more business for her restaurant and cement her reputation as a talented local chef. But Tony wants his niece's celebration—and his own talent—to outshine the rest.

Can competing chefs teach each other a few lessons about cooking, culture—and love?

For more information, please visit http://bit.ly/SouthBeachLove.

Copyright Notice

---

1.   http://www.caridad.com/

About the Author

C aridad Pineiro is a transplanted Long Island girl who has fallen in love with the Jersey Shore. When Caridad isn't taking long strolls along the boardwalk, she's also a NY Times and USA Today bestselling author with over a million romance novels sold worldwide. Caridad is passionate about writing and helping others explore and develop their skills as writers. She is a founding member of the Liberty States Fiction Writers and has presented workshops at the International Women's Writing Guild, RT Book Club Convention, and the Romance Writers of America National Conference as well as various writing organizations throughout the country. You can connect with Caridad at www.caridad.com[1] or at:

Instagram at https://www.instagram.com/CaridadPineiro/

Twitter at https://twitter.com/caridadpineiro

Facebook at https://www.facebook.com/Caridad.Author

Pinterest at http://pinterest.com/caridadpineiro/

Goodreads at https://www.goodreads.com/Caridad_Pineiro

Caridad also sends out a newsletter to her friends! To subscribe, please visit www.caridad.com[2].

---

1. http://www.caridad.com

2.   http://www.caridad.com

Other Books by Caridad

Additional Books by the Author Writing as Caridad Pineiro
Books in At the Shore Contemporary Romance Series
ONE SUMMER NIGHT[1], #1, October 2017 Sourcebooks Casablanca
WHAT HAPPENS IN SUMMER[2], #2, June 2018 Sourcebooks Casablanca

Novellas in the Take a Chance Military Romance Series
TAKE A CHANCE Box set[3], #1 to #6, December 2015
TAKE A CHANCE Box Set[4], #3 to #6, February 2016
ONE NIGHT OF PLEASURE[5], March 2015
STAY THE NIGHT[6], December 2014
TAKE A CHANCE Box set[7], #1 to #3, November 2014
ONE LAST NIGHT[8], October 2014
ONE SPECIAL NIGHT[9], August 2014
JUST ONE NIGHT[10], June 2014
Books in The Gambling for Love Romantic Suspense Series

1. https://www.caridad.com/books/at-the-shore/one-summer-night/

2. https://www.caridad.com/at-the-shore-2/what-happens-in-summer/

3. http://www.caridad.com/books/military/take-a-chance/

4. http://www.caridad.com/books/military/take-a-chance/

5. http://www.caridad.com/books/erotic/one-night-of-pleasure/

6. http://www.caridad.com/books/erotic/stay-the-night/

7. http://www.caridad.com/take-a-chance/

8. http://www.caridad.com/books/erotic/one-last-night/

9. http://www.caridad.com/books/erotic/one-special-night/

10. http://www.caridad.com/books/erotic/just-one-night/

THE PRINCE'S GAMBLE[11] November 2012 ISBN 9781622668007 Entangled Publishing

TO CATCH A PRINCESS[12] August 2013 ISBN 9781622661329 Entangled Publishing

Books in The Sin Hunter Paranormal Romance Series

THE CLAIMED[13] May 2012 ISBN 978-0446584609 Forever Grand Central Publishing

THE LOST[14] August 2011 ISBN 978-0446584616 Forever Grand Central Publishing

STRONGER THAN SIN[15] November 2010 ISBN 0446543845 Forever Grand Central Publishing

SINS OF THE FLESH[16] November 2009 ISBN 0446543837 Forever Grand Central Publishing

Other Novels by Caridad

SNOW FALLING[17] from Jane the Virgin, writing as Jane Gloriana Villanueva, November 2017, Adams Media

THE FIFTH KINDOM[18] July 2011 ISBN 9781426891885 Carina Press

SOLDIER'S SECRET CHILD[19] Dec 2008 ISBN 0373276109 Silhouette Romantic Suspense

Other Novellas by Caridad

GHOST OF A CHANCE[20], paranormal short story November 2012 ISBN B00AUGV89G

---

11. http://www.caridad.com/books/suspense/the-princes-gamble/

12. http://www.caridad.com/

13. http://www.caridad.com/sin-hunters/the-claimed/

14. http://www.caridad.com/sin-hunters/the-lost/

15. http://www.caridad.com/books/paranormal/stronger-than-sin/

16. http://www.caridad.com/books/paranormal/sins-of-the-flesh/

17. https://www.caridad.com/books/snow-falling-by-jane-gloriana-villaneuva/

18. http://www.caridad.com/books/suspense/the-fifth-kingdom/

19. http://www.caridad.com/books/suspense/a-soldiers-secret-child/

20. http://www.caridad.com/

HER VAMPIRE LOVER[21] October 2012 ISBN 9781459242289 Nocturne Cravings Novella

NIGHT OF THE COUGAR[22] June 2012 ISBN 9781459231153 Nocturne Cravings Novella

THE VAMPIRE'S CONSORT[23] April 2012 ISBN 9781459222731 Harlequin Nocturne Cravings Novella

NOCTURNAL WHISPERS[24] February 2012 ISBN 9781459221437 Harlequin Nocturne Cravings Novella

AMAZON AWAKENING[25] December 2011 ISBN 9781459282766 Available Harlequin Nocturne Cravings Novella

WHEN HERALD ANGELS SING[26] novella in A VAMPIRE FOR CHRISTMAS October 2011 ISBN 0373776446 HQN

AZTEC GOLD[27] January 2011 ISBN 9781426891045 Carina Press Novella

Crazy for the Cat in MOON FEVER[28] Oct 2007 ISBN 1416514902 Pocket Books

UNDER THE BOARDWALK[29] July 2016

Books in THE CALLING/THE REBORN Vampire Novel Series
VAMPIRE REBORN[30], April 2014
DIE FOR LOVE[31], December 2013
BORN TO LOVE[32], November 2013
TO LOVE OR SERVE[33], October 2013

---

21.   http://www.caridad.com/books/erotic/her-vampire-lover/

22.   http://www.caridad.com/books/erotic/night-of-the-cougar/

23.   http://www.caridad.com/books/erotic/the-vampires-consort/

24.   http://www.caridad.com/books/erotic/nocturnal-whispers/

25.   http://www.caridad.com/books/erotic/amazon-awakening/

26.   http://www.caridad.com/books/paranormal/a-vampire-for-christmas/

27.   http://www.caridad.com/books/paranormal/aztec-gold/

28.   http://www.caridad.com/books/paranormal/moon-fever/

29.   https://www.caridad.com/charity-pineiro/under-the-boardwalk/

30.   https://www.caridad.com/books/paranormal/the-calling-is-reborn/

31.   https://www.caridad.com/books/paranormal/the-calling-is-reborn/

32.   https://www.caridad.com/books/paranormal/the-calling-is-reborn/

33.   https://www.caridad.com/books/paranormal/the-calling-is-reborn/

FOR LOVE OR VENGEANCE[34], September 2013

KISSED BY A VAMPIRE[35] (formerly ARDOR CALLS) October 2012 ISBN 9780373885589 Harlequin Nocturne

AWAKENING THE BEAST[36] Collection featuring HONOR CALLS October 2009 ISBN 0373250940 Silhouette Nocturne

FURY CALLS[37] March 2009 ISBN 0373618077 Silhouette Nocturne

HONOR CALLS[38] February 2009 ISBN 9781426828362 Nocturne Bite

HOLIDAY WITH A VAMPIRE[39] December 2007 ISBN 0373617763 Silhouette Nocturne

THE CALLING COMPLETE COLLECTION[40] October 2008 ISBN 9781426807657 Silhouette Includes Darkness Calls, Danger Calls, Temptation Calls, Death Calls, Devotion Calls, and Blood Calls–as well as the online read Desire Calls.

BLOOD CALLS[41] May 2007 ISBN 0373617631 Silhouette Nocturne

DEVOTION CALLS[42] January 2007 ISBN 0373617550 Silhouette Nocturne

DEATH CALLS[43] Dec 2006 ISBN 0373617534 Silhouette Nocturne

TEMPTATION CALLS[44] Oct 2005 ISBN 0373274602 Silhouette Intimate Moments

DANGER CALLS[45] June 2005 ISBN 0373274416 Silhouette Intimate Moments

---

34.   https://www.caridad.com/books/paranormal/the-calling-is-reborn/

35.   https://www.caridad.com/books/paranormal/the-calling-is-reborn/

36.   https://www.caridad.com/books/paranormal/the-calling-is-reborn/

37.   https://www.caridad.com/books/paranormal/the-calling-is-reborn/

38.   https://www.caridad.com/books/paranormal/the-calling-is-reborn/

39.   https://www.caridad.com/books/paranormal/the-calling-is-reborn/

40.   https://www.caridad.com/books/paranormal/the-calling-is-reborn/

41.   https://www.caridad.com/books/paranormal/the-calling-is-reborn/

42.   https://www.caridad.com/books/paranormal/the-calling-is-reborn/

43.   https://www.caridad.com/books/paranormal/the-calling-is-reborn/

44.   https://www.caridad.com/books/paranormal/the-calling-is-reborn/

45.   https://www.caridad.com/books/paranormal/the-calling-is-reborn/

DARKNESS CALLS[46] Mar 2004 ISBN 0373273533 Silhouette Intimate Moments

Romantic Suspense Series

SECRET AGENT REUNION[47] Aug 2007 ISBN 0373275463 Silhouette Romantic Suspense

MORE THAN A MISSION[48] Aug 2006 ISBN 037327498X Silhouette Intimate Moments

Additional Books by the Author Writing as Charity Pineiro

NOW AND ALWAYS[49] June 2013 ISBN 1490362770

FAITH IN YOU[50] July 2013 ISBN 1490412697

TORI GOT LUCKY[51] December 2013

THE PERFECT MIX[52] March 2013

TO CATCH HER MAN[53] April 2014

TAMING THE BACHELOR[54] April 2015

SECOND CHANCE AT PERFECT[55] October 2015

ROOKIE OF THE YEAR[56] October 2015

---

46. https://www.caridad.com/books/paranormal/the-calling-is-reborn/

47. http://www.caridad.com/books/suspense/secret-agent-reunion/

48. http://www.caridad.com/books/suspense/more-than-a-mission/

49. http://www.caridad.com/

50. http://www.caridad.com/

51. http://www.caridad.com/

52. http://www.caridad.com/

53. http://www.caridad.com/

54. https://www.caridad.com/books/charity-pineiro/taming-the-bachelor/

55. http://www.caridad.com/charity-pineiro/second-chance-at-perfect/

56. https://www.caridad.com/books/charity-pineiro/rookie-of-the-year/

Made in the USA
Monee, IL
08 January 2021